T0123246

Everybody's Business

CHARLOTTE RAYBON

authorHOUSE

AuthorHouse™
1663 Liberty Drive
Bloomington, IN 47403
www.authorhouse.com
Phone: 1 (800) 839-8640

© 2018 Charlotte Raybon. All rights reserved.

No part of this book may be reproduced, stored in a retrieval system, or transmitted by any means without the written permission of the author.

Published by AuthorHouse   10/15/2018

ISBN: 978-1-5462-6294-7 (sc)
ISBN: 978-1-5462-6293-0 (e)

Library of Congress Control Number: 2018911764

Print information available on the last page.

Any people depicted in stock imagery provided by Getty Images are models, and such images are being used for illustrative purposes only. Certain stock imagery © Getty Images.

This book is printed on acid-free paper.

Because of the dynamic nature of the Internet, any web addresses or links contained in this book may have changed since publication and may no longer be valid. The views expressed in this work are solely those of the author and do not necessarily reflect the views of the publisher, and the publisher hereby disclaims any responsibility for them.

This is a work of fiction. All of the characters, names, incidents, and dialogue in this novel are either the products of the author's imagination or are used fictitiously.

Contents

Acknowledgements

To read is to escape, to write is to re-imagine, to create the possibilities into realities of making a dream or two come true.

Thank you Marlene Moore-Glass, Project Director of AARP-SCSEP Program; Elenore Bobrow WDIY Radio; Dr. Charles Ludivico, M.D.,F.A.C.P., Dr. Nona Edward- Thomas, M.D.; F.A.C.D.G., Maxine Billings, Author. Michael Davis, Jr. Veronica Patterson, Nereida Quinones, Penny VanTassel, Robert L. Wilkes, for empowering, inspiring and encouraging me to re-imagine my life as an author.

Chapter 1

Paris Benson sat on the front porch with her overnight bag at her feet waiting for the gas and electric company while she enjoyed the summer breeze; it was a warm and comforting evening. She sat there admiring the burning bushes that Edwin Benson, her husband, had planted in the front of the house and reminiscing about how her mother, Emily Love, lying on her death bed had told her not to move out of New York. When Paris asked why; her mother had refused to give her an answer. A week later, Emily Love went into a diabetic coma and died. Her mother always made statements and never explained them; so how could she take anything her mother said seriously?

Paris's life was filled with uncertainties from childhood. The rumors in the projects where she grew up were that Paul and Emily Love weren't her parents and that she was adopted. Paris grew up with the whispers that her mother didn't really love her and Paris didn't have any brothers or sisters. Emily Love had two sisters who claimed all the time that Paris was not Emily's child. Around the holidays when they got together, Paris had to hear about how her complexion had a hint of red tones. Emily's two sisters would sit around and take Paris apart. "Look at her eyebrows and eyelashes her hair. She doesn't look like one of us."

The words would echo through Paris's mind days after the holidays were over. Paris is forty years old, dark brown complexion with hazel-brown eyes and long thick wavy sandy brown hair and dimples in her cheeks. When she'd met Edwin, Paris had known right then and there that Edwin was the man for her; her heart would throb every time he called her or when he entered a room. Edwin is forty-eight years old and five foot eleven, light skin freckles, and had dark brown hair and with light brown puppy dog eyes. *Paris had wanted a new and different life away from the whispering idiots and her gossiping aunts.*

Paris still loved Edwin; but the passion had faded away with all the drama and insanity that came from Edwin's mother Inez and his sister Corona. Edwin and Paris left New York City as soon as their son Anthony graduate from high school and moved to the mountains of Pennsylvania to a little town called Hidden Valley. Anthony looked like Edwin except for the freckles and he was a proud young man but humble at the same time.

Edwin's father Bradford died two years after Paris' mother died and his father left his entire estate to Edwin because he is the oldest of three children. The estate that Edwin had inherited came from Bradford Benson's grandparents under the "Forty Acres and a Mule" law whereby slaves had a right to own land as long as they stayed and worked after the Civil War. Bradford was an uneducated man; he couldn't read or write, nor could he count money. So Bradford never knew he had inherited land. It was after his death that Edwin looked into his father's paperwork and found that his father owned ten acres of land in South Carolina. Edwin sold the land.

When Paris first met Bradford she couldn't understand a word he said. When Paris was telling her friends about him they explained to her that he was a Geechee and that how the old- timers from South Carolina spoke. It took Paris forever more than a day to understand him, but she was never one hundred percent certain.

Edwin gave his sister Corona money who is was six foot one in her stocking feet. Paris always thought of Corona as a dufus or Big Ethel from the Archie comics because she walked bent over. However, Corona was a beautiful dark- skinned woman with shoulder- length black hair. It was just that Corona at times lacked common sense.

Edwin also gave his brother Steven money. Exactly how much, Paris didn't know. She felt it was stupid for Edwin to hide that he gave his family money. Paris knew she would have done the same if her parents were living and if she had siblings.

When Edwin mentioned moving to Pennsylvania, at first Paris was against the ideal and then she thought it would give them a new beginning and it would give them enough distance from her demon-in-laws. Besides Paris didn't have any blood relatives that she knew of other than her son.

As Paris sat there on the porch watching the sun slowly going down and the neighborhood children skating back and forth on the road she now knew the answer to the question she asked her mother. As soon as they moved out of New York, Edwin flipped the script on her and she wasn't far enough away from her demon-in-laws. Or had he? Maybe he hadn't flipped the script at all. In New York Paris was much more active working temporary, more active in church than she was now, and she had more friends that she spent time with. And then there were Paris's hobbies. Paris loved to paint and she would create stories about her painting. During spring time she would enter her paintings in art contest and donate her paintings and drawings to charities to raise money for whatever the causes might be for the events. Edwin wasn't happy about Paris' hobbies and claimed that her hobbies were interfering in her serving God and their marriage. So Paris stops painting when they move to Hidden Valley.

Paris spent most of her time at home when she wasn't working her part-time job. Paris hated living in Hidden Valley because it was too slow. Paris missed the hustle and bustle of New York. She hated Hidden Valley almost as much as she hated her last name. She preferred her maiden name Love which she hyphenated. Paris Love-Benson sounded kind of funny; but Paris did love Edwin Benson. But her love for him couldn't grow as much as she would like it to because of Edwin's mother and sister. Edwin's mother Inez needed a lot of attention because she was a paranoid bipolar schizophrenic, and no one was good enough for her except of course Edwin. Edwin was not only Inez's son, but in some kind of way Inez worked up in her mind that Edwin was her man even though she was married to Bradford which she claimed he abused her.

There were times Paris did believe Inez and there were other time she couldn't help but doubt her. A lot of Paris and Edwin marital problems stemmed from Inez's mental illness. Unfortunately, Paris didn't learn about Inez's mental illness until her son was born and Paris insisted on meeting her doctors. When Paris found out that Inez was a paranoid bipolar schizophrenic she asked Edwin why he hadn't told her. Edwin claimed he didn't know and that his mother and father told him that she went into the hospital for high blood pressure. Paris kind of believed that Edwin's parents told him that. "But they don't lock you up behind bars if you have high blood pressure." Edwin said he just didn't know. Paris believed him; because she knew as a child you believe anything and everything your parents told you from Santa Clause to the tooth fairy.

Chapter 2

Edwin came storming out of the house with a shopping bag that held his tooth brush and one pair of underwear. "What is taking them G.E.C. people so long?" He walks over to Paris.

"I don't know how you can sit here so calm when we have a carbon and monoxide leak".

Paris took a deep breath. "You don't know if it is a carbon monoxide leak; because you can't smell carbon monoxide. Besides this is the fourth time that you have called G.E.C. within the last two months."

Finally the G.E.C. Company arrives as Edwin was pacing back and forth on the porch. The men went through the same procedure of checking for carbon monoxide and they check for gas leaks.

Their diagnosis was the same as it had been the last four times.

"Mr. Benson we found no carbon monoxide leak and no gas leak. Perhaps you and your family will be better off getting a room in a hotel just to be on the safe side," said the inspector from the G.E.C. Company who smiled and wiped his hands with a rag.

Paris felt good about going to a hotel; because on Saturday morning, she could get up early, get dressed, dine out for breakfast, and go do volunteer work at the church. This way she would be free from all the hum-drum household chores that came along with Saturday mornings.

"You seemed to pretty happy" said Edwin as he merged onto the highway.

"Did you call Anthony let him know that we will be staying at a hotel?" ask Paris.

"Yeah I called him and then I heard his cell phone ringing in family room where he left it last night; so I called Keith's house and his mother answer the phone. She said they went to the gym to run ball." said Edwin.

"Good." said Paris as she put on her lipstick. "I tell you that boy would lose all of his body parts if they were not attached. So what hotel are we staying at?

"I forgot the name; but I know where it's at." exclaims Edwin; frowning and looking at Paris. "And how many times I have to tell you not to put make-up on in my car?"

"Oh please" said Paris. Rolling her eyes and putting her lipstick back in pocket book.

"I will call her back when we get to the hotel to let Anthony know where we are staying. Did you book a room for Anthony or do you think he want to spend the night with the Warren family?" Ask Paris

"Yep, I did and I hope he calls back soon. I don't want to lose money on a hotel room" Said Edwin.

"Did you tell Betty about the carbon monoxide leak?" asked Paris, turning her head to look out the window so Edwin couldn't see her facial expression.

"Nah." said Edwin "I didn't have time; I just told her to give Anthony the message to call me and besides I was too busy trying to get out of the house. I was scared I might pass out."

Paris couldn't figure out why Edwin just didn't go outside the house and call Betty from his cell phone instead of calling from the house phone since he was so scared of passing out. She didn't dare ask because she knew the question would just lead to an argument.

"Believe me Edwin that was hardly unlikely" said Paris grinning and still with her face turned looking out the window. When they arrived at Motel 8 Paris could not believe her eyes.

"You mean to tell me you actually decided to stay at a cheap motel?" Ask Paris with a surprise look on her face.

"Yeah; it just for one night" Said Edwin as he pulls into the motel's parking lot.

"Well that certainly didn't stop you before from staying at the Holiday Inn and the Hilton. And remember the last time you ran us all the way to New York City to stay at the Waldof Astoria for one night?" Ask Paris looking around the motel's parking lot.

"What wrong you don't want to stay here?" ask Edwin with his eyes budging out is his sockets.

"Oh no" said Paris batting her eyelashes. "This is fine with me; I'm just surprised it's not the Ritz."

After checking in the motel, Edwin and Paris got on the elevator and went to the second floor and walked down to the end of the hall and finally reaching room 201. Edwin slid the card key in the door lock and entered the room. Edwin walked into the room and Paris followed closely behind him

"I can't stay in this room" shouted Edwin

"What's wrong with this room, it seems alright to me." said Paris as she inspected the room.

"I smell smoke and someone has been in this room smoking. I am calling downstairs to the front desk." said Edwin, he walked over to the night stand and picking up the telephone receiver and pressing zero.

"Hello front desk, this is Mr. Benson from 201 my wife and I just checked in and we smell cigarette smoke and we want another room."

"I am sorry for the inconvenience Mr. Benson. I did give you a key to a no-smoking room. You and your wife can come back to the front desk and I will be happy to exchange the room."

"Thank you. We will be right down." said Edwin he hung up the receiver on the phone. Turning around and walking pass Paris as if he didn't see her and exited out the room. "Come on Paris" let's go we are getting another room."

Paris followed behind Edwin as they walked to the nearest exit and walked down the stairs to lobby.

"I am Mr. Benson and I just spoke to someone about changing our room because we smell cigarette smoke." Edwin tosses the room key on the concierge desk and paces back and forth telling the hotel clerk all about his personal life and how important he is.

"Yes I do remember speaking with you Mr. Benson; here is another pass key to room 209. I believe you will find this room to be more comfortable and it is a non-smoking room." said the hotel clerk.

Paris followed Edwin back on the elevator to the second floor and to room 209. Edwin opens the door and Edwin walks in the room a head of Paris.

"Now, this is more like it" said Edwin and he sat down on the bed and Paris stood in the doorway.

"Well, come on in Paris why are you standing in the doorway?"

"Are you sure Edwin that you are comfortable with this room?"

"Yeah it's fine" said Edwin.

Paris sat her overnight bag down on the bench at the end of the bed and kicked off her shoes; before Paris could say another word she heard Edwin on the phone.

"Is this the front desk?" ask Edwin.

"Yes it sir."

"This room isn't right either." shouted Edwin.

"May I ask what is wrong with the room Mr. Benson?" asked the desk clerk.

"My wife and I find that the bed is too hard!" yells Edwin as he sat down on the bed.

"I am sorry for the inconvenience Mr. Benson. I will send someone right away to escort you another room." Said the desk clerk annoyed with Edwin.

Edwin slams down the receiver on the phone and stands up and walks across the room and looks out the window.

"I don't understand why we can't get a decent room" said Edwin. Turning around and walking to the foot of the bed and sitting down.

"I don't understand Edwin. Whenever we go to a hotel you always have to change rooms a hundred times before we can settle down." Said Paris leaning on the dresser with her arms folded across her chest.

"What are you trying to say Paris; that I am crazy or something?" yells Edwin.

"No, I don't think you are crazy Edwin. I just believe you have some serious issues that need to be addressed" said Paris.

The conversation was interrupted by a knock at the door and Edwin walked over and opened the door and there stood the maid holding out the pass key to their next room. Paris quickly slipped on her shoes and hurried out the room behind Edwin carrying her overnight bag and Edwin's shopping bag.

After changing rooms two more times because Edwin found a

ring around the bath tub. The last room they went into the window was facing the front of the hotel which was too noisy for Edwin. But Edwin told the clerk it was his wife that wasn't satisfied with the rooms. Once they finally settle in a room Paris was able to call Betty.

"Hi Betty this is Paris, how are you and the family?"

"Oh hello Paris, I am okay. I just feel like I am coming down with a cold. Said Betty coughing

"I am sorry to hear that." said Paris; not feeling like having a conversation with anyone especially after she just finished playing musical rooms with Edwin. "Have the boys come back from the gym yet?"

"No they are not back yet." said Betty sounding hoarse and clearing her throat.

"Okay, please tell Anthony to call me. It's important."

"Oh is everything okay?" asked Betty

"Yes everything is fine; just tell Anthony to call me."

"Okay, will do." said Betty.

Betty hung up and Paris was glad the conversation was over with. Paris didn't bother telling Betty about the carbon monoxide leak since Edwin didn't mention it and besides Betty was just another person she saw at church on Sundays.

Edwin was already sitting up in the bed with two pillows behind his head and leaning back on the headboard. He had shoes kicked off with his feet on the bed and holding the remote control in one hand; and surfing the channels on the dingy television set that was on the dresser and holding a restaurant menu in his other hand.

"I gonna order some food; what cha want to eat?" asks Edwin.

"At this point I have no idea. I have to see the menu." said Paris taking a deep breath and just feeling tired. "We can order later; right now I want to talk to you about these carbon monoxide episodes you be having."

Paris went to sit down on the bed next to Edwin. But before she could say another word Edwin's cell phone rang and he picked it up on the first ring.

"Hi Mommy, how are you?"

Edwin went into telling his mother about his carbon and monoxide episodes. Paris straightens up because she never sat down on the bed before the phone rang; so she decided to go into the bathroom and washed her face. She knew that Edwin would be on the phone with mother for at least an hour. It didn't matter where they went or what they were doing when his mother would call. Edwin would stop in the middle of everything to talk to his mother. He even stopped one time while they were having sex. Anthony was in first grade and it was around one thirty in the afternoon and Edwin had taken the day off and he wanted to have sex.

"It's almost two o'clock and I have to go and pick Anthony up from school" said Paris "and why on earth would you wait until now to tell me you want to have sex and you been sitting around here all day doing nothing?

"Aw come on" begged Edwin. You have plenty of time to get dress and make it to the school house."

After Edwin begged and begged and tickled her onto the bed; then Paris gave in. Mid-way through the love making session; Inez called and Edwin answer the phone while he was lying on top of her. Paris pushed Edwin off of her; it was no way on God's good earth was she going to lie up under this fool while he talks to his mother. From that day forward Paris felt like Inez was the other woman. Inez wasn't a monster-in-law she was more like a demon-in-law.

If Paris could write Inez's biography the book stores would label it fiction and placed in between Alfred Hitchcock's novel "Psycho" and Steven King's novel "The Shinning." Inez was a paranoid bipolar schizophrenic; to put it in layman's terms Inez was just a full blown nut waiting for the right moment to cause major damage in Paris and Edwin's marriage.

There were times when Paris would feel sorry for Inez and she tried to understand her illness. When Paris told the doctors about some of Inez's behavioral patterns that was really taking a toll on their marriage the doctor explained to Paris and Edwin that the things she was doing had nothing to do with her illness. She also asked the doctor about all the times Inez would run away from home claiming her husband was abusing her? The doctor claimed that was part of Inez's illness. But Paris wasn't so sure if the doctor was right about his mother not being abused.

Paris asked Edwin did he think his father was abusing his mother; Edwin said not anymore he use to when they were kids and Edwin ended the conversation. Edwin had this rule when he didn't want to discuss things any longer the conversation was over. Paris felt like she had married in a third-world country where the women were seen and not heard. She had married into this dysfunctional family that she would swear only existed in the Twilight Zones.

Then there was the devils' spawn. Edwin's sister Corona she was a whole story by herself. Corona's biography would be entitled "Wicked Just Wicked." Corona would lie, steal, and scheme at the drop of a hat. Corona would lie about things that didn't make any sense to lie about. Edwin's brother Steven was too busy making babies up and down the east coast to be bothered with their foolishness. In fact Edwin and Corona would plot together on how they would get Steven's money on Fridays when he got paid. Steven was just about Steven, and he had very little to do with Inez; in fact

Steven didn't like Inez and neither did he try to pretend he like her. She was just a woman that gave birth to him and he kept his life moving as far was away from Inez as possible.

When Paris came out of the bathroom Edwin was still on the phone just as she knew he would be. She managed to ease the remote out of Edwin's hand while he was engrossed in a conversation with his mother. Paris sat on the bed scanning through channels until she came across the Planet of the Apes movie marathon and decided to watch it until Edwin finished talking with his mother. Paris was determine to take advantage of this carbon monoxide episode and enjoy herself before going back to work on Monday. Paris' cell phone ranged. She picked up her cell phone from the nightstand and pressed the button and then held the phone up to her ear.

"Hi Anthony; where on earth is your cell phone?" Acting like she didn't know.

"I forgot it and left it at the house." Said Anthony trying to remember where he left his phone.

"Your father and I are staying at a motel"

"Why are you all staying at a motel?" ask Anthony.

"Your father smelled carbon monoxide again."

"Oh..... Oh okay....Did dad get me a room?" ask Anthony.

"Yes, it's right next door to ours." said Paris.

"So, is the house safe to go in?" ask Anthony.

"Yes, it's safe. But the man from the G.E.C Company suggested that we stay at the hotel just to be on the safe side. Even though he found no signs of carbon monoxide and no signs of a gas leak, you know, just like the other four times." Said Paris as she stood up and walked to the foot bed and sat down because Edwin kept talking louder and louder as he heard her talking to Anthony.

"Okay, I'll get some games and come over."

"That sounds great and make sure you bring the tennis and the basketball games" Said Pairs

"Okay....I will be over as soon as I drop by the house and pick up the games; oh by the way." asks Anthony "should I pick up some food?"

"Nah, we are going to order room service as soon as your father gets off the phone with his mother. I will tell him to wait until you get here."

"Okay is it anything else you need from the house?" asked Anthony.

"Nope, I have everything, but I am going over to the church in the morning after breakfast to do some community work. If you want to come make sure you bring a change of clothes with you." Said Paris hoping Anthony would agree to go with her.

"Yeah okay, by the way what hotel are we staying at? Ask Anthony.

"It's the cheap section 8 motel". said Paris laughing.

"The section 8 motel.....Where's that at?" ask Anthony frowning.

"It's the Motel 8 Anthony here in Hidden Valley on River Road." said Paris.

"Well I didn't know Mom." "Why dad picked a cheap hotel this time?"

"I am not a mind reader Anthony; just hurry up and get here so we can have time to hangout."

"Okay; I will be there as soon as I pick up the things from the house." Said Anthony

Edwin got off the phone as soon as Paris hung up from talking with Anthony.

"Was that Anthony?" asked Edwin.

"Yeah, he is on his way as soon as he soon as stops by the house to pick up some things." Said Paris; sitting at the foot of the bed.

"Anthony is going to the house?" yelled Edwin with eyes bulging out of his eye sockets.

"Yes he is going to pick up some things and then he is coming here to the motel." said Paris

"Didn't you tell him I could smell carbon and monoxide?" Ask Edwin.

"Yes I told him; and I also told him what the man said from G.E.C. Company said too. They found no signs of carbon and monoxide in the house; just like the last four times." Said Paris feeling annoyed with Edwin's line of questioning.

"Well I hope he will be alright; you should not have sent him there." yell Edwin.

"Why don't you go meet Anthony at the house to make sure he is alright?" suggest Paris.

"Well if he isn't here in a half hour I will go see about him." Said Edwin, reading the menu trying to figure out what he wants to order for dinner.

"Let's wait for Anthony before we order that way we can all eat together and we don't have to order room service a second time and tip twice." suggest Paris.

"I don't want to wait. I want to order now. Do you want anything?"

"No; I will wait for Anthony." said Paris as she kicked off her shoes and lay down at the foot of the bed to watch television. "But I still want to talk to you about your carbon monoxide episodes."

"Yeah okay, right after I placed my order, then we can talk. Said Edwin; reading the menu.

Before Paris could answer Edwin, his cell phone rang again. "Can't you just let the phone ring?" asked Paris.

Edwin never order his food and neither did they have a chance to talk because it was the other demon-in-law, his sister Corona called; and Edwin had to go through the whole carbon and monoxide series again. In fact Edwin was the king of drama; him and his mother and sister. Paris moved further down to the foot of the bed and turned up the volume on the ape movie which at the time was the most exciting thing. Thirty minutes later a knock at the door and Edwin gets up from the bed and runs to the door while he is still on the phone with Corona.

"Who's there?" yells Edwin; opening the door.

"It's Anthony"

"Man what took you so long; I almost starved to death waiting for you." yells Edwin, as he swings the door open. "Hey Corona, I have to get off the phone I talk to you later."

"Let's order food." said Edwin walking back over to the bed and picks up the menu. "I'm ordering steak." said Edwin passing the menu to Anthony who order burgers and fries and Paris order the Caesar salad.

"Hey mom; there is a game room down stairs you want to check it out?"

"I thought you brought the X box?" ask Paris.

"I did but I want to check out the game room first; then we can come back and play the X box"

After dinner Paris and Anthony invited Edwin to come down stairs to the game room but the phone rang and it was Inez again.

So Paris and Anthony went down to the game room and played table hockey, ping pong and the arcade machines.

"I am hungry." said Anthony.

"Anthony, how could you possibly be hungry we just had dinner?"

"That was the only thing I ate all day." said Anthony."

"You want to order more room service?" ask Paris.

"Nah lets go out to a deli." said Anthony.

"Okay that's sounds good if we can find one open."

They ended up at Arby's and order corn beef sandwiches and sodas and Paris sat there and listening to Anthony talked about cars and telling his old corny jokes. Anthony leans back and laughs sounding like Herman the monster; which Paris swore one day would land her in the I.C.U later unit in the hospital because she didn't think she could stand another one of Anthony's corny jokes.

"So what you want do you now?" ask Anthony.

"I think it's time we head back to the motel. I want to get up early so I can help out at the church in the morning. Are you going with me?"

"Yeah I go." said Anthony; reluctantly standing up from the table.

"Good cause I am going to need a ride." said Paris as she stood up to leave the restaurant.

When they got back to the motel room Edwin was still on the phone; but this time he was talking with his friend Bruce. Paris picked up the key from the dresser and gave Anthony his room key. "I'll see you in the morning at seven thirty." said Paris.

"Why so early? Ask Anthony standing in the doorway.

"We are having breakfast at the Waffle House before going to the church. So good night Anthony, I will see you in the morning at

17

seven thirty sharp." Said Paris closing the door after Anthony says good night and walks next door to his room.

Paris went into the bathroom and took the hottest shower she could stand. When she came out of the bathroom Edwin was already sleep. "Unbelievable" was the only word that she could think of that could possibly describe her day. She didn't get to talk with Edwin about his carbon and dioxide as Edwin would call it. She turned the lights out and passed out.

Chapter 3

It was about 12 midnight and Edwin check to see if Paris was asleep. Edwin got up and dressed. He slipped out the hotel room and ran down the stairs through the lobby and out the front exit and got into a car with a light complexion black woman who dyed her hair blonde. She was 35 years old and slender. Edwin had met Jennifer on the job; she had own a vacation spot in Pennsylvania through the time share company that Edwin worked at. When she came for her two week vacation she decided to go to meet Edwin whom she had spoken with several times on the phone. So Jennifer showed up with her 13 year old son and they had a so-called family day together. Edwin kisses Jennifer on the lips and then told her to drive him home. Once inside the house they went upstairs to the master bedroom and made passionate love.

An hour later Edwin rolls out of bed ripping the covers off his part-time lover Jennifer who lies there all sweaty and relaxed after an hour of making pretend it was all good. "I just want to sleep for an hour before I go back to my sister's house. I wish you would come and spend some time with my family in Detroit Edwin."

"I will." said Edwin balling the sheets up. "You know I have to deal with my bipolar wife. As long as she stays on her meds I should be able to get away." Said Edwin as he exits the bedroom and running down the steps to the basement and putting the sheets in the washer. Edwin goes back upstairs to the kitchen and make sandwiches for him and Jennifer and he goes into the family room and takes a bottle of Gin out the globe bar that Paris brought him for their fifteenth anniversary. He goes back into the kitchen and he takes two paper cups from the cabinet and pulls a can of coke from the refrigerator. Edwin can hear Paris telling him how disgusting Gin and Coke taste mixed together. Who drinks that Paris would ask and then she would tell him that he drinks too much.

"Edwin what are you doing?" asked Jennifer now fully dressed walking into the breakfast nook.

Edwin walks over to the kitchen table "I was just making us some sandwiches while I am washing the sheets." said Edwin as he set two plates of sandwiches on the table.

"I don't understand you Edwin;" said Jennifer sitting down at the kitchen table.

"What do you mean, you don't understand me? ask Edwin with a puzzled look on his face.

"I mean why you go through all these changes with your wife, why don't you just get up and leave. After all, your son is grown and your wife has a job; it's not like you have to support her."

"You just don't get up and leave because someone is mentally ill." said Edwin as he got up and went back into the family room to pour more Gin in his glass. He came back to the table and finished off his sandwich.

"You such a good man Edwin to care for your wife the way you do. Your wife doesn't deserve you. Said Jennifer eating her sandwich; and then she takes a sip of her drink and she starts choking.

"Why on earth do you mix Gin and Coke together this is nasty?" ask Jennifer, getting up from the table and going over to the kitchen sink and throwing out the drink. Edwin looks at Jennifer with disgust written all over his face; she reminded him of Paris.

"Yeah right." said Edwin standing up and walking to the basement door. "I got to go downstairs to put the sheets in the dryer."

When Edwin came back upstairs he saw Jennifer sitting at the table drinking orange juice out of a glass that she had taken out of the kitchen cabinet that was a part of a set of glasses that belonged to Paris's mother. Paris never allowed anyone to use her mother's dishes unless of course it was a special occasion.

"What are you doing with that glass?!" yelled Edwin.

"I just wanted a glass of orange juice. Is something wrong with me drinking a glass of orange juice?" Jennifer asked sarcastically.

"Let me tell you something Jennifer; I am the man in this house and you don't put your hands on anything unless you asked you me first. Do you understand me?!" yelled Edwin with his eyes budging out of his eye sockets; he snatched the glass off the table and spilled some of the orange juice on the floor. He walked over to the sink and threw the orange juice down the drain and washes the glass, dries it off with paper towel and places back in the cabinet.

"I'm sorry," said Edwin wiping the orange juice off the floor with a paper towel. "It's just that Paris drives me crazy. She went to visit her mother in New York City and she is always complaining when she comes back that I don't keep the house clean."

"Why don't you ask her for a divorce?" ask Jennifer wiping her mouth with a napkin.

Edwin sat back down at the kitchen table and Jennifer reached over and held Edwin's hand and she looked over into the family room at the family portrait that hung over the fireplace.

"She sure doesn't look like anything is wrong with her." said Jennifer.

"I tell you my wife invented the word crazy. She has done everything from laying up with men to beating up a few men and she is always running away from home. The last time she ran away we couldn't find her for months. Let's just say I don't like being around her when the moon comes out." Said Edwin as continue to lie; he knew he was really talking about his mother.

"Have you tried putting her away?" Ask Jennifer; not understanding why fine men like Edwin that has everything from good looks to a good job would stay married to a crazy woman.

"Well;" said Edwin standing up and stretching as he ignores Jennifer's question. I think the sheets should be dry. He went back down to basement and brought the sheets back upstairs.

It was five o'clock Saturday morning when Jennifer dropped Edwin back at the motel. Jennifer asked why he was staying at the motel. Edwin explained the time-share company that he was working for was closing a contract with the motel and the company wanted him to spend the night to check out the accommodations. And Paris had friends that worked at the motel. The truth of the matter was the thrill of having another woman in his wife's bed is what he couldn't explain to Jennifer after all she might not like the ideal.

Jennifer told Edwin that she would be staying with her sister for the rest of the week. Edwin kissed Jennifer and told her that he would meet-up with her before the weekend was over.

Edwin had managed to enter the room and undress and slip back into bed without waking Paris. She had not moved since he had left the room. He knew once Paris falls asleep he could count on her to sleep all night; in fact he could rearrange the furniture and Paris would sleep right through it. He remembered when they first moved into their newly built community the builders was dynamiting in order to lay a new foundation to build another house and he had to wake Paris up to tell her to get up because the builders was dynamiting. Paris laughed about it because she couldn't believe she slept that hard and the builders was dynamiting right outside her bedroom window. Edwin still laughs about the time Paris came home three hours late from work because Paris ended up in the train yard. She went to sleep on the "A" train in New York. The conductor was mad and yelled at her because he had to turn the train around at the end of his shift to let Paris off in the station and the conductor had to work an extra shift.

Chapter 4

At six-thirty the alarm rings from Paris's cell phone. Paris reached over to the night stand and picked up her cell phone and shuts off the alarm.

"Why you set your alarm clock?" asked Edwin, rolling over facing Paris as he stroked her leg. "I'm not leaving until noon and besides I want to get some cookies; we might as well make good use of the room."

Paris just ignored Edwin's advances to have sex. Paris lifted his hand off her leg with one pinky held in the air and threw his hand over on the bed like it was a nasty rag. Paris couldn't stand being intimate with Edwin. The thought of having sex with him made her feel like she wanted to throw up something she never ate; because of his relationship Inez and Corona. Too many times in the past when Edwin would finish talking with Inez on the phone they would end up in an argument and he would physically attack her. And Edwin always would dip into their savings and give their money to Corona. Paris got wise to Edwin giving money to Corona when several hundred dollars was missing from their savings account. Paris opened up another account in a different bank.

Paris was angry with herself for having an affair but she couldn't take it anymore; she had lost all soundness of mind. She allowed her husband and her demon-in-laws cause her to sin against God and herself; because she lacked faith, courage and the strength to get up and walk away. And she made all the excuses in the world for not leaving; one reason was her son he needed a father. Edwin was a good father even if he wasn't a good husband. The other reason Anthony was always sick going in and out of the hospital with his asthma attacks and she didn't have a full time job; she only worked temporary assignments as a secretary in order to be home with Anthony.

Paris knew Edwin would kill her if she left with Anthony and it was no way she would leave Anthony with her dysfunctional in-laws. Paris was also scared of being homeless; where would she go? She was very depressed after her mother had died. She felt like her whole world ended and she didn't know which way to turn and she had no other relatives to turn to; so she just lost all soundness of mind.

Almost; anyway, the man she had the affair with said that he would beat Edwin up for her and put him in the hospital for beating her up. But Paris told him no she felt that because she was already in the wrong it was no point in adding to her sin list. Paris rolled out of bed and called Anthony and her call went into voicemail.

"I bet Anthony has his phone on vibrate and he knows I want to go to church this morning." said Paris as she made her way to the bathroom.

A half an hour later Paris came out the bathroom dressed and ready to go. She looked over at Edwin watching television. Edwin would never go and does volunteer work at the church even when he was ask to; he would always find some excuse for not going.

"Did Anthony call?" asked Paris; looking over at Edwin lying in the bed watching the travel channel.

"Nah he never called." said Edwin picking up the menu. "I going order breakfast; you want something?

"No." said Paris. She picked up her cell phone off the nightstand and called Anthony again; this time he picked up and Paris could tell Anthony was just waking up.

"Anthony, wake up you said you coming with me to church this morning to do volunteer work."

"I'm sorry Mom" said Anthony yawning. "I will be there in twenty minutes."

"Okay" said Paris taking a deep breath of relief.

"Ask Anthony if he want me to order breakfast for him." yell Edwin.

"Yeah, okay" say Paris ignoring Edwin's offer to order breakfast for Anthony.

"I be knocking on your door in twenty minutes, make sure you be ready. By the way is Dad going to order breakfast? "Anthony asked before hanging up.

"We are going over to the Waffle House so hurry up" said Paris. She clicks off the cell phone and slid it in her pants pocket and sat down in the chair and looked over at Edwin.

"Edwin we need to talk about your carbon and monoxide episodes. Now I just want to know what makes you think you smell carbon monoxide and you know it's odorless."

Edwin turns over on his side facing Paris; "I don't know I just know I smell it and it has a strong odor."

"You know Edwin I could understand if, it was a gas leak and you being confused; but you are smart enough to know carbon monoxide does not have an odor. So what on earth is going on with you?" asked Paris leaning on the arm of the chair.

"I'm telling you Paris I am smell carbon monoxide and it has a bad odor."

"Edwin, you need therapy. This is your fourth episode and I

can't take it. said Paris nonchalantly; and knowing Edwin is going to disagree with her.

"I'm not going to see some nut cracker!" said Edwin shouting.

"And what is wrong with therapy Edwin?" ask Paris.

"My mother goes for therapy and it's not doing anything for her. I'm just not going." shouted Edwin.

"Well I agree with you on that note that it's not working on your mother; but your mother needs more therapy or a different type of therapy then the ones she has been receiving." said Paris.

"Don't talk about my mother!" Edwin screamed like madman and his eyes bulging out of his eyelids.

"I am not talking about your mother; in fact, you are the one that brought your mother into the conversation. I am just trying to help you to understand that it is important to take care of your mental health, just like you need to take care of your physical and spiritual health. Good Lord, you are a trip! I tell you what Edwin; you have one more of those carbon and monoxides episodes and I am going to 9.1.1 your butt in the nearest asylum; because I can't take it. And I am not going to allow you to run me crazy." Paris thought to herself not this time she I won't sin against God or myself.

It was 7:45 and their conversation was interrupted by a knock at the door and it was Anthony and he was on time and dressed to work. "Hi Anthony, said Paris as she open the door. "Are you ready to go?"

"Hey man" Edwin called out. "You want me to order you some breakfast."

"Nah Dad. We are going out to the Waffle House." Said Anthony he walks into the room. "Why don't you join us?"

"Nah man, it's too early for me to be going out." Said Edwin sitting up in the bed and pick up the menu off the nightstand. "I am going hang-out here; until check-out time."

As soon as Paris and Anthony left the room Edwin picked up his cell phone and hit the speed dial number; the phone rang three times before Jennifer answered.

"Hey baby, why don't you come on over to motel and rock with me? ask Edwin sitting up on the side of the bed.

"I thought you didn't want the workers to see me." said Jennifer.

"You can come through the back door. Call me when you get here and I let you in." Said Edwin.

"Okay order me some breakfast." Said Jennifer I will be there in an hour.

It was now three o'clock and it had start to rain and they finished their work at the church. "Hey mom we all going over to Shelia's for pizza you want to come?" asked Anthony.

Paris felt tired after a long day and thought about going home; but if she went home she would just be doing laundry. She also thought about Edwin being home hollering and yelling about nothing.

"Hey that sounds good; will Shelia need us to pick some up stuff from the store?"

Shelia was a year older than Anthony. She love herself some Anthony but Anthony didn't love Shelia. He said Shelia was too flaky and she was always running up on every single guy she could meet and she refused to go to work or further her education. So, on that note Anthony was only interested in Shelia as a friend. Paris liked Shelia but she felt Anthony had good reason for keeping Shelia only as a friend.

Sheila's gathering ended early. It was seven thirty when Anthony dropped Paris at home.

"Are you coming in?" Asked Paris?

"No I am going to the movies with the guys." said Anthony.

"Okay; don't you stay out too late we have church in the morning." Said Paris as she got out of the car and walked through the garage. Paris came into the house through the kitchen and walked into the family room. Edwin had the television on and the volume was up so loud the walls were vibrating and he was on the phone growling and barking like wild animals. Paris almost asks Edwin who was he on the phone with but she realize it was his brother. It was unbelievable; whenever Steven would call they never said hello and how are you, like normal people, they just went to making wild life noises, barking, howling and growling like a bunch wild animals out in woods somewhere or like they were in a horror movie rated "I" for idiots on the loose.

"Edwin could you please turn down the television and stop making those animals sounds; good lord don't you and Steven know how to hold a conversation?"

"Okay man, she home I holler at you later." said Edwin getting off his recliner and, clicking off his cell phone, turns off the television and went into the kitchen where Paris was putting on the teapot on the stove.

"So how did it go at the church today?" ask Edwin leaning on the snack bar as Paris took a coffee mug out of the cabinet.

"We got everything done." said Paris waiting for the water to boil."

"My mother and Corona wants to come up for next weekend." said Edwin. Grinning from ear to ear, waiting for Paris to agree with his decision.

Paris felt like she was going to faint and on that note she went into the family room and open up Edwin's globe bar and pull out a bottle of brandy.

"Oh so now you got to have a drink because my family coming up for the weekend?!" asked Edwin screaming at the top of his lungs.

"No, I got to get a drink because I came home to you the Horror Drama King." said Paris walking pass Edwin back into the kitchen.

"That's okay Paris you think you funny. "said Edwin as he walked over and her grabbed hair and twisted it around his hand and pulled her closer to him. "My family is coming next weekend."

He released her hair and walked in front of her and then he pushed her forehead so far back Paris fell backwards down to the floor and hit the middle of her back on the kitchen cabinet door handles. He went back into the family room and turns the television back on and this time the volume was even louder. Paris set on the floor and started to cry and then she got up and finishes making her tea and went up stairs to the guess room. Paris cried so long that her face and eyes swelled up and nose was stopped up. There has to be a way out; but Paris knew it wasn't going to happen. She turned on the television and started watching the surreal television show with Mr. T visiting this white family and helping to solve this family's problem as he walked around saying "I pity the fool." She imagine Mr. T visiting her family and Edwin standing up laughing and hanging out with Mr. T and then watch Mr. T cold clock Edwin. Paris finished her tea with her brandy and she cried again until she fell asleep.

Chapter 5

Sunday morning the sun was shining bright and blazing through the bedroom window. Paris heard Anthony and Edwin down stairs talking. So she decided to get up and go downstairs and she went into the breakfast nook and saw they were having breakfast.

"Where is my breakfast?" Ask Paris with a puzzled look on her face.

"You were asleep and I told Anthony just to get breakfast just him and me; I figured you wouldn't want anything." said Edwin.

"Yeah so you both just forgot me altogether; neither one of you thought about me?" ask Paris.

"Mom; I'm sorry but you were sleeping and I didn't want to wake you up."

Paris went into the powder room at caught a glance of her face in the mirror she couldn't believe how red and puffy her eyes were and the left side of her face was swollen. Paris felt like she had a lump in the middle of her back which ached with a dull pain. Anthony didn't even notice and she felt so listless. After using the bathroom she came out and Edwin asked was she going to church. Paris just looked at Edwin and wonder why he was going and why he bothered to asked. Paris didn't answer she turned around and went to go upstairs when Edwin followed behind her and pulled her by her arm.

"Look Paris I'm sorry about last night and it just that I had too much to drink and I thought you didn't want my family to come for the weekend."

"Let me ask you something Edwin." As she snatched her arm away from his grip and turning around to face him. "Have I ever denied your family from visiting?"

"No" said Edwin looking down at the floor like he was sorry.

"Well, they can't come next weekend; because you invited your homeboys and their wives over for a barbeque; so tell them next month; because it is going to take that long for me to get over last night." said Paris.

"But that is a whole month from now!" Scream Edwin. "Why can't we have them come the following weekend?"

Paris walked up the steps and didn't bother to look back.

"NEXT MONTH!" Yelled Paris as she went back into the guest room and slammed the door and went to back to bed.

Anthony and Elwin went to church; and Paris popped a couple of muscle relaxers that she had gotten from the doctor last winter when Edwin had a fit out in the street and cussed her out. He accused Paris of looking at some man and pushed her down on the ice and causes her to tear ligaments in her right ankle and she had to take a leave of absence from her job because her ankle was in a cast for six weeks. Paris decided to watch a noir movie until she went back to sleep. When she woke up it must have been about three o'clock and the house was quiet. The phone rang and Paris jumped out of bed and bent over and grabs her back; she forgot about the horrible pain that was throbbing in middle of her back. She made her way to exit the guest bed room; she opens the bedroom door stumping her little toe into bedroom door as she opens it. The phone continues to ring and she stumbles into the master bedroom to the nightstand and answer the phone.

"Hello" said Paris clearing her throat because her voice was hoarse.

"Hi Paris" answered Edwin

"Oh hi Edwin"

"Are you alright?" asked Edwin"

"Yeah I am fine." "What do you want?"

"Anthony and I are going to the rib shack in Queens, you want anything?" ask Edwin.

"Yeah, I want the barbeque chicken dinner."

"Okay you want anything else? asked Edwin

"Yeah, and get me the bread pudding." Paris felt like she at least deserve that and that wasn't much to ask for considering what she had been through.

"Okay, we will see you in a little while." said Edwin.

Paris knew a little while would be five or six hours before they would get back; because she knew he was going to stop by Corona's apartment in Harlem and he wouldn't be home until real late and that was great. Paris took a shower and when she looked in the mirror this time the swelling on the left side of her face went down and her eyes had cleared up. Even though she looked better she was still hurting on the inside and her back still ached.

Since Paris had left New York she didn't have many friends. And didn't try making friends either; so there was no one she could call and tell what Edwin had done to her. Paris life was going to church and going to work and returning home. In reality her family was her whole life and what would she do without Edwin? This crazy deranged man was Paris' whole life. Paris couldn't think about him any longer it was just making her feel more depressed. She went down stairs and made a picture of ice tea and fixed herself some cheese and cracker and put some grapes on her plate and found an old Joan Crawford movie "Mildred Peirce" that she has seen it a thousand and one times. Paris wishes she had family or a close friend she could visit just to get away from Edwin and his dysfunctional family.

She had one friend that she cherished in New York who was old enough to be her mother; Belinda. She met Belinda through some of her church friends in New York and Belinda would baby sit Anthony when she would work on temporary assignments as a secretary; so she called about two months ago and asked Belinda could she come and visited for the weekend and Belinda told her no because she just didn't want to be bothered. Belinda had her share of drama; so Paris understood and didn't bother asking anyone else.

Paris motto was: "just don't think about it, just keep it moving." As her mama use to say "Keep moving that way they can't bury you." When Paris asked her mother who was "they" of course as usual she didn't give Paris an answer.

Monday morning came pouring in with the thunderstorms and lighting striking the bedroom window panes. Paris awakens by the storm jumped up out of a deep sleep and sitting up in bed and gasps for air. The nightmare of being smothered was so real; she looked next to her were Edwin would be lying but he wasn't in the bed. She looked around the room. No Edwin. She then got out of the bed and walked toward the bedroom door which Edwin had left wide open and she heard Edwin saying goodbye to Anthony as he exited the house. Seconds later she could hear Anthony setting the alarm system on the door.

"Bye Anthony, have a good day." yelled Paris as she walked out into the hallway and looking over the balcony stairs.

"Bye Mom." Anthony called out as he exited out the back door.

Behind the nightmare and drama and she had went through over the weekend; Paris just didn't feel like going to work. Sleeping in the bed with Edwin last night and disgusting feeling that cover her body again when she thought about how Edwin bounce up and down on top of her. She needed to call the office it was now eight-thirty but first she had to wash the disgusting remains off her body. She would have done it last night but Edwin always felt insulted when she got up after their so-called love making sessions and took a shower.

Paris went into the bathroom and step into the shower stall. She spent for a good twenty minutes scrubbing her body down and washing her hair; then she step out of the shower stall and walked over to the bathtub and filled it with water and adding essential oils to make a bubble bath. She sat in the bathtub for thirty minutes. She couldn't help but to remember the nightmare, the nightmares that seemed to come more often. After sitting in the tub for thirty minutes she decided to wash get out of the tub. She then returned to the shower and spent another twenty minutes scrubbing and washing. When Paris finally finished in the bathroom washing, primping and then cleaning the bathroom it was now ten o'clock. She couldn't believe the how the time flew by. Paris threw on her bathrobe and called the office and Mr. Bonds her manager answer the phone.

Hi Mr. Bonds this is Paris. Paris didn't bother trying to sound sick...... she was sick of her whole situation.

"Hi Paris, are you alright?" ask Mr. Bonds.

Paris very seldom if ever called out sick maybe twice out of the two years she worked for him and one of those times was when Edwin knocked her down and gave her a black eye. Paris worked as a part time administrative assistant and the pay wasn't much but it beat a blank as her mama would say. And as of lately Paris could even apply that saying to her husband; Edwin had become a blank as far as Paris was concern.

"No I am not feeling well Mr. Bonds. I will be out until next week; my back is hurting me. I will be back next Monday."

"Okay Paris; you take care of yourself and I see you back at work on Monday." said Mr. Bonds.

Paris wasn't physically sick. Her back was a little stiff with some pain; but more than anything else she was sick and tired of her situation and needed a brake just to breath. Paris went downstairs and made oatmeal for breakfast and made herself a cup of coffee. She sat at the table thinking about the nightmare of someone smothering her and it seemed so real. Paris decided to put the nightmare out of her mind and she wouldn't dare tell anyone. She figured that folks would think she was crazy. The house phone rang and Paris got up from the kitchen table and walked over to the snack bar and looked at the indicator on the telephone and saw it was Inez calling. Paris started not to answer the phone. Why was Inez calling the house phone? Inez had Edwin's cell phone, the phone rang the fifth time and Paris decided to answer.

"Hello." answer Paris trying to sound like she didn't who was calling.

"Oh hi." said Inez surprised that Paris answer the phone.

"Hi Inez, How are you?"

"I am fine; I am calling looking for Corona."

What makes you think she here? asked Paris

"She didn't come home last night and she left the kids with some of the church members." said Inez.

That wasn't a surprised to Paris. Corona had a history of disappearing and leaving her two children anywhere and with anybody.

"So where are the kids?" asked Paris

"They are with me. I went and picked them up Saturday night." said Inez

"Well Edwin had just spoken with her Friday night. So she just is missing since Saturday night?"

"Yeah, you sure you haven't seen or heard from her?" asked Inez.

"No I haven't. Edwin was in New York Sunday; you should give him call."

"Okay" said Inez and hung up the phone to call Edwin.

Paris labeled her Corona Queen Dufus because was always doing something stupid. She even made a mistake and hit herself in the head with a cast iron frying pan because she was trying to put the frying pan in the cabinet on the top shelf instead of putting it in the lower cabinet. The frying pan slipped off the top shelf and hit Corona on her forehead leaving a lump the size of a plum. Corona walked around all week with a big lump in the middle her forehead covering it with an ice pack complaining that she had a headache and when she removed the ice pack she put a Band-Aid on it and started popping Tylenols. When Paris suggested that she should go to hospital; Corona mumble something about how Paris needs to mind her own business. On that note Paris fell out in laughter and she laughed until she cried.

Paris sat back down at the kitchen table and finished her coffee. Paris felt like she needed to get out of the house; but where would she go and who could she visit. Paris remembered meeting Virginia. Virginia had just move to Hidden Valley with her husband who was an aviation technician and for the most part his job took him out of town and her two twin daughters they were seventeen years old and they could be left alone for a couple of hours while they hangout. Virginia would make the perfect friend; she hadn't been in Hidden Valley long enough to make friends with anyone or even long enough to bother with any gossip from the church members. Not that they could say anything about Paris who went to church and said hello and amen and out the door; except for the times she would go and do volunteer work at the church. Paris went upstairs and looked through several handbags before she found Virginia's phone number. She picks up the receiver and dialed her number, after four rings Virginia answered.

"Hello." answer Virginia

"Hi Virginia, this is Paris. I was thinking about you and I decided to call you since I have taken the day off from work."

"Oh that is so nice of you. I was just about to clean up the breakfast dishes and do some more unpacking before the kids come home from school." said Virginia.

"Okay." said Paris interrupting Virginia. "Well how about we do lunch?" Paris didn't offer to help Virginia unpack being that her back was stiff and ached from Edwin pushing her into the kitchen cabinet doors handles.

"It's just that I have to do so much work around here, I hate to go out and leave all these boxes unpacked." said Virginia; she wanted to go to lunch with Paris but at the same time she felt obligated to finish unpacking.

"We can have lunch at that new café that open up in town. I think it open up the same week you moved in." said Paris.

"Oh yes." said Virginia "we have one of those cafes back home."

"Okay, so you know it a déjà vu kind a thing that we must go and eat there. I will pick you up at one o'clock my treat." Paris hung up the phone before Virginia could protest.

Paris checks her bank account and she saw that she had enough money for lunch and to make it through to her next pay day. Paris looked in her closet and saw that the blouse she wanted to wear was dirty. She looked at the clock and it was just eleven o'clock. She decided since she missed doing the laundry over the weekend due to Edwin's carbon monoxide episode, she would wash a load of clothes. Just as Paris finished loading the washing machine she heard a car drive up in the driveway. She ran upstairs from the basement to the front of the house and she and saw Edwin getting out of the car. Paris wished she was dressed so she could run out the back door. Paris could hear her mother saying "Get up and put your clothes on cause you never know when you will have to run out." When Paris asked her mother why she would have to run out; she didn't get an answer to that question either. It wasn't until after her mother died and she had to go through all the paperwork and saw the year her mother was born in. Emily Love was born in the 1910 that meant that Paris grandmother had to been born at the end of slavery and her great grandmother had to be in slavery. And that would explain all the crazy sayings. That's if her mother was really her mother.

Paris opens the door and step outside and she watches Edwin walking up to the front door.

"What are you doing home?" Edwin had beat Paris in asking the question.

"I'm not feeling well; my back is still hurting." Said Paris as she stepped back out of the doorway and held the door open for Edwin to enter the house.

"So what brings you home?" Paris was almost afraid to ask because she just had a feeling it was going to be horror-a-rama time.

"I got a called from my mother looking for Corona." said Edwin going into the den and opening the desk drawers.

"Yes I know." said Paris following behind Edwin. "Your mother called here early this morning looking for Corona. Have you heard anything about where she might be?"

Paris tried to look concerned as she sat down on the sofa in the den. She can't remember if she turned on the washer or added the detergent. But she just wanted Edwin to get what he came for and get out.

"You got any money?" asked Edwin looking through his desk like the mad-man that Paris suspected him to be.

"No, what do you need money for?" ask Paris.

"For Corona, she is in jail." Said Edwin; still looking the desk for his checkbook.

"What is Corona doing in jail?" Paris is really concern now even though Corona was her dufus demon-in-law she didn't want to see anything happen to her.

"You sure you don't have no money Paris?"

"You know if I had some money I would give it to you." Paris lied and she had promised herself that she wouldn't let Edwin and his dysfunctional family causes her to sin again; but at times it just seemed impossible and this was one of those times. Paris didn't care if Edwin needs money to get Corona out of jail or if they needed a plumber to pull a plunger out of Corona's backside she wasn't giving up any money for Corona the dufus who landed herself in jail.

"Would you mind telling me why Corona is in jail? asked Paris and wondered why she even bothered to ask.

Edwin walked over and sat down on the coach next to Paris and starring at her as if he was trying to read her mind.

"Corona is in jail for arm robbery." said Edwin.

"Oh my God!" said Paris. Covering her mouth and voice inside of her said run Paris run.

"That can't be true; it must be some kind of mistake." Exclaims Paris standing up and walking backwards and she turned around and walked out the room into the foyer.

"You got any money?" ask Edwin following closely behind her.

At this point Paris wanted to run outside but she only had on her see through night gown. Paris turns around facing Edwin and wiping her face with both of hands trying wipe away the fear as she could see the rage in Edwin's eyes.

"Edwin what happen?" Paris asked in a soft tone.

"Corona and her boyfriend broke into some old woman's home up in Harlem and took the woman's social security money." said Edwin.

"I thought her boyfriend was still in jail." said Paris turning away from the Edwin and walking toward the stairs.

Edwin grabs Paris by the arm and spun her around to face him. "Look Paris all I need to know from you is money, do you have any?"

Paris snatching her arm away from his grip. "I don't have any money; and how much is Corona's bail."

"I don't know." shouted Edwin.

"Wait a minute, you don't know?!" ask Paris trying to easing herself up the steps away from Edwin. "Well don't you think you ought to find out the exact amount before you go asking for money?"

Edwin eyes were filled with rage with hate for Paris and he slapped Paris with the back of his hand and Paris fell backwards. She grab onto the handrail managing not to hit the steps. The phone rang in kitchen and Edwin jumped down three steps and ran down the foyer to the kitchen to answer the phone.

"Hello, hello" screamed Edwin as he paced back and forth in the kitchen.

Hey Corona, what's going on? Where are you?

Paris put her hand up to her mouth and felt the blood dripping from her lower lip.

"Good, I am glad you are out." said Edwin.

Paris made her way up the stairs and went into the bathroom and took a wash cloth and ran cold water on it and pressed it on her lower lip. Then she came out of the bathroom and went to the closet and put a black t-shirt dress and a pair of low heel shoes; just as she was coming downstairs Edwin met her at the bottom of the steps.

"I am sorry" said Edwin "I was just so upset over Corona."

Paris ignores Edwin's apology as she walks down the stairs into the foyer, and walks over to the bench and picking up her handbag. She walks pass Edwin down the foyer to the kitchen and opened the freezer and pulled out an ice cube and wrapped it in a paper towel and places it on her lower lip where Edwin had hit her.

"Are you alright?" asked Edwin trying to sound like he cared and he walked over to Paris to give her a hug. Paris step away from Edwin and took the ice away from her lower lip.

"No, I am not alright" said Paris speaking slowly. She threw the ice cube wrapped in the paper towel into the sink and then walked to the back door that opens up into the garage. "If you ever put your hands on me again I will 9.1.1 your sick derange behind all the way to Lewisburg State Prison and believe me I will press all the charges that the law will allow against you. Don't put your hands on me again."

Paris turned and walkout slamming kitchen door behind her. Paris could still hear Edwin still apologizing for hitting her. He had slapped her all the way from New York to the mountains of Pennsylvania. He had slapped her out of one century right into a new century. Every time he spoke to his mother or had to deal with Corona's drama, Edwin would attack her. Paris was hurt and tired of Edwin and his dysfunctional derange family. She couldn't forgive him and she prayed for God to help her to escape the insanity.

"What happen to your lip?" asked Virginia.

Paris didn't know what to say; she couldn't tell Virginia that she bumped into a door knob that was the excuse for a black eye.

"If I told you" said Paris grinning "you wouldn't believe me."

"Go ahead and try me" Virginia said smiling.

"You ever seen that commercial on television where the bird is flying and it bumps into a window?" asked Paris.

"Yeah." said Virginia.

"Well that's what happened to me." laughs Paris.

"You got to be joking" said Virginia laughing. "How did you manage to do that?"

"I went into the gas station to pay for gas and I turn around and walked right into the window and busted my lip; for some reason I thought the door was open. I guess I had a bird brain moment. Laughs Paris.

"Well Sister Paris that sure sound like a bird brain moment to me and you kissed the door!"

They both laughed about the made up story and they went into talking about all their unbelievable "when nobody was looking moments." Paris couldn't believe she sat there and told that outrages lie and Virginia seemed to she believed it. But Paris was sick to her stomach about the whole situation and having to deal with her husband and his family from another planet. An hour and a half had passed and Virginia thanked Paris for lunch and promised the next lunch date would be on her. She rushed out of the café to pick up her daughters from school.

Paris stopped by the supermarket to pick up something for dinner. She decided to make Edwin's favorite meal for him as his punishment. She would be quiet the whole week and make all of Edwin's favorite dishes and he would be scared and accused her of poisoning him. Funny thing is Edwin would eat anyway and in spite of his fears of being poison and yet he never hit Paris. Only when Inez would call or when Corona had drama. But Paris couldn't stop talking for a whole week; this week with company coming over for the weekend.

The house was quiet and the pitter patter of the raindrops against the window pane just made the tears rolled down Paris's face as she prepare Edwin's favorite meal fried chicken, collard greens and baked macaroni and cheese with cornbread. And of course when Edwin came home he was surprised about having his favorite dinner and he made remarks about how he hopes Paris wasn't poisoning him. He washed his hands and made his favorite drink. Paris made his plate and sat it on the table and as usual Edwin picked up his plate and went into his man-cave and turned on the television. Paris went into the living room and pickup her bible and started to read feeling satisfied because she knew Edwin had felt some kind of fear.

Chapter 6

The barbeque was just what her idiot husband wanted. He embarrassed her before their company. This was the first time, by calling her a liar when she was talking about the changes the church was going to make throughout the winter months. This was the first time Virginia had been to their home. Paris glanced over at Virginia; Paris could see the smile pasted on Virginia's face. It was as if Virginia had seen something that night and she was concealing it with a smile. Paris wrapped up a lot of the barbeque and gave it to her guest to take home. Paris would always end up throwing out most of the food. When Edwin found out the next morning he yelled at Paris.

"What's wrong with you Paris giving all our food away?" yelled Edwin he slammed the refrigerator door shut.

"We always end up throwing out most of the food." Said Paris sipping her tea and she let out a little giggle. "Yeah I guess I did give away too much food; but it's plenty left over for dinner."

Edwin pulled out the left over barbeque chicken and ribs and put the food in the microwave.

"Well" said Paris getting up from the kitchen table. "There goes dinner."

She left the kitchen and went downstairs in the basement to wash clothes and she saw a box where she had all her painting supplies. Behind the box stood one of her paintings that she was going to hang up but never did because she knew it would upset Edwin. Paris dusted off the painting of a child kneel down at the bedside praying in her pajamas. The painting was one of Paris best paintings; in fact she won first place award for it in New York.

"What you got there?" Paris was startled by the sound of Edwin's voice and she turned around and she was angry that he interrupted her memory of a moment of success; but that wasn't anything new he always managed to take the "O" out of her joy and made her feel bad.

"A painting" said Paris and she could see Edwin's eyes were raging with hate and anger.

"I thought I told you to get rid of that thing." yelled Edwin. You shouldn't have painting of people praying to gods in the house.

"Edwin it's just a picture of a little girl saying her prayers before she goes to sleep." said Paris as she held the painting in her arms. Edwin snatches the painting and threw it to the floor, stomping it; and picks it up and then he turns and went up the stairs. He walks through the kitchen to the back door and out into the garage and threw painting behind the trash can. He came back in the house and slammed the door. He went into the kitchen took his plate out of the microwave and made himself a drink. He walked over to his man cave and sat down and turned on the television. Paris was so angry she had to stop and prayed not to cuss him out.

"God please help me....help me to control myself, my thoughts because right now all I want to do is kill him." The tears rolled down Paris' face as she walked up the stairs to the guest bedroom where she cried and pray for a release from her crazy husband. She prayed and asks God to help her not to hate Edwin because she knew hate would make her kill him. Hate would end both their lives; even her son's life. Paris cried herself to sleep and when she woke up it was about three o'clock in the afternoon. Paris went downstairs where she found Edwin and Anthony playing video games in his man cave. Paris felt listless and hungry so she opened the refrigerator door finding only the left over potato salad from the barbeque.

"Hey Mom what are we having for dinner?" asked Anthony.

"Soup and sandwiches." said Paris taking out the lunch meat and mayo from the refrigerator.

"I don't want that" yelled Edwin.

"You don't have to eat it" Paris yelled back. "Do you want soup and sandwiches, Anthony?" "Nah." said Anthony sounding sad. "I'll just go to the store and pick something up."

"Anthony you need to learn how to cook. It's all a part of survival" said Paris making herself a sandwich speaking in soft tone; she felt sorry for Anthony; but she was too tired to cook.

"Yeah I know Mom. said Anthony.

"What cha going to get from the store?" asked Edwin playing video games.

Paris picked up her sandwich and her cup of soup and went up stairs to her office where she would sit and play games on her computer. She really didn't feel like hearing the ritual of Edwin and Anthony trying to make up their minds about what they were going to eat. It always ended up ordering KFCs because there were very few places to eat out in Hidden Valley. By ten o'clock Paris was in bed Edwin and Anthony were still playing video games.

"Paris is you going to work today?" Ask Edwin standing in front the snack bar drinking orange juice.

"No" said Paris. I'm staying home today; in fact I am thinking of quitting because I haven't been feeling well lately.

"Well you should look into getting disability before you quit". Said Edwin putting his glass in the sink and placing the bottle of orange juice back into the refrigerator; he walked over to the table were Paris was sitting and looked over her shoulder.

"What are you writing?" Ask Edwin

"I am writing out a shopping list" said Paris turning around looking at Edwin. I'm trying to figure out what to make for dinner when your mother and Corona come.

"Let's make a turkey dinner" said Edwin.

"Why don't you cook dinner for a change Edwin; your mother always has something negative to say about my cooking."

"She does not." said Edwin growing angry

"Yes she does and besides no one can make a better turkey than you" said Paris smiling. "And you can make all the sides you like as well. I bet your mother will complain about the food if she thinks I cooked it."

"Yeah okay I'll cook and I'm telling you Paris; you are wrong." said Edwin taking his keys off the key rack and going out the garage door. "I see you this evening"

"Bye" said Paris and she was happy because she didn't have to cook dinner for her crazy in-laws. She got up and walked over to the snack bar and picked up the receiver and called her job and left a message on the answering machine that she wasn't coming in. Paris went upstairs and took a shower and put on one of Edwin t-shirts and a pair of her sweat pants.

All of a sudden Paris was feeling on top of the world. She prompted herself upon the banister to go downstairs and slid down hollering "Wee". Then she fell off the banister onto floor and tumble over and hitting her leg on the grandfather clock. She got up laughing and rubbing her right leg and started limping to the kitchen; when the house phone rang.

Hello ..... Hello......hello sang Paris leaning on the snack bar.

Oh hi Paris this is your mother-in-law. Sister Benson.

Paris just took a deep breath and rolled her eyes up to the ceiling as she thought to herself. "Now she is Sister Benson....... Lord please, help me to be good."

"Hello Sister Benson; how are you?

"Oh I am doing just fine and how are you feeling today Paris?"

All of a sudden Paris started to feel sick and she didn't bother to answer because she knew Inez would have been just thrilled to see her drop dead.

"I was just calling to tell Edwin that I don't know if I will be coming this weekend; 'because I don't have a way back home and I don't want to be going home in the dark. whined Inez.

"Well did you try calling Edwin on his cell phone?" asked Paris as if she didn't know the real reason why Inez called the house. Inez always called before her scheduled visits and pretended that she didn't want to come for a visit in order to lay out her plans.

"Inez." said Paris clearing her throat. "Excuse me Sister Benson you always spend the night when you come for a visit and Edwin always picks you up and drives you back home; so I don't see why there would be a problem with you coming this weekend.

"I have to see. I have to call Edwin to see if he can come and pick me and Corona up from New York and bring us back home. I'm getting too old to be riding up and down on buses and trains. Bye." said Inez.

"Why......oh why did I listen to my mother and marry into this left back, jackass, crazy family?" Paris asked herself as she slammed down the receiver on phone. She picked up her pocketbook and took out her keys and then headed out to the supermarket. Paris could not help but to think about Inez as she did the grocery shopping; one minute Inez is a nice quiet pleasant woman and then the next minute the woman is a living nightmare. And Corona always lying and scheming; it was obvious to everyone that knew Corona that her god and father was the devil. And these was the folks she had to spend the next two days with including Edwin and that was a life time sentence.

Edwin came home that evening slamming the door and screaming. Paris where are you?

"I am here in the kitchen." said Paris frowning. "Why are you screaming; what is wrong with you?"

Next thing Paris knew she was holding her mouth with blood gushing out. Edwin had backed hand in her mouth again. "I told you to watch what you say to my mother, you no good black whore.

Paris ran upstairs and ran into master bathroom and got a wash cloth and held it on her mouth and she cried and cried because she knew she had no one that cared anything about her. Paris knew she had nowhere to go. She was stuck in this hell hole with these crazy people. She left out of the bathroom and went into the guest bedroom and lay across the bed and cried until she felt Edwin standing over her.

"Hey Paris," said Edwin sitting down on the side of the bed "I'm sorry for going off on you like that but I was just upset because I wanted my mother and Corona to come up for the weekend; can you forgive me?"

Paris couldn't answer all she could do is cry and she cried and Edwin lay across the bed next to Paris and holds her in his arms. You know Paris, sometimes we are going to have arguments but it doesn't mean we don't love each other. Paris just could not stop crying and never spoke a word.

"Come on Paris are you going to stop crying?" Edwin sat up easing Paris off his arm. "You mean to tell me you are not going to forgive me?

"I'm calling the"......said Paris but she was interrupted by Anthony coming home.

"Hey Dad, Hey Mom where is everybody at?

"We are upstairs" yelled Edwin standing up walking into the hall way "We are coming down stairs." He turns around and looks at Paris.

"Fix yourself up and come on downstairs you can keep me company while I prepare the food for tomorrow." said Edwin and by the way I want you to make a cake.

"I thought your mother and Corona wasn't coming" said Paris. Sitting up and sliding her slippers on.

"Oh they are coming, I am going to pick them up at the park and ride in town and then I am going to take them back home on Sunday." Said Edwin smiling as though he did nothing wrong.

"So why did you come home yelling and screaming for and slapping me in my mouth?" ask Paris now standing up and walking toward Edwin.

"I had a bad day at the office and on top of everything else mommy called nagging me about picking her up. Said Edwin grinning like it was all a joke.

"I am calling the police on your crazy ...." said Paris

Anthony came running up the stairs yelling at the top of his voice interrupting Paris. "Hey Dad....hey Mom. I am going back to college. I got accepted at a college in California to design cars".

"That is great Anthony" Paris walked over to Anthony and hugged him. "I am so happy that you decided to go back to school and do something you like. After all you love art and you love cars, what a great combination!"

What happen to your lip Mom? Ask Anthony looking concern.

"Your father tripped and back slapped me in my mouth" said Paris covering her mouth with her hand.

"Don't pay your mother no mind; she always joking." said Edwin. "Besides you don't need to go to college Anthony." Walking down the stairs with his arm wrapped around Anthony's shoulders. And besides can't you find a college to go here in the states?

"Edwin California is in the states.....why are you trying to discourage Anthony from moving on with his life? ask Paris walking down the stairs behind Edwin and Anthony as she held a tissue on her lower lip to stop the bleeding.

"I meant the state of Pennsylvania okay!" yell Edwin walking into the kitchen throwing his hands up.

"Anthony needs to move on and make a future for himself; after you are dead and gone what do you expect him to do?"

Edwin ignored Paris's question and in all the excitement of Anthony's announcement Paris forgot about calling the police on Edwin. They spent the rest of the night talking about Anthony moving to California and laughing and joking about Anthony's car designs as they prepared the food. At that moment they were a happy family. Well at least it was to Anthony.

Nine o'clock the next morning Edwin had the turkey in the oven and Paris was putting the chocolate icing on the cake and Anthony was still in the bed asleep. Corona called several times that morning and twice she called to ask if her kids could stay the week; claiming it would be like a summer vacation.

Paris walked over to Edwin while he was on the phone with Corona and told Edwin no.

"I have not been feeling well" and I have doctor appointments all next week" Said Paris.

"Oh God, please forgive me about lying about those doctors' appointment." Paris prayed again for forgiveness for lying.

"Paris is not feeling well and she has doctor's appointments lined up all next week; I have to go Corona. I'll talk to you later." said Edwin hanging up the house phone.

Paris was happy Edwin stuck to his decision about not letting the kids come for the week. Edwin had missed his calling in life he should have been a lawyer or an actor. Once Edwin would think up a lie he had no problem living up to the lie. Paris had never seen or knew anyone like Edwin or his immediate family for that fact. When it came to lying they were all experts and they would lie and believe the lie till they died.

Chapter 7

An hour later Corona called back asking could she bring one of her friends for dinner and Edwin told her no. Corona and Inez called several more time before they got to Pennsylvania. By three o'clock they had arrived at the house and Corona and the kids were loud and rowdy as usual and even though this was their normal behavior Paris still could not get use to them. Edwin did an excellent job as usual in cooking the turkey dinner.

"Ah Paris the food was alright" said Inez but the turkey was a little dry and tough and the collard greens were gritty and the stuffing was too watery!"

"Oh really Inez, but I didn't cook." Paris smile and look over at Edwin.

Well who cooked? asked Inez; looking surprised as she stands up and steps away from the table.

"I cooked." said Edwin with a disgusted look on his face.

"Well it sure enough was good." said Inez laughing.

"When did you learned to cook?" asked Corona also standing up and walking away from the table.

"I taught Edwin to cook when we first got married." said Paris as she cleared the dishes off the table.

"Aunt Paris can we have some cake now?" ask Tince, licking her lips.

"Of course you can Tince" said Paris. "Would like to go a get the dessert plates for me off the snack bar?"

"Sure." Said Tince; getting up from the table and running out of the dining room into the kitchen.

"Tell me something Corona why on earth do you have Tince wearing all that bling-bling around her neck and hair extension and she is only seven years old?" asked Paris.

"That is what all the kids are wearing up now Paris." Said Corona looking at Paris crossed eyed.

"I told mama that Tince was too young to be wearing that junk; that's why my sister thinks she is grown." said Butch passing his dinner plate to Paris.

"Thank you Tince' said Paris as Tince put the desert plates on the table. "You know Corona you should be educating your daughter not to be like the kids in the streets and you should be teaching her about God and seeing that she gets a good education."

Corona rolled her eyes and looked across the room at Edwin sitting at the end of the table eating.

"What do you want to be when you grow up Tince?" asked Paris.

"I wanna do hair" said Tince twisting her braids.

"Oh please" said Butch "you can't even do your own hair."

"Now Butch that is not being fair. She will be doing her own hair soon. Said Paris as she passed Butch a slice of cake. "Now you all sit back down and have some cake"

"I wanted to be a nurse before their father stopped me; that would be a good job for you Tince. said Inez sitting down next to Edwin.

"I want to do hair!" exclaimed Tince.

"Tince being a cosmetologist is a very good career and you can make a very good salary at it too; but you are not going to succeed at anything if you don't study hard in school and keep your eye on the Christ so he can direct you in everything you do."

"Yes I know Aunt Paris." Said Tince; sitting down at the table.

"Well don't you forget it and don't let no one steal your thunder. said Paris.

"What's my thunder?" asked Tince.

"Your thunder is your dream of becoming a cosmetologist." said Paris smiling as she passed Tince a slice of cake.

They all sat around the table eating chocolate cake and ice cream and Inez asked Edwin did he make the cake too and when Edwin said no and Inez said the cake taste like corn bread with icing on it.

"Yeah okay Inez" said Paris shaking her head and laughing.

"Thank God for a dishwasher" said Paris and no one paid her any attention as they all exited from the dining room through the kitchen into the family room also known as Edwin's man cave. Anthony went out to hang out with his friends and Tince and Butch ran upstairs to Anthony's room to play video games. After Paris finished with the dishes she felt like going to bed but she thought it might appear that she was just being rude; so she decided to join her family as they were all sitting around relaxed with the television on.

Paris heard Inez talking. At first Paris didn't understand what Inez was talking about. Edwin and Corona didn't have anything to say. Paris started listening to what Inez was talking about and she couldn't believe what she was hearing. Paris looks over at Edwin and then at Corona and they seemed to be comfortable with the conversation; however they wasn't saying anything. Inez was talking about the devil and his demons as if she had a personal relationship with them.

"I don't know what wrong with you Inez, but we are Christians and our thoughts are God's thoughts. We only talk about our relationship with God and the Christ. And here you call yourself a Christian and you sitting up here talking about the devil." Paris felt like telling Inez to get out but she knew that wasn't going to be in her best interest. All three of them might jump on her and beat her to death. "You go to bible classes three times a week and evidently it don't mean a hill a beans to you because you are sitting here talking about all the things the devil can do."

It made Paris sick to her stomach; she felt like she could throw up something she never ate. "Let me explain something to you Inez." Said Paris angry and upset as she was sitting on the edge of the couch. "In the Bible at Proverb chapter 2 verse 4 let us know that we are supposed to keep searching and seeking for the things of God, like silver that we may understand the fear of God and understand the knowledge of God; and He will give us wisdom and discernment." Paris looked across the room at Edwin reclining in his chair drinking his gin and coke and then Corona who was sitting at the other end of the coach looking like a full blown idiot watching television. They were all crazy demonic idiots as far as Paris was concern.

"I know what the bible says." Said Inez clearing her throat. "but the devil has his plans of..."

Paris got up and left the room before Inez could finish her sentence and she went and pick up her bible off the table in the foyer and walk outside and sat in the rocking chair on the front porch and of course the flies were out but Paris felt better outside with the flies; than inside in the house with those disgusting, deranged, demonic things that was supposed to be her family. Then the conversation that she had with Inez's minister came back to her from several years ago when they use to live in New York. Brother Little called to speak to Edwin about Inez.

"Hello" said Paris wiping the sweat from her forehead. It was a heat wave that day and the last thing Paris wanted to be bothered with someone calling who was rude and didn't know how to speak on the telephone.

"Hello" repeated Paris with her hand on her hip.

"Ah Hello...is Brother Edwin in?" Asked Brother Little

"No" replied Paris. Paris didn't recognize the voice of this so-called brother that didn't even greet her over the phone with a decent hello.

"May I ask who is calling?" asked Paris

"Um... I need to speak with Ed....Edwin...........this is Brother Little."

Paris then knew who she was talking to and she didn't care for the little short, fat, bald headed, ugly man that was always up in Inez's business and telling her what to do as if Inez didn't have a husband; so what if Edwin's father didn't go to church that didn't give Brother Little the rights over Inez or her household."

"Oh hi Brother Little this is Paris" She paused for a second but Brother Little never greeted her back." Paris figured it was because Inez told Brother Little all kind of lies about her.

"How are you and your family?" asked Paris; trying to overlook this rude so-called Christian Brother.

"We are fine thank you." said Brother Little stuttering and clearing his throat. "I was calling to talk to Edwin about his mother."

Paris did not want to hear anything about Inez. It was just too hot to be bother with Inez's drama. "Well Brother Little." said Paris taking a deep breath "Edwin is not home right now; I can ask him to call you back?"

"I just wanted to tell Edwin that his mother is demonic." said Brother Little.

"Well" said Paris. "Just because she is mentally ill doesn't mean she is demonic.

"Just give Edwin the message. He has my number and he can call me whenever he gets in." Brother Little just hung up without even saying good bye.

When Edwin came home from work that evening; Paris was angry.

"Brother Little called Edwin to speak to you about your mother."

Edwin didn't seem to be concern about the phone call. "Yeah what did he have to say?" Asked Edwin going into the refrigerator as he took out a can of Coke-Cola and took a bottle of Gin from the cabinet and sat it down on the counter and then went to the freezer and took out the ice tray. Edwin never said a word and he had no facial expression.

"Well." said Paris leaning on the entrance of the kitchen wall with her arms folded across her chest. "Brother Little wanted to tell you that your mother is demonic."

Edwin acted as though Paris wasn't there and he had not heard a single word she said. Edwin put the ice tray back in the freezer and walked past her into the living room and sat down in his recliner and picked up the remote control, turned on the television and start surfing the channels. Paris followed behind Edwin and she didn't get any response from him.

"Well Edwin, I think that is a terrible thing to say about your mother; just because she suffers with a mental illness and then for Brother little to leave such a horrible message with me to give to you." said Paris standing in the living room waiting for Edwin to respond.

"What can I say Paris....... he said it."

"Yeah, that's right Edwin he said it, now are you going to call him back?" asked Paris.

"I call him tomorrow" said Edwin. As far as Edwin was concern tomorrow never would come because he had no intentions of returning Brother Little's phone call. And as far as Paris was concern it was just another crazy horror-o-mama moment in the Benson Family.

Paris sat there on the porch with tears in her eyes and she opens her bible and read Isaiah 40: 10 "Do not be afraid for I am with you. Do not be anxious for I am your God. I will fortify you, yes I will help you. I will really help you. I will really hold on to you with my right hand of righteousness." All Paris could do is cry and pray. She had never felt so alone in her life. Paris managed to get up and go back into the house and get 2 blankets and a pillow from the hall closet. Edwin, Inez and Corona was so busy laughing and talking they didn't hear Paris enter or leave the house. She went back outside and laid one blanket out on the swing bench and laid the pillow on top and then she laid down and covers herself with the second blanket. Paris prayed and prayed that God would help her to escape this insanity that surrounded her. She prayed and cried until she fell asleep.

"Wake up Mom, wake up." Anthony was standing over Paris tapping her shoulder.

"Oh what's going on?" Said Paris rubbing her eyes and her bible slipped off the side of the swing bench on to the porch floor.

"You slept out here all night?" asked Anthony looking surprised

"Oh my God" said Paris I must have fallen asleep out here reading my bible.

"Where is everybody?" asked Anthony; as he bended over and picked up the bible and helps Paris up from the bench.

"Oh my God I am stiff." said Paris holding her back trying to stand up. "Whew, Rigamortis must have set in."

"Rigamortis Mom?" Ask Anthony looking confused. "That is what happens to people after they died."

"Well that is how I feel." said Paris.

"Mom I can't believe you slept out here all night, and dad or no one else came out here to look for you." said Anthony helping Paris walk to the front door.

"I am so tired Anthony, I don't even want to discuss it. And by the way where were you last night?" asked Paris.

"I called dad last night and told Dad that I was spending the night at Carl's house."

Anthony and Paris walked in the house and they saw Edwin, Inez, Corona and the kids sitting at that kitchen table.

"So what cha cooking for breakfast Paris?" Ask Edwin.

Paris and Anthony looked at each other. Anthony had the look of fear in his eyes. Paris stop dead in her tracks and her inner voice came to her "Control yourself Paris; you know you have a very nasty temper. Seek peace and pursue it."

"Well." said Paris as she pasted smile on her face. "Let me go upstairs and take a shower and I'll come back down and whip you all up some pancakes, eggs and sausages.

"Well excuse me" said Inez laughing "I didn't think you had it in you after you slept outside all night."

Edwin, Corona and the kids all joined in laughing at Paris.

"Well I tell you Sister Benson it's nothing like sleeping under the stars; you all should try it the next time you all come for a visit." said

Paris yawning as she slowly walks up the stairs thinking about how she would like to curse them out. Then she would have to pray for forgiveness; it just wasn't worth it. But now Paris knows that Inez is not only insane but she is also demonic so the less Paris has to say to her the better off she felt and the very thought of sleeping in the same house with her made Paris's skin crawl. As far as Paris was concern they were all insane except for her and Anthony.

Paris went into the bathroom and took a long hot shower. The hot water felt so good running down her stiff, aching back. Paris cried and cried. Edwin had the audacity to ask her to cook breakfast after she slept out on the porch all night and Edwin or no one else came out to see about her? The thought occurred to her while she making for breakfast them, she could put arsenic in their food and kill all of them. Except for Anthony; after all she love Anthony and he had to live in order to make a dream or two come true. Paris toy around with the ideal of killing them and then thought about how that would also end her life. She imagined herself being put to death by lethal injection. Paris told herself the Benson family wasn't that important to die for. She got out of the shower and dried off and brushed her teeth, and then she slipped into her night shirt and tied her hair up in a scarf and took out a bottle of aspirins out of her night stand and popped two aspirins in her mouth. She went back into the bathroom and cups her hands under the faucet and drank the water. She dried her hands off and went back into the bedroom, got into bed and fell asleep. Fifteen minutes later Edwin came upstairs with Anthony following closely behind him.

"Man look at your mother; I can't believe your mother came up stairs and went to sleep and had us waiting for her to make breakfast." said Edwin standing in the doorway of the master bedroom looking at Paris sleeping.

"Well Dad she did sleep outside all night" said Anthony walking to his bedroom.

"I should wake her up" laughed Edwin

"I wouldn't advise you to do that Dad." Said Anthony, as he turned around and walked back into the foyer toward Edwin. "Besides, I thought you all were going to stop off at I Hop for breakfast on your way back to New York."

"Yeah I guess you're right man; I'll let her sleep. Said Edwin walking down the steps; ten minutes later Edwin, Inez, Corona and the kids had left the house.

It was a bright Sunday afternoon and Paris felt refreshed after her long nap; however, she felt guilty for missing church for the second time in the month. Paris went into the closet and pulled out one of Edwin's old tee-shirts and she pull out a pair of sweat pants from the dresser drawer. She went downstairs and was happy to see that Edwin and his horror-a-rama family had left. She went into the kitchen and saw dishes piled up in the sink.

"Now wait a minute, I know that I washed dishes before I went out on the porch last night." Said Paris to herself; she stood in front of the kitchen sink with her hands on her hips looking confused.

"Hey Mom, how are you feeling?" asked Anthony; walking into the kitchen and carrying a basketball under his arm.

"I don't know" said Paris looking confused "I know I washed dishes last night."

"They ate twice; Mom." said Anthony.

"Where are you going?" asked Paris still in a state of confusion and turning around looking at Anthony.

"I am going to Pocahontas Park to run some ball." said Anthony walking toward the back door.

"You are not going to stay and help me clean up?" asked Paris feeling deserted.

"Mom I only have a couple more weeks to go before I head out to California and I want to spend as much time as I can hanging out with my friends." said Anthony looking pitiful.

"Understood, but could you take out the garbage." said Paris as she went around the kitchen and in the family room picking up empty cans and bottles.

"Here Anthony put these in the recycling bin and don't forget to drag it out to the sidewalk along with the garbage cans." said Paris.

Anthony set his basket ball down on the floor in the garage and in five minutes Anthony had the garbage cans sitting out on the sidewalk; he ran back in the house and picked up his basketball and got into his car and waved goodbye to Paris.

By seven o'clock that evening Paris manage not only to clean up the kitchen but she also strip all the sheets off the beds that her in-laws slept on and washed the linen and made up the beds and cleaned all four bathrooms. Paris forgot to eat and it was no way in the world was she going to cook. Paris changes her clothes and went to KFC's for dinner.

Chapter 8

"Hey Paris is that you?" said a man standing on line behind Paris in KFC.

Paris turned around and looked; she could hardly believe her eyes. The man standing behind her was medium built, he was five nine and had a smooth dark brown complexion with jet black short curly hair; with dark brown eyes. He had a trimmed mustache and a shadow beard. He was smiling from ear to ear and that brighten up Paris's day.

Hey Papa, how are you doing?" said Paris as she fell into the man's arms and they embraced each other.

"Papa it is so good to see you; what are you doing here in Left Back City?" That was Paris nickname for Hidden Valley being that just about everyone she met in Hidden Valley appeared to be behind in time.

"Wow Paris you look great." said Papa.

Papa and his brothers and sister lived next door to Paris and her family. They all went to the same church and the same schools and they were always in each other's apartments. Papa real name was Daxton Williams. Daxton acquired the nickname Papa because when his father died from a car accident and Daxton took on many responsibilities by getting a part-time job and then he started acting like he was everybody's father. In fact Daxton had become Paris's older brother as well; he always looked out for her at school. Then Daxton's mother decided to move to New Jersey and that liked to have killed Paris; she felt deserted that her family had left her behind and she never saw them again.

Paris and Papa got a table together and they talked about old times. Papa had been married and divorced twice and he had 2 daughters by his first wife and 3 sons by his second wife. And now he was on the road all the time pushing tour buses throughout all the east coast of the United States and into Canada. Paris told Papa how she was married for 25 years and had one son; but she didn't bother to go into telling Papa about her crazy demonic husband and in-laws. He might think she had lost her mind.

"Wow its nine fifteen." said Paris looking at her watch. "Boy time sure does goes by fast when you are having a good time. How long are you going to be in town?" Asked Paris getting up from the table and putting her pocketbook on her shoulder

"I have to leave tomorrow morning I am heading up to Rochester and Utica NY and then into Canada." said Papa. Standing up and picking up the trays carrying them over to the garbage cans.

"Wow" said Paris following behind Papa. "I am sorry we won't be able to spend more time together."

Papa and Paris exchanged phone numbers and email addresses. Papa promised he would call her the next time he was back in Pennsylvania. They hugged and said their goodbyes. Paris wondered how Edwin would take to Papa. After all Edwin was a jealous insane man; but she had to tell him about Papa because she was going to stay in touch with Papa whether Edwin liked it or not.

When Paris arrived at home she saw Edwin's car in the drive way. It had started to rain so Paris ran into the house from the garage into the kitchen.

"Where were you?" yelled Edwin the minute Paris stepped in the house. "I have been home for hours wondering where you were at."

"You were home for hours?" asked Paris kicking her shoes off at the door "What time did you get home?"

"I been back home since four o'clock and there is nothing in this house to eat." yelled Edwin.

"Where were you in the house at four o'clock because I didn't see you?" asked Paris.

Paris walked down the foyer away from the kitchen and up the stairs leaving Edwin downstairs mumbling his lies about what time he got home. By eleven o'clock Paris was washed up and had her PJs on and in the bed.

Paris woke up panting and coughing and waving her arms and kicking the covers off her. She was having those nightmares again that someone was smothering her. She looked over at Edwin and he was asleep. As soon as Paris regained her composure the phone rang. Paris looked at the clock and saw it was one o'clock in the morning and wondered who could be calling.

"Hello" answered Paris.

"Who is on the phone" asked Edwin sitting up in the bed.

"This is Nurse Walsh from Bellevue hospital in New York City; may I speak with Mr. Edwin Benson" the nurse spoke in a nasal tone.

"Ah, just one minute" Paris handed the phone receiver over to Edwin.

Who is it? Edwin asked again.

"It's a nurse from Bellevue hospital." replied Paris.

"Hello." answered Edwin.

"Hello is this Mr. Edwin Benson? asked Nurse Walsh.

"Yeah this is him" said Edwin getting out of the bed.

"I am calling in reference to Mrs. Inez Benson your mother; she was brought into the hospital by the police at 12 am this morning because she was running down the street in her night gown on Eighth Avenue and 125th Street. She asked that you come to the hospital."

"Can it wait until morning? asked Edwin getting out bed. "I live in Pennsylvania."

"You will need to sign some papers in order for her to be admitted into the hospital. She won't admit herself sir." said Nurse Walsh, becoming impatient with Edwin.

"Yeah okay, I will be there in a couple of hours."

Edwin told Paris he had to go admit his mother in the hospital.

"Why can't Corona admit her?" asked Paris

"She doesn't trust Corona." said Edwin.

"Just be careful driving." Paris knew it was nothing else to say; it was the same old story. When the seasons would change Inez would stop taking her meds and lose her mind. In fact Paris couldn't wait until Edwin would leave so she could relax and have a cup of tea.

"I'll be back as soon as I can" said Edwin leaving out the kitchen door and going into the garage. As soon as Paris heard Edwin drive off she filled up the tea kettle and put it on the stove.

Chapter 9

Edwin's cell phone rang and he saw it was Jennifer's number. "Hey Jennifer baby how are you? Why are you calling me at two in the morning?"

"I will be landing in JFK airport in New York later on this morning. Why don't you come and meet me."

"Hey that will be fine...I am going into New York I have to go and admit Paris in Bellevue hospital."

"Really, is she okay?" ask Jennifer trying to sound like she was concerned.

"Yeah she is alright; the police picked her up running down the street butt naked in over in East Harlem." said Edwin laughing.

"What!" said Jennifer laughing hysterically. "Listen I got to go we are hitting air pockets I call you soon as I land."

As soon as Edwin clicks off his cell phone; he calls Corona.

"Hello Corona." Edwin could barely hear Corona when she answered the phone.

"Yeah" said Corona sounding like an old man waking up out of a deep sleep. "Why are you calling me before day in the morning?"

"Mommy is back in Bellevue Hospital can you meet me there?" asked Edwin

"What time are you going to get there?" asked Corona

"I am on my way to the hospital now. I should be there around three thirty or four o'clock" said Edwin.

"Okay" said Corona, call me when you get to the hospital.

Edwin became frustrated and anxious driving around the hospital for an hour looking for parking; he finally gave up and drove five blocks down to the nearest parking garage. To Edwin's surprise when he entered the hospital it wasn't crowded as he approached the information desk.

"Excuse me can you tell me where I can find Mrs. Inez Benson she was brought into the emergency room last night?"

"Yes sir." said the receptionist looking up at Edwin. "You said the person's name is Mrs. Inez Benson?

"Yeah that's right." said Edwin becoming annoyed.

"Mrs. Benson is on the fifth floor and has been admitted to room 501; however, visiting hours is not until eleven o'clock sir.

"What do you mean admitted; I came all the way from Pennsylvania to sign her in the hospital."

"I m sorry for the inconvenience Sir, but she has already been admitted." said the Receptionist.

"Who admitted her?" asked Edwin.

"May I ask Sir what is your relationship to the patient?" asked the Receptionist.

"She is my mother." said Edwin lowering his voice and leaning on the information desk.

"Perhaps you would like to speak with her doctor." suggested the Receptionist, giving Edwin a slip of paper. "Turn to the right at the end of this corridor and you will see a bank of elevators; take the elevator to the fifth floor and then make a left to the nurse's station."

After Edwin went through the whole ordeal of stopping at the nurse's station on the fifth floor; he sat in the waiting room nodding for forty five minutes waiting to speak with Inez's doctor.

"Hello Mr. Benson." said the Doctor

"Yes" said Edwin standing up.

"I am Doctor Keller and your mother was brought in the hospital at 12 am this morning and admitted by the arresting officer. Right now she is medicated and resting."

"What was she arrested for?" asked Edwin with fear in his eyes of what he might hear.

"Please have a seat Mr. Benson" said Dr. Keller.

Edwin sat down on the couch and Dr. Keller sat down in the chair directly in front of Edwin.

"Mrs. Benson was arrested for indecent exposure. She was running through oncoming traffic her nightgown talking loudly disturbing the peace; so an officer arrested her and admitted her into the hospital."

"So why did the nurse call me to come in to have her admitted to the hospital" asked Edwin looking dazed and confused. Edwin was angry and just thinking about how Jennifer was going to be in town and he was going to have to spend his day looking after his mother.

"Mr. Benson the nurse called you because your mother asked that you be informed that she was the hospital" said Dr. Keller speaking softly and slowly.

"The nurse could have waited until a more decent hour to call." yelled Edwin jumping up off the coach and went to pacing back and forth. "And besides that nurse said nothing about the officer admitting my mother into this hospital; you all should have a better system in contacting people; I came all the way from Hidden Valley, Pennsylvania" yelled Edwin with blood shot eyes and wiping the sweat from his forehead with his hand.

"Mr. Benson I understand that you are upset. But your mother is safe and she is going to be okay" Said Dr. Keller. "Please come with me Mr. Benson so I can speak with you in private."

Dr. Keller walked in a nearby examining room and Edwin followed behind her. "I want just want to take your vitals and speak with you in private; so please have a seat."

Edwin sat down on the exam table as the doctor the check his blood pressure and his heart rate. "Mr. Benson is you taking medication for high blood pressure?"

"Yes I take Bystolic 20 milligrams once a day." Said Edwin

"When is the last time you took your medication?

"About a several weeks ago" said Edwin looking worried.

"Your blood pressure is 160 over 100" said Dr. Keller as she stood up from her laptop and walked over to Edwin and held onto his risk while she looked at her watch. After she finished listening to Edwin's heart she asked Edwin a series of other health questions and Edwin answered no to all of the doctors' questions.

"You have hypertension stage 2 which means you need to take your medication on a daily basis."

"Do you use any form of drugs?" asked Dr. Keller typing notes on the computer.

"No" said Edwin. Why are you asking me all these questions?

"I am going to have my nurse to come in and give you 20 mgs of Bystolic and that should bring your blood pressure down and I will also write you a prescription that you can fill at your local pharmacy."

"Okay thank you Dr. Keller, but you never did finish telling me about my mother."

"Your mother is going to be fine. I am going to hold her here in the hospital where we can regulated on her medication and give her psychiatric therapy. I see here on her chart she has you as well as sister as persons I can discuss her illness with and you probably already know that she is a Paranoia Bipolar Schizophrenia.

"Yeah I already know" said Edwin looking down to the floor and then looking back up at the doctor. "How long will you be keeping her in the hospital?"

"We usually hold the patient no longer than 3 months and if she makes good progress we will send out on a day pass. If she continue to do well we will release her to go home. I can discuss this with you after we get your blood pressure down to normal. My nurse will be in to see you shortly." said Dr Keller as she left the room.

Shortly after; the nurse came in and asks Edwin for his name, address and medical insurance. She checked his Edwin's blood pressure again and then gave him the medication.

"Dr. Keller will be back in to speak with you Mr. Benson before you go home." Said the nurse and then she exited the room leaving Edwin resting on the exam table.

"Mr. Benson, wake up Mr. Benson." Dr. Keller stood next to the exam table looking down at Edwin.

"Oh huh....Said Edwin sitting up on the side of the exam table. "I must've fallen asleep while I was waiting."

"Hold your arm out." Said Dr. Keller; wrapping the blood pressure cuff around Edwin's arm.

"Well you probably need the rest" Said Dr. Keller removing the cuff from Edwin's arm.

"Your blood pressure is 140 over 90" said Dr. Keller as she walked back over to her computer to make a notation of Edwin's blood pressure.

"How is my mother doing?" asked Edwin.

"Your mother is doing fine; we have put her back on the lithium medication and we may have to adjust the milligrams but we are going to do some blood work and exams to get her stabilized on her medication." explained Dr. Keller.

"What time is it?" asked Edwin

"It's twelve o'clock" said Dr. Keller looking up from her computer screen and handing Edwin the prescription for his medication..

"Oh my God, I have to call my job." Said Edwin as he jumped down off the exam table, and running toward the door. "I have to go; you have my number if you need to get in touch with me; thank you doctor."

Edwin ran passed the nurses' station down the corridor to the bank of elevators. Edwin was still a little dazed and confuse over having to get up before day in the morning to go see about his mother. The elevator came. Edwin looked in the elevator before getting on; he could still hear Paris telling him how it is important to look in the elevator before you get on; because the elevator may not be there.

"That is the craziest thing I ever heard; if I see the elevator I know it's there.

"That is not necessarily so; you know there is a difference between the mind's eye and the physical eye. The mind's eye sees one thing and the physical eye sees another thing" said Paris sitting on the swing bench and swinging back and forth. "Haven't heard of elevators doors opening but the elevator wasn't there and people getting on because they thought they saw the elevator and ended up at the bottom of the elevator shaft dead? That was Paris; Edwin thought to himself. She was always coming up with some story. Once on the elevator Edwin wasn't quite sure what to press the G button or the L button. He certainly didn't want to end up in the morgue, not alive anyway. He decided to press the L button and once he left the elevator and started walking through the lobby and through the emergency room he felt more relaxed. Edwin remembered he left his car five blocks away from the hospital in a garage. On his way to the garage he decided to called his job and found out Paris had already called and told them about his mother being ill. He could always depend on Paris because she was so perfect and he could not stand her for being Ms. Perfect except for that time he got on her nerves so bad that she cheated on him. That was not enough; she still had that "I am that Ms. Perfect air about her." Paris's mother was the same way. They could do no wrong. Good thing her mother was dead, and it is just a matter of time that Paris would be dead too. Just few more times of smothering her and she would be gone. Just the way he and Corona had planned it. Edwin picked up the phone and call Paris.

"Hello" answers Paris

"Hi Paris, its me." said Edwin

"How are you doing Edwin?" asked Paris

"I'm okay." said Edwin

"How is your mother?"

"She is okay." said Edwin.

"What did the doctor say?" ask Paris.

"The same thing they always say Paris, they are going to keep her in the hospital until they can get her back on her medication and then they going to release her."

So Edwin did you get to talk to her? ask Paris.

No, the doctor said I couldn't see her; she was sleeping when I got there."

Edwin's phone rang he looked at his phone and saw it was Jennifer.

"I got to run." said Edwin.

"I called your job for you Edwin. said Paris

"Yeah I know; thanks a lot. I got take this call from Corona.... I will call you later.

Edwin saw that Jennifer's call fell into voice mail.

"Hey Edwin give me a call I have landed and I am staying at the Radisson Hotel near JFK. Call me Sweetie."

Edwin heard a man saying something in the background to Jennifer, but he couldn't make out the conversation. He quickly pressed speed dial to call Jennifer but there was no answer. Then he pressed another number and called Corona.

"Hey" Corona answered the phone. "What's going on, I tried to call you."

Edwin knew Corona was lying but he didn't have time to go into Corona nonsense.

"Hi Corona, I called to tell you Mommy is okay and she is in Bellevue Hospital on the 5th floor."

"Did you see her?" asked Corona.

"No, she was asleep; but I am not going home tonight and Jennifer is here to visit me so if Paris calls you tell her I am with you and I went to the store or something. Okay?"

"She never calls me." said Corona.

"Yeah, I know but just in case" said Edwin. Edwin's phone rang again and it was Jennifer.

"I got to go, talk later" said Edwin pressing a button and switching over to Jennifer's' call.

"Hey baby, I was trying to call you." said Edwin.

"I'm sorry I missed your called." said Jennifer. "My cell phone was in the bottom of my pocketbook and I didn't hear it."

"So are you checked in at the Radisson in Queens? asked Edwin as he approached the parking garage.

"Yep. I am all checked in and ready and waiting to shake, and rattle your world big boy!"

"I heard that and I will be there as soon as I get my car out of the garage." Said Edwin

"Did they keep your crazy wife?" asked Jennifer. "After all I don't want her on the loose while I am in town."

"Don't worry about her." said Edwin as he rushed into the garage. "In time I will have her buried under the nut house."

Edwin gave his keys to the attendant in the parking garage. "My phone is ringing, said Edwin looking at his phone and he saw it was Paris calling back. "I see you in about an hour baby."

"Yeah," said Edwin answering the phone.

"I was just wondering how you were doing and what time are you coming home?" asked Paris

"I won't be home until tomorrow because Corona is taking care of some of Mommy's affairs and she wants me to help her out."

"How long are you going to be in New York and don't forget you have to go back to work tomorrow?" asked Paris.

"I will leave from New York early in the morning and come home and change and then go to work." Said Edwin feeling annoyed with Paris for asking.

"Oh okay Edwin, if you need anything or even if you need to talk you know you can call me anytime.

"Yeah, thanks Paris, but I think I will be fine." Said Edwin clicking off his phone before Paris could say goodbye.

"Okay bye." said Paris she clicked off her phone and whispered "Good".

Chapter 10

Paris was beside herself with joy with Edwin not coming home. She sat at her desk trying to figure out what she could do for entertainment. The sad thing was Paris didn't have any friends in Hidden Valley except for Virginia and she knew Virginia would be busy with her family. At four o'clock just as Paris was about to rush out the door her when the manager Mr. Bonds stopped her.

"Paris, I wanted to speak with you concerning the fair that is coming up next month" said Mr. Bonds pulling out the chair from her desk.

Paris turned around and walked back to her desk and reluctantly sat down. "What about the fair? ask Paris.

"Paris you know the fair is to raise money for women and their children who are in Hidden Valley Haven for Women due to domestic violence and we are to donate monies from selling some of the artwork from local artist but this year we don't have enough artist that are contributing this year." said Mr. Bonds with his arms fold across his chest.

"Wow, I thought we had enough from all the phone calls and letters I sent out to the artist here in Hidden Valley." said Paris frowning and feeling disappointed.

"Some of the artist have moved and others are just not able

donate as much this year. You know the economy has not been doing well." Said Mr. Bonds

"So what are we supposed to do now Mr. Bonds?"

"I want you to paint" Said Mr. Bonds with a smile on his face.

"Oh no!" said Paris standing up and walking toward the door.

"Why not?" asked Mr. Bonds "I have seen some of your paintings; you are great artist."

"My husband doesn't like me taking time away from the family with my painting." said Paris.

"He doesn't have to know" said Mr. Bonds. "Look, you can paint here in the evenings and on the weekends and your husband will never know."

"Oh please, like he won't notice I am gone?" asked Paris trying to make her way out the door.

"Just tell him you are working extra hours at the store." said Mr. Bonds following behind Paris.

"Mr. Bonds. I always get in trouble when I lie because I'm just not good at lying." Said Paris

"You won't be lying." said Mr. Bonds; he walked over to Paris and whispered to her. "Don't say no to women and children that need your help Paris."

"Let me think about it and I let you know." said Paris.

"You have until tomorrow morning to let me know." Said Mr. Bonds

"Good night." said Paris.

"Don't forget Paris, tomorrow morning you will have my answer" Said Mr. Bonds as he watch Paris shake her head and rolled her eyes as she walks out the door.

"Why....why, why did Mr. Bonds have to hit me with this mess tonight?" asked Paris as she drove home on the busy streets and wondering how she was going to deal with Edwin finding out she is painting again.

When Paris got home Anthony was in the family room watching television.

"Hello Mom." said Anthony.

"Hi Anthony; how was your day? asked Paris.

"It was okay." said Anthony getting up and walking into the kitchen. "I am going to need some money to buy some things before I leave for California."

"Well," said Paris washing her hands. "How much do you think you going to need?"

"Several hundred dollars" said Anthony sitting down at the kitchen table.

"I think I'll make some hamburgers." said Paris drying her hands with paper towel and taking ground beef out of the refrigerator. Paris walked over to the kitchen cabinet and pulls out a bowl and put the ground beef in the bowl and started adding bread crumbs and seasonings.

"Did you tell your father you needed money?" asked Paris.

"Yeah, but he said he didn't have any money." said Anthony looking sad.

"Do you have money to get you to California?" asked Paris as she put the frying pan on the stove and look over at Anthony.

"Yeah I have enough." said Anthony.

"You have enough for what Anthony?" asked Paris growing tired and impatient.

"I have enough to get to California and enough for the first couple of weeks until I find a part time job." said Anthony.

"I will let you have some money Anthony and we will talk with your father when he comes home tomorrow." said Paris as she put the hamburgers in the frying pan. "You know Anthony if you told your father you had enough money; you should have known he is not going to give you any money. You have to learn how to ask for money."

"Where is dad anyway?" asked Anthony walking over and sitting down at the snack bar.

"Oh you haven't heard; his mother is sick and he had to go to New York to see about her." Explains Paris as she flips the hamburgers over.

"Is she alright, what's wrong with her." asked Anthony.

"She is alright and she is in Bellevue Hospital; and she will be home as soon as they get her back on her medication."

"I'm sorry to hear that." said Anthony. Anthony knew he didn't have to ask any more question he had heard enough horror stories about his grandmother going in and out the hospital and he knew Bellevue hospital specialized in mental health.

After dinner Anthony went to his room and Paris was so tired that she didn't have a chance to think about Mr. Bond asking her to do the paintings for the women's shelter.

Paris took a shower and thought about calling Edwin to ask how he was doing; but she decided not to. She got in the bed and just laid there thinking about painting. What would she paint she was so depressed and tired lately she really didn't think she had the strength to paint. Her cell phone rang and she answered the phone without looking at it.

"Hey, Paris what going on....what's happening?

"Hey Papa, you back in town already?"

"No, I am in Canada; you will never guess who I bumped into?"

"No, I never will; so do tell." said Paris rolling over on her stomach and kicking her feet in the air.

"I saw Robin" said Papa there was a long pause.

"You saw Robin Connors?" asked Paris.

"Yep, I couldn't believe my eyes." said Papa

"Where did you see her? asked Paris rolling over and sitting up in the bed.

"I saw her up in Toronto, Canada.

"Wow." Does she live there now?

"No she lives in Albany, New York. said Paris.

"Wow. That is so great to hear; you have to give me her phone number."

Hey Paris, I have another call coming in I have to call you back." said Papa

"Not tonight." said Paris yawning. "I am going to sleep."

"Okay, I call you when I get back into Pennsylvania"

"Okay. Good night." said Paris hanging up the phone and as soon she hung up the phone she slid down under the covers and fell asleep.

Chapter 11

The next morning Paris sitting at her desk drinking her coffee still trying to decide whether or not to do the paintings for the women shelter when Mr. Bonds came over to her.

"Paris I need you to go over to the women's shelter to discuss the project we are going to do for them in September." said Mr. Bonds as he stood in front of her desk with a look of authority on his face.

"To be perfectly honest with you Mr. Bonds;" said Paris taking a deep breath. "I haven't made up mind if I want to take on this project."

"Well you can make up your mind on your way over there." said Mr. Bonds. He reached into his shirt pocket and pulled out a card and hands it to Paris. "This is the address to the shelter; you have to go and get all the details of how they want the artwork set up in Central Square Park in September and don't forget to discuss a rain date."

"Can't you send someone else I have tons of work to do here before Friday?" asked Paris.

"No; you have to go Paris and you need to talk to her about the types of paintings she want to display and exactly how many. Said Mr. Bonds walking back into his office and sitting down at his desk. "Now get going; they are expecting you.

As soon as Paris got into her car she pulled out her GPS and tapped in the address. The roads were long and winding and she started to fill a little anxious because it was a cloudy day and she was driving on the back roads that led into the woods. Then she turned down a steep road. When she reached the bottom of the hill, Paris stops the car and pulled out her cell phone and then she had to search for the business card in her pocketbook and then she searched the passenger seat. She found the card on the floor. Paris called the shelter and a woman answered the phone in a very low voice.

"Good Morning Hidden Valley Haven for Women. How may I help you?" whispered the lady.

"Good Morning said Paris. I have an appointment with Ms...." Paris paused and looked down at the card "With Ms. Collins this morning but I am having a problem finding the shelter."

"Where are you?" Whispered the lady on the other end; the woman's voice made Paris feel uneasy and she couldn't understand why the woman was whispering. Paris wondered what kind of place is this that women have to whisper?

"I am at the bottom of the hill but I don't know where to go from this point."

"Make a left and then keep going until you see an under path. Take the under path and then make a sharp right and go across the bridge. Then make another sharp right and you will see a mountain. Then make a left at the mountain. The shelter is behind the mountain." whispered the woman.

"Okaaaaaaay!" said Paris taking a deep breath and stepping on the gas pedal.

Paris made the left and the scenery was beautiful; she drove another two miles before she came to the under path. She made a right turn and crosses the bridge then came to the road where the mountain stood tall. Paris picked up the phone and called the shelter again.

"Good Morning Hidden Valley Haven. How may I help you?"

Paris could tell it was the same lady that answers before.

"Hello." Said Paris "I spoke with you a few minutes ago; I am at the mountain could you tell me do I go to the left or to the right of the mountain?"

"Go to the left and you will see a curve come down that curve and you will see the shelter." Whisper the lady

"Thank you." Said Paris clicking off her phone and she drove to the left of the mountain and the curves was so deep she found herself driving down on the side of the mountain and all she could do was pray. Paris was relieved when she finally pulled up in front of the shelter and saw children running and playing outside in front a 2 story red house with white shutters and a white door that was open with a welcoming mat at the entrance. There were two girls sitting on the steps drawing pictures as Paris walked in. Paris spoke to the girls but they didn't look up and they didn't speak.

Paris walked in and to the left was a large room with coaches, chairs, tables with lamps and plants in the corners; and the floors was covered with a Russian rugs. The walls were painted light green color and there were the tiny little fragile white lady with short blonde hair about five feet three and must have weighed a 100 pounds sitting behind a desk with white flowers in a glass vase. Paris thought to herself no wonder she was whispering; if she talked loud she would probably break a bone.

"Hello I am Paris Benson. Looking down at the card she had in her hand as she walked to the desk. "I am here to see Ms. Becky Collins."

"Oh yes." Whisper the lady. "I am Ms. Sarah, Ms. Becky's

assistant. "You must be the one I just spoke to over the phone. Ms. Becky is expecting you. Would you like a cup of coffee while you wait?"

"Yes," said Paris relieved that Sarah asked. "I will take it black with two sugars."

"Have a seat and I will get your coffee and let Ms. Becky know that you are here." whisper Ms. Sarah and rushes off to the back of the house.

Shortly after middle aged white woman that look like she could have been in her mid-forties with reddish brown hair. She had to be around 130 pounds and must have been about five feet and ten inches tall approached Paris with a smile.

"Hello you must be Ms. Paris, I'm Becky Collins." Ms. Becky greeted Paris with a warm handshake.

"Hello Ms. Collins; it's nice to meet you."

"Please call me Ms. Becky. We address everyone here as Ms. and by their first name."

"Here is your coffee." whispered Ms. Sarah, and handing Paris her coffee in a paper cup.

"I see you have met my assistant Ms. Sarah. She came to us ten years ago and been with us every since because she has so many good skills and talents. She has done a wonderful job in helping us keeping the shelter on the move." Ms. Becky turned and looked at Ms. Sarah. "That will be all for now Ms. Sarah." said Ms Becky as she nodded with a smile and then turning her attention back to Paris. Ms. Sarah smiled, nodded and tipped toed out the room.

"If you don't mind me asking, is it something wrong with Ms. Sarah's throat?" asked Paris

"Ms. Sarah whispers because her husband only allowed her to whisper when speaking and Ms. Sarah is still trying to learn how to speak up for herself. We have high hopes for her and she has proved to be a real treasure to us here at Hidden Valley Haven; she is very knowledgeable and talented. "So how was your drive coming here?" asked Ms. Becky?

"Well I must say it was most challenging" said Paris sipping her coffee.

"Yes it is. We like this location just for that reason; we don't want the abusive husbands or boyfriends to be able to find us so easily or at will." said Ms. Becky she sat down in a chair across from Paris sitting on the coach.

"Are you originally from Hidden Valley?" asked Ms. Becky.

"No, I am from New York." said Paris smiling

"So do you have any family here?"

"I have no extended family here; it just my husband and my son." said Paris

"Oh, that's nice. How old is your son?"

"He is 20 years old." Said Paris wondering why she is being questioned about her personal life.

"How long have you worked at the art gallery?" ask Ms. Becky smiling.

"About two and half years." said Paris.

"Do you like it there?" asked Ms. Becky.

"Oh yes, very much so." said Paris still sipping on her coffee.

"So tell me Ms Becky what type of paintings would you like me to paint for the shelter?" asked Paris.

"Paintings?" asked Ms. Becky. "I didn't ask for any paintings."

"Mr. Bonds told me to come here because you wanted me to create some paintings for your fundraiser in September." said Paris frowning. "And he had me sending out letters and making phone calls for donations for your shelter."

"Oh you must be mistaken dear; Mr. Bonds called me and told me that you were interested in receiving some counseling" said Ms Becky. As far as the donations we did receive them and we are most grateful for all your hard work and for the donations that we received."

"I can't believe Mr. Bonds did this!" said Paris standing up and placing her cup on the coffee table in front of her and starts walking to the door.

"Wait Ms. Paris, your employer must have thought you needed help otherwise he would not have called to set this appointment for you. said Ms. Becky, standing up and walking over to Paris.

"What right do he have to interfere in my personal life; he ought to mind his business" said Paris turning around and looking at Ms Becky.

"It is his business Ms. Paris if you are being abused." said Ms. Becky walking closer to Paris. "It's everybody's business if you are being abused and you need to tell everybody for your own safety. The more people that know that you are being abused the safer you are."

"Excuse me" whispered Sarah tip toeing the room. "Lunch will be ready in an hour should I set an extra place at the table?"

The room became darken as lighting struck the house and the window panes shook and the children came running in the house screaming and yelling.

"Calm down children it's just rain" said Ms. Becky walking over to the front door and closing it.

"Ms. Sarah please takes the children up stairs and make sure they change into some dry clothes. Also set an extra place at the table. Ms. Paris will be staying for lunch."

"Yes Ms. Becky" whispered Sarah as she guided the children upstairs.

"And you come with me Ms. Paris; because you are not going anywhere in all this rain." said Ms. Becky putting her arm around Paris's shoulders. Paris felt like she had been bamboozled but she knew she was not up to driving in the rain with all that thundering and lighting.

"Come let sit over here on the coach and tell me what is going on with you and perhaps we can figure out why Mr. Bonds felt that you needed counseling."

"Well what did he say to you?" ask Paris sitting down on the sofa.

"He said that you miss a lot of time from work and that sometimes you come to work not looking well. said Ms Becky.

"I have been missing a lot of time from work because I haven't been sleeping well." said Paris.

"What do you do when you wake up and can't go back to sleep?" asked Ms. Becky.

"I don't know." said Paris. Paris felt guilty for lying, but she could not possibly tell this woman about her being smothered in her sleep. The woman would think she was crazy.

"So tell me what does your husband do for a living?" ask Ms. Becky.

"My husband sells time share and he also does collections as well." Paris felt maybe she should just give in and talk about Edwin. She has never told anyone about the madness and the insanity that she has been dealing with for the last 25 years. Maybe this is God's way of helping her.

"You know, Ms. Becky; I am not in an abusive marriage at least I don't think I am anyway." said Paris. "But I am dealing with insanity within the family."

"Really," said Ms. Becky sitting back on the coach and crossing her arms over her chest. "Tell me who in the family is ill?"

"My mother-in-law, she is a paranoid bipolar schizophrenic and it's really takes a toll on our family. At least on my husband and me even though my son knows his grandmother is ill he has never seen her ill, you know when she refuses to take her medication and have to go into the hospital." said Paris taking a deep breath and looking down at the floor. "They always lock her up behind bars in hospital; so I never let my son visit her in the hospital. I don't want him to see his grandmother like that." Paris looked back up at Ms. Becky. "I don't want him to ever to see her like that or to remember her as a mad woman."

"So what exactly happens when your mother-in-law goes off her medication? asks Ms Becky

"She runs away and no one can find her for weeks and then sometimes she just run from one person house to another and calls all times during the night. Then Edwin gets up and goes running to find her."

"So tell me how long Edwin has been dealing with his mother's illness?"

'Every since he was two years old; that what Edwin would say anyway." said Paris.

"That must be really rough on him." said Ms. Becky

"Oh yes it is; on the both of us." replied Paris

"What about Edwin's father?" asked Ms. Becky with her head tilted to the side frowning and trying to understand the madness she was hearing.

"Edwin's father passed away some years ago. He was a strong man but at the same time he wasn't strong because he was illiterate; he couldn't even read numbers." said Paris.

"That is very sad" said Ms. Becky. "It must have been very hard for your husband growing up; did he have any brothers and sisters?"

"Yes, Edwin has a brother and a sister; but Edwin is the main one that looks after his mother and his sister helps. Edwin and his brother and sister grew up very poor and life was very hard for them having a mother with a mental illness and an illiterate father. Tears started to flow from Paris' eyes and Ms Becky reached over and passed a box of tissues to Paris.

"I just wanted to help Edwin; he was such a nice and warm hearted man when I first met him. I love Edwin." said Paris as she wiped the tears away. Ms. Becky waited for Paris to stop crying before she asked her next question.

"Did you know your mother in-law had a mental illness before you married him?"

"No, I didn't." said Paris clearing her throat. "No, I had no idea; it was a well kept secret."

"So Ms. Paris, when your mother-in-law stops taking her medicine; how does your husband deal with it?" asked Ms. Becky now sitting on the edge of her seat.

"First he acts like he has everything under control and he will go and see about his mother; but when he comes back home for days he will walk around mad and he yells and curses at me and sometimes he will push me and slaps me."

"And you don't think he is abusing you?" asked Ms Becky

"To be honest with you; I never really thought about it. I was just so caught up in this snare of the insanity I just never thought about it. At first I was all about helping Edwin; trying to help him understand that he could have a better life. I just felt that he was having problems dealing with the insanity I never looked at it as abuse. Now I just want to get away from the insanity. But I just don't know how to escape; being that I have nowhere to go and no one to help me. I am afraid of being homeless and poor." said Paris.

"Yeah....well that is understandable." said Ms. Becky nodding in agreement.

"Lunch is now ready." whispered Ms. Sarah.

"Thank you Sarah" said Ms Becky standing up "Come Ms. Paris we can talk more after lunch.

Paris followed Ms. Becky and Ms. Sarah in kitchen where the children was seated at a large wooden table with a red and white checked table cloth. The kitchen look like a farm house kitchen; the walls was paint light orange color with the red and white boarders. There with a white potbelly stove, double sinks and with a red brick fire place. There were pictures on the walls that the children had painted of houses, flowers, and animals and a large picture window where you could see out in the back yard. There were several cabins, picnic tables and there was a tree house.

"Wow, this is really beautiful." said Paris sitting with Ms. Becky at separate table from the children in front of the picture window. Paris could see several log cabins and a few picnic tables and swings in the backyard.

Sarah and another woman served grill cheese sandwiches and vegetable soup and milk and for desert they had cup cakes. Sarah came over to the table where Paris and Ms. Becky was sitting and served them their lunch which was the same as the children.

"What would you like something to drink with your lunch Ms. Paris?" whispered Sarah

"I would like a cup of tea, thank you" said Paris.

Sarah poured Ms. Becky a cup of coffee.

"So Ms. Becky" said Paris smiling and looking out the window "How did you come about establishing this place?"

"I grew up in this house." Said Ms. Becky and so did my mother.

"Wow this is a big house; did you have brothers and sisters?" Asked Paris; looking around the kitchen.

"I had two brothers and a sister." Said Ms. Becky cutting her grill cheese sandwich in half

"Here is your tea." Whispered Ms.Sarah; setting a small tea pot, and a cup and a saucer on the table in front of Paris.

"Thank you Ms. Sarah.

"So where are they now? asked Paris.

"My father use to work on the railroad and he was a drunk and he fell out drunk on the train tracks one night and got ran over by a freight train." Said Ms. Becky taking a sip of her coffee

"Wow, I am so sorry to hear that. That must have been devastating for you and your family." said Paris sipping her tea.

"Actually, it was a relief to us all. You see my father abused all of us and the memories were so bad that my brothers and sister won't even come back to this house for a visit."

"That is really sad." said Paris.

"It's okay. said Ms. Becky they are still my family and we have our family reunion once a year."

"So why do you stay here?" asked Paris

"Mama started the shelter back in 1974 for abused women and children and I guess being the youngest child I was left behind and just decided to stay and help mama with the shelter. After Mama died I just decided to stay on and keep the shelter up and running and I am glad I did." said Ms. Becky.

It had stop raining and Ms. Becky took Paris on a tour of the shelter and of the 10 cabins that she had renovated after her mother died.

"You know Paris, "said Ms. Becky. Mr. Bonds had an excellent ideal about doing an art show; but I think it should be something more than an art show. Let's go back to the house."

Ms. Becky walks over to her desk and picked up her day planner "Hum, October is "Domestic Violence Awareness Month" and we can have you display your art work at that time. And there are ladies here that do some fine sewing, and knitting and they can sell their work.

"That is a great ideal" said Paris.

"We can also bake bread, cakes, cookies, and pies to sell and it will help raise money for the shelter. How about we get together next week and make all the plans. We have to work fast because this is already the first week of August." suggested Ms. Becky

"That sound just great" said Paris picking up her pocketbook and fishing for her car keys.

"I have to get back to the office" said Paris looking up at the clock on the wall. It was already three o'clock. "Thank you for everything Ms. Becky."

"It was nice meeting you Ms. Paris and tell Mr. Bonds I said thank you. I look forward to seeing you next week. Ms. Becky gave Paris a hug. "I want you to know Paris; you now have a new beginning." Paris smiled and thanked Ms. Becky again and got in her car and made it back to the office.

Paris realized that she really didn't want to go back into the office because Mr. Bonds invaded her privacy and she really didn't know how she was going to approach him about it. Paris sat in her car in front of the office just thinking how over whelming the day had been; everything from Edwin leaving home to admit his mother in the hospital to taking that long drive out to Hidden Valley Haven and discovering that Mr. Bonds was aware of her marital problems. Paris backed out of the parking space and drove and the at first stop light she came to she called Mr. Bonds

"Hello Mr. Bonds."

"Hi Paris" said Mr. Bonds; in a surprised tone of voice to hear Paris. "Are you on your way back to the office?"

"No." said Paris it has been a very long day; and my mother in law is ill and I decided to go home.

"I'm sorry to hear that." said Mr. Bonds, clearing his throat. "So how did it go at Hidden Valley Haven?"

Paris decided not to mention anything about the conversation that she had with Ms. Becky concerning her personal problems.

"Everything went just fine and we are going to get together next week to make plans for the festival that is going to take place in October which is "Domestic Violence Awareness" month.

Oh really! Said Mr. Bonds; sounding surprised. So Paris you are actually going to paint?

Well, that is the reason you sent me there right? asked Paris

"Oh yeah....yeah that's right." said Mr. Bonds.

"Well, I will see you in the morning." said Paris clicking off her cell phone."

Chapter 12

Paris pulled up in the drive way she could see that Edwin was home. Paris took a deep breath and said a prayer before getting out of her car. Tears started to weld up in her eyes; she felt so exhausted and really didn't feel like dealing with the insanity. She opens her pocketbook and took out a tissue and wiped her eyes and then she decided to refresh her make-up by powdering her cheeks and adding on some more lipstick. She got out of the car and slowly walked up the driveway and as she approached the house she could hear Edwin talking on the phone. She paused for a moment taking another deep breath and then unlocked the door. When she opens the door she could hear Edwin talking loud on the phone talking to his sister about his mother. Paris walked down the foyer into the family room where Edwin was.

"Hi Edwin." said Paris.

"Hey Corona," Said Edwin "I'll call you back later; Paris just came in."

"Hey Paris," said Edwin laying his cell phone down on the coffee table. "Where have you been?"

"I went to work. How is your mother?" asked Paris; as she walks out of the family room into the kitchen.

"She is alright; but by the time I got to the hospital they already had admitted her." Said Edwin

Paris was not sure how that could happen being that the nurse called and said she needed Edwin there to admit his mother; but Paris thought better not to ask.

"So what did the doctor say?" asked Paris.

"It's the same old story" said Edwin getting up walking into the kitchen.

Paris washed her hands at the kitchen sink while she was listening to Edwin and dries her hands and then took a bottle of water out of the refrigerator and then reached up in the cabinet and took out a bottle of Pamprins.

"Oh so it's that time of the month?" asked Edwin in a sarcastic tone

"Yes it is" said Paris. Lord forgives me for lying but I just got to get away from this fool tonight. "And I got to go lay down; I am just so bloated, tired, and achy. Paris walks by Edwin down the foyer going to the stairs and the house phone rang.

Edwin walked over to the snack bar and answered the phone.

"Hello" said Edwin. "Oh hello Brother Miller; how are you."

Paris was relieved for that phone call; she went upstairs and took a hot shower and she felt confused about where to sleep. She didn't know whether or not to sleep in her own bed or in the guest room. She just felt so uneasy; so nervous and restless. It was actually too early to go to bed it was only five o'clock. Paris decided to take her nap in her own bed; besides the walk across the hall to the guest room seem like it was miles away. Paris woke up at 9 pm and the house was quiet; as she went down stairs she could hear the television playing in the family room. As she went to the family room and saw Edwin was sleep in the recliner. Paris decided not to wake him and she went into the kitchen and took out a bottle of water out of the refrigerator and went back upstairs; but this time she decided to sleep in the guest room and she locks the door.

The next morning Paris woke up late. It was half pass nine and she jumped out of bed and ran into the master bedroom and notice that Edwin was already gone to work and that was a good thing; the less she saw of Edwin the better she felt. She picked up the phone on the night stand and called the job and left a message on Mr. Bonds' voice mail and told him that she had over slept and would be at work at twelve thirty. Paris knew she would probably be in earlier; but it gave her a more time to get herself together without rushing. The phone rang just as Paris was going to step off into the bathroom.

"Hello" answered Paris

"You know something Paris" shouted Edwin you left me downstairs sleeping in the recliner and you didn't even wake me up and then you had the nerve to go upstairs and go into the guest room and lock the door; so tell me what's up with you?"

"I am late for work." said Paris. "I got to go. We can talk when you come home."

"No we are going to talk now!" exclaimed Edwin.

"Well I just got out of bed and I got to go pee, bye." Paris slammed down the phone and ran into the bathroom.

By ten thirty Paris was dressed and as soon as she opens the front door Edwin stood there with his keys in hand.

"I came home to talk to you Paris, to find out what is going on with you." said Edwin

"What's going on with me is I got to get to work, I'm late." said Paris, pushing by Edwin.

Edwin grabs hold of Paris' arm and squeezing her arm tightly. "Let me tell you something you don't push me aside when I am talking to you."

"Let go of my arm; you are hurting me." said Paris

"Not until I am finish talking to you." said Edwin squeezing Paris's arm tighter.

"If you don't let go of my arm I am going to scream!" said Paris trying to pull her arm out of Edwin's grip.

Edwin pushed Paris away causing her to trip and falling down the front steps outside the house and then his cell phone rang and pulled it out of his jacket pocket

"Hello" said Edwin

"Hey Edwin, what cha doing tonight?" ask Jennifer

"I don't know." said Edwin as stepped over Paris still lying on the steps. Edwin went and got in his car and drove away.

Paris stood up and brushed herself off and then she start to walk toward her car and realized she had sprung her ankle and decided to go back into the house. She called the office and told Mr. Bonds that she had sprung her ankle getting out of the shower and she wouldn't be able to make in.

"Is there anything I can do to help Paris?" asked Mr. Bonds.

"No, Mr. Bonds." said Paris with tears in her eyes. "Thank you for asking I should be in tomorrow morning."

"Okay Paris." said Mr. Bonds. "Call me if you need anything."

Paris hung up the phone after thanking Mr. Bonds and managed to hop in the downstairs bathroom. She prepared a foot bath with Epson salt. She pulled down the lid to the toilet seat and sat on it and soaked her foot and cried.

At that point Paris came to the realization of how alone in the world she was and there was no one that cared with whether she lived or died. She had no family or friends that she could turn to help her out of this insane dysfunctional marriage. And all she could do was cry; she didn't even have the strength to pray and ask God to help her.

Chapter 13

"Yeah baby that was good." Said Edwin; he sat up in the bed, with Jennifer lying next to him. "You really know how to rock it"

"Well you need somebody to make your world go round for you honey; especially after all you go through dealing with your demented wife."

"Well Jenn, I have to do what I have to do. I feel sorry for her that is why I try to help her and be there for her." Said Edwin

"Wow," said Jennifer sitting up in the bed laying her head on Edwin's chest. "You are some kind of man Edwin most men would have walked out on her a long time ago."

"Let's not waste our precious moments talking about that nut case" Said Edwin. "Why don't you serve me up right one more time baby?"

"Oh I am sorry. I got to run." Jennifer managed to get out of the bed; away from Edwin and put her clothes on. "I have to meet my sister to help her take care of some business I will call you this evening" said Jennifer blowing Edwin a kiss as she ran out the door.

Edwin was speechless as he sat there in the bed and watching Jennifer run out the door and he was furious. He got up and got dress and went downstairs in the hotel lobby to the bar and sat down and drenched himself in Gin and Coke. Edwin got so drunk and loud at the bar he had to be escorted back to his hotel room.

"Shoot" said Edwin waking up in the hotel room and looking

at his watch; it was two in the morning and he had been to work but left early to tell Paris off about sleeping in the guest room. He forgot to call into the office to say he wasn't coming back to work and hadn't called home to find out what Paris was doing after he had knocked her down. He got up and went in the bathroom and splashed cold water on his face. He looked in the mirror and saw his eyes were blood shot red.

"Paris won't notice she will be sleep." said Edwin.

He left the room and took the elevator to the lobby and he stopped at the front desk and paid the bill in cash. He gave the parking attendant his car keys. As soon as the parking attendant pulled up Edwin tip the attendant five dollars and jumped in the car and took off in a road rage.

Chapter 14

The next morning Paris was at work bright and early and in a good mood and the swelling in her ankle had gone down. She slept peacefully all night and had not heard a word from Edwin. It was strange that he had not called all day or night. That was not like Edwin not to call or come home. He always came home. Paris hoped that nothing happen Edwin; what would she do without him? The thought of him laying up dead somewhere brought on mixed emotions. So she just decided to enjoy the day and worry about Edwin when she got home. More than likely he would be calling her before the end of the day.

Paris talk about her plans to work with Ms. Becky in October.

"Wow" said Mr. Bonds. Raising his eyebrows and staring Paris in amazement and smiling. "So you are really serious about getting back into painting.

"Well" said Paris that is reason you sent me out there isn't it?

"Yep that's why I sent you out there." Said Mr. Bonds smiling and whistling as he got up from his desk carrying his coffee cup to the other side of the office to get more coffee.

Paris decided not to say anything to Mr. Bonds about butting into her personnel life; perhaps she needed someone to take notice and care enough to butt in. After all like Ms. Becky said when someone is being abused it is "everybody's business."

Paris' cell phone rang and she ran over to her desk; but she missed the call. She checks the number and it was a New York number; but she had no idea who the call was from. She decided to call voice mail.

"You have one missed call." "Press 1 to hear the message."

Paris press 1 on her cell phone.

"Hi Paris, this is Steven."

"Just as Paris was listening to the message; her phone rang again."

Paris clicks over to the phone call. "Hello" said Paris

"Hi Paris, this is Steven did you get my message?"

"I had just picked up my cell phone when you called." said Paris; taking a deep breath and looking up at Mr. Bonds who was now standing in front of her desk looking at her.

"I was just calling you to tell you that Edwin was in car accident last night and he is now in the hospital." said Steven.

"Oh my God." said Paris. "Is he alright, what hospital is he in?"

"Yeah he is going to be alright; he had a slight concussion to the head and the doctors are going to release him from the hospital tomorrow morning.

"Where did he have a car accident at?" asked Paris now sitting down in shock

"He was down in Philly." said Steven

"What was he doing down in Philly?" asked Paris

"I have no idea." said Steven. "You have to ask him that when you see him."

"So why are the doctors keeping him until tomorrow if he only had a slight concussion to the head?" asked Paris frowning

"They just want to run more test on him" said Steven. "Look I will bring him home tomorrow when they release him, I got go to work."

"Wait Steven what hospital is he in?"

"He is in Philadelphia General Hospital".

"Thanks for calling me." said Paris clicking off her cell phone and she just sat at her desk and stare into space.

"Is everything alright Paris?" asks Mr. Bonds still standing in front of Paris's desk.

"Oh yeah, my husband was in a car accident and he has a slight concussion to the head; but he will be alright, they going to release him from the hospital tomorrow."

"Do you want to leave and go to the hospital?" asked Mr. Bonds

"Paris, do you want to go to the hospital?" Mr. Bonds asks the second time.

"Oh no" said Paris. "I am going to get busy on those paintings."

Paris clears off her desk and rushed over to the supply closet and start pulling out all the art supplies that she needed to start the project for the shelter. Mr. Bonds stood and watch Paris racing back and forth from the supply closet to her desk with art supplies.

"Excuse me Paris" said Mr. Bonds; stepping aside as Paris rushes by him with an arm full of paint and paint brushes. "I know this is none of my business; are going to call your husband to see how he is doing?" Paris dropped the paint and paint brushes on her desk and dropped down in her chair and lean on her desk with elbows and her hands covering her mouth laugh hysterically; the tears rolled down her cheeks. Mr. Bonds reached over and pulled a tissue out of the tissue box on Paris' desk and hands it to her and he walks over and put his arm around Paris' shoulders.

"Are you alright Paris?"

Paris took the tissue and covered her mouth coughed and then wiped away the tears from her eyes. "Yes I am fine Mr. Bonds. I don't know what came over me; I will call my husband right away."

Paris was embarrassed as she pushed away from Mr. Bonds embraced and stood up and open her desk drawer and took out her pocketbook.

"Please excuse me while I go and call my husband" as she walked out of the office into the parking lot.

"Take all the time you need Paris" Said Mr. Bonds shaking his head.

Paris could not believe how she acted; but the reality of it all Paris was glad she was going to have another day and night without Edwin. She was glad he wasn't hurt too bad or dead but she just wanted to celebrate a day without Edwin. Paris pulled out her cell phone and calls Edwin.

"Let me pick this up" said Edwin sitting up in the hospital bed. "Do you mind giving me some privacy Jennifer I have to take this call?"

"No problem" said Jennifer but I still want to know why you had to come all the way down to Philly?" asks Jennifer walking out room

"Close the door behind you" yelled Edwin.

Edwin click on his cell phone "Oh my head." said Edwin.

"Hi Edwin how are you?" asked Paris as she walked over to her car and lean against it.

"Yeah, I am alright Paris; I just had a car accident. I have a slight concussion but the doctors want to run some more test on me and they also want me to see a psychologist." said Edwin sounding sad.

"Really, said Paris. Trying to sound like she was surprise but it was about time someone else made the suggestion besides her.

"Well, I think that would be an excellent idea; being that you were in a car accident; it has to have some physiological affect on you. Did the doctor say anything about your behavior doing or after the accident that cause him to believe that you needed to see a physiologist?" Paris walked out of the parking lot to sit on bench in front of the office building.

"The doctor thought my reaction to me totaling the car was a bit extreme." Said Edwin

"You lost the car....what on earth were you doing in the car for you to have an accident; was you drunk again?" asked Paris.

"Well I was drinking." admitted Edwin.

"I have told you a million times not to drink and drive; you are nothing but a low down dirty functioning drunk and furthermore......" yelled Paris.

Edwin room door open and Jennifer stood in the doorway. "Hey Paris, I have to call you back the nurse is here to take my blood pressure." Before Paris could say another word Edwin hung up the phone.

"Paris" said Jennifer walking over to his bed. "I thought she was in the nut house?"

"Yes she is. And don't yell at me my head hurt." said Edwin with his hand on his forehead.

"Well how did she fine out you were here?" ask Jennifer standing next to the bed and looking down at Edwin.

"She didn't know I was here; she called me to tell me that she will be coming home soon." said Edwin; looking up at Jennifer.

"Wow that is going to be really hard on you." said Jennifer as she sat down on the side of the bed and holding Edwin's hand. "Did you tell her about the car accident?"

"No" said Edwin. I am glad you didn't get hurt Jennifer; it's amazing you didn't get a scratch.

"Well, that's because I had my head down. I still don't understand why you felt like you had to pull off and drive."

"It was all for thrill of it." said Edwin looking down and holding his head.

"Well because of the "thrill of it all" you jumped the divider and ran head on into an oncoming car and totaling your car and getting a concussion. You could have killed us; and by the way I checked on the other driver and he is alright too. He is an illegal immigrant without a driver's license. So they will be sending him back to wherever he came from." Said Jennifer she stood up and started pacing back and forth in front the bed. "We came out on top of this time. I mean with the guy being an illegal immigrant and us not getting killed and your wife being in the nut house; so we don't have to be worried about her showing up today."

"I wish you would stop talking about my wife being in the nut house; she is in the hospital." said Edwin still holding his head. "She can't help being sick."

"Yeah okay Edwin...now you all sensitive about your wife being a nut, by the way; I just wanted to give you this."

Jennifer opens her pocketbook and pulls out a safety pin and hands it to Edwin.

"Here is your safety pin that was holding up your drawers" said Jennifer laughing. "Didn't your mamma teach you not to wear raggedy drawers outside? Didn't she tell you to change your drawers? Don't be chasing me down for some sex with holes and safety pins in your drawers. I can't believe you live in a big house and you walking around with a safety pin holding up your drawers. Man your wife need to hurry up and get out the nut house so she can sew up your drawers!"

"Could you do me a favor Jennifer?" ask Edwin.

"Anything for you baby" said Jennifer kissing Edwin on his forehead.

Edwin sat up on side of the bed and looked up at Jennifer and screamed. "GET OUT!"

"Don't get mad at me because you are using safety pins to hold up your drawers! said Jennifer backing away from Edwin and turns on her heels and walked out the room laughing.

Edwin threw the safety pin at Jennifer and misses her as she leaves the room.

Edwin's cell phone rang and he saw it was Paris calling back.

Hi Paris, I was just getting ready to call you back. cries Edwin.

"Edwin is you crying?" asked Paris.

"Yeah, I can't help it. said Edwin crying.

"Well, I'm sorry you had the accident; but crying is not going to solve your problem. said Paris Standing up and pacing back and forth in front of the bench. What are you crying about, is it because your head is hurting or are you crying about losing the car?

"I just was in a car accident and on top of everything else my co-worker that was in the car with me at the time brought me the safety pin I had holding up my drawers."

"What?!" asked Paris. "A safety pin you had holding up your drawers?"

"Yeah, the elastic on my favorite pair of drawers had worn out and I put a safety pin in them to hold them up." cries Edwin.

Paris sat back down on the bench and laughed. "I have you told you a hundred and one times to throw those old raggedy drawers away; I told you I would buy you another pair with a picture of Goofy on it; but no you couldn't wait for me to buy you another pair of Goofy drawers. So tell me Edwin, is this so-call co-worker that you were in the car with; are they alright?"

"Yes he didn't get a scratch." Said Edwin; still crying and wiping his face.

"What about the other driver Edwin?" asked Paris impatiently.

"Oh he was an illegal immigrant and he didn't have driver's license."

"Well did he get hurt?"

"I don't know." Said Edwin

"You don't know Edwin," said Paris pausing and taking a deep breath. "It would be a good idea for you to go and see that psychologist."

"No way, you see how those doctors drug my mother."

The thing is Edwin when you go and see a psychologist he is different from a psychiatrist.

"They are all the same" said Edwin lying back in the bed.

"They are not the same Edwin." said Paris shaking her head rolling her eyes and thinking to herself what an idiot. "The difference is Edwin is that a psychologist does not prescribe medication; he talks with the patient and sees if he can help the patient work through their problems and if he sees that the patient has more serious issues to deal with then he will refer the patient to a psychiatrist to prescribe medication."

"So why the psychologist wouldn't just go ahead and prescribed the medication?" asked Edwin turning over in the bed.

"Because a psychologist is not licensed to prescribed medication." said Paris losing patience with Edwin as she stood up and walking back to the entrance of the office building. "Look, I have to get back to work, what time do you think you will be released from the hospital?"

"Sometime tomorrow morning;" Said Edwin wiping his face with hands. "Steven is going to pick me up and bring me home. I'll call you and let you know when I am on my way.

Okay, if you need to talk or you need anything give me a call?

Thanks Paris. I just feel so bad. said Edwin.

"Well that is to be expected you were in a bad car accident and you are in the hospital with a concussion and you totaled your car. But you will be alright and back on your feet in no time."

I love you Paris. cried Edwin

I love you too; and stop crying and I will see you in the morning. Said Paris clicking off her cell phone and walking back to the bench and sitting down to collect her thoughts. "I love you Paris echo in her mine." Paris couldn't help but to feel sorry for Edwin; he sound so pitiful and he doesn't have anyone to cry on but me because whoever she is would just laugh at him. She went back into the office and saw that Mr. Bonds was in his office on the phone. Paris stopped at the supply closet and picked up an empty box and walked over to her desk and started placing the art supplies in the box and then she picked up the phone and called the shelter.

"Good Morning, Hidden Valley Haven for Women. How may I direct your call?" whispered Ms. Sarah.

"Good Morning Ms. Sarah;" Paris recognized Sarah voice right away. This is Ms. Paris is Ms. Becky available?"

"Oh yes; she is standing right here."

"Good Morning Ms. Paris, how are you; it is so good to hear from you so soon."

"I am fine." said Paris. "I am calling to set up a time to come over to work on the paintings for the fair you are having for Domestic Violence Awareness month."

"Oh, that is so wonderful." Said Ms. Becky; "Are you available for Wednesdays, and Fridays afternoons after lunch?"

"Okay." Said Paris "could you hold on and let me check with Mr. Bonds?"

Paris looked up and saw Mr. Bonds standing over her desk looking at her.

"Oh Mr. Bonds, I didn't see you standing there." Paris presses a button and places the call on hold. "I have Ms. Becky on the phone and she wants to know if I can come over on Wednesday and Friday afternoons to work on the project.

"Why can't you do it here?" asked Mr. Bonds.

"Because I will need Ms. Becky's input." explained Paris.

"Well I need you here Paris; you can do it on your own time." said Mr. Bonds.

"Mr. Bonds this was your idea that I go over to the shelter because you said this was a company project; so how come I have to do this on my own time?" asked Paris.

"Oh yeah, I did tell you that; okay, but I expect you to make up the hours"

"Mr. Bonds, if this is a company project why do I have to make up the hours?" ask Paris.

"Okay....okay you don't have to make up the hours." said Mr. Bonds.

"And are you going to pay me for painting at the shelter?" ask Paris smiling.

Mr. Bonds smile and nodded yes and walks away.

"Thank you, Mr. Bonds." said Paris. After going over all a few details with Ms. Becky; Mr. Bonds called her into his office.

"Paris." said Mr. Bonds clearing his throat "How is your husband?"

"Oh, he is doing okay." said Paris rolling her eyes and looking around Mr. Bonds' office.

"Are you sure you are going to be able to take on this project at this time; I mean with your husband coming home after having an accident?"

"First of all Mr. Bonds, I just want to thank you for your concern." said Paris, folding her arms across her chest. "This is first time in a very long time I feel like I am alive and this project is just what I need to motivate me to move on and make the needed changes."

"What about your husband Paris?" ask Mr. Bonds.

"What about him, Mr. Bonds?"

"Well you have told me he doesn't like you painting and with him being in a car accident he is going to be requiring a lot more attention." said Mr. Bonds, staring at Paris as he tried to read her facial expressions.

"My husband is fine and he is coming home from the hospital in the morning and furthermore I don't give a good-ca-hoot how he feels about me painting for the women's shelter. Said Paris raising her eyebrows and shake her head. "Now if you excuse me I have to get back to work."

Paris turned around and walked out of Mr. Bonds' office and back to her desk.

Mr. Bond smile and whispers, "Ms. Paris you are on your way to living again."

Chapter 15

After work Paris went to the bank and withdrew five hundred dollars and calls Anthony and asked him what he wants to do for dinner.

"I don't know Mom; what do you want to do?"

"Let's go to Cracker Barrels for dinner." said Paris."

Paris met Anthony at Cracker Barrels and when they finish eating dinner Paris gave Anthony five hundred dollars.

"Here you go Anthony you take this money and use it for whatever you need for school; don't blow it." said Paris taking a deep breath and feeling exhausted.

"Thanks Mom; I really appreciate it." said Anthony smiling from ear to ear.

"I will have more money for you next week before you leave; did you hear from your father today?"

"No I didn't, I notice he didn't come home last night. said Anthony sipping his soda through a straw. "What's up with dad?"

"Your father was in a car accident; but he is alright." replied Paris.

"He was in a car accident....is he alright?" ask Anthony.

"Yes, I said he is alright, Anthony." said Paris.

"Why didn't you tell me before?"

"Because he is alright." said Paris. "He just has a slight concussion;

your uncle is picking him up tomorrow morning from the hospital and bringing him home."

"I'm going to call dad." said Anthony pulling out his cell phone from his jacket.

Paris waved to the waitress for the check.

"Hi Dad, Mom told me you were in a car accident; are you alright; what hospital are you in?"

The waitress came over and gave Paris the check. "Anthony, said Paris tapping Anthony on the hand I will see you at home. I got to run." Paris left a tip on the table and went to pay the cashier. But then she decided to wait for Anthony outside the restaurant. Anthony finally came out with head hanging down.

"Hey Anthony" said Paris "How is your father?"

"He alright" said Anthony. "I just don't understand why you didn't call me and tell me earlier that dad was in a car accident."

"Anthony didn't your father tell you he was alright?" ask Paris.

"Yeah; but you should have still told me earlier." said Anthony.

"Look Anthony I told you that your father is fine. If he had been dying I would have called you so you could have gone to hospital to see him. I apologize for not calling you right away. So let's be happy that is he is alright. Okay!"

"Yeah okay Mom, but I just wish you had told me earlier." said Anthony.

All Paris could do was shake her head as she stood there watching Anthony pouting about her not calling him.

"Anthony, why don't you go shopping for school and I will see you when you get home." said Paris smiling.

"Okay Mom," said Anthony sounding more up in spirits.

Anthony and Paris both walked away from the restaurant in

opposite directions to their cars; Paris stopped and looks back; watching Anthony getting into his car and driving away from the restaurant. Paris walks several more steps to her car unlocked the door and gets in and turned on the engine; but she just had to stop and say a prayer thanking God for her son and asking for His protection for her son's and herself. When Paris got home she just wanted to talk to someone but there was no one. She took a shower and then went down stairs and made a cup of tea; but this time she went into the family room and lift open the globe bar she had brought for Edwin for their tenth anniversary and pick up a bottle of brandy and went back into the kitchen and pour some into her tea and went upstairs and turned on the television to the smooth jazz music station and sipped on her tea and she sat up in her bed relaxing to the music until she fell asleep.

"Hey Mom" yelled Anthony. "Dad is home."

Paris woke up and looked at the clock it was ten o'clock in the morning. She jump out of bed and ran out the bedroom into the hallway and looks over the balcony stairs and saw Anthony going out the front door.

"Oh my God, I over slept." said Paris.

She ran into bathroom and took a shower and when she came stumbling out of the bathroom; she saw Edwin sitting on the foot of the bed waiting for her.

"Oh, hi Edwin;" said Paris as she tried to look surprised to see him.

"Oh hi Edwin is that all you have to say to me?" asked Edwin sitting at the foot of the bed with his head still bandaged up from the car accident.

"Well you told me you were going to call me before leaving the hospital." said Paris rushing to the dresser and opening the drawers and pulling out her underwear. Edwin sat on the bed the whole time watching Paris getting dress complaining how she didn't care about him or love him after all he had done for her.

Paris didn't say anything to Edwin. When she finished getting dressed she gave Edwin a hug and then she ran out of the bedroom and down the stairs and pick up her pocketbook off the bench ran and out the front door. Edwin slowly followed behind Paris; by the time Edwin got to the front door Paris was in her car and nowhere to be found.

"I am so sorry I am late; Mr. Bonds. I over slept and Edwin just came home this morning from the hospital." said Paris walking over to the coffee pot and pouring herself a cup a coffee.

"I'm happy you made it in. "said Mr. Bonds.

Paris had a good day at work especially since she had not heard from Edwin.

Chapter 16

"I'm telling you Corona, I have tried everything with Paris." said Edwin laying in the bed talking on his cell phone. "She just doesn't care about me the way Jennifer does. I am going to keep trying what you suggested; she sleeps like a dead animal and nothing seems to work. I can't tell whether she is dead or alive half the time."

"Did you try the carbon monoxide? Ask Corona popping her chewing gum.

"Yeah Corona, but the carbon monoxide thing didn't work either" Said Edwin. You know every time I plan the carbon monoxide leak by calling the electric company to have them check for the leak; and then the following week I make sure Anthony and I are out of the house and I make sure I set off the carbon monoxide to leak; Paris gets up and leaves. I tried everything from poisoning her to smothering her. It's like she is clairvoyant or something. I don't care what I try Paris walks right through it or by it. Nothing seems to kill her."

"Do you think she suspects anything?" Asked Corona

"No, Paris is too dumb to suspect anything and too busy trying to be right with the God.

"There has to be a better way to kill her Edwin; are you sure you are smothering the right way?" Ask Corona sounding impatient.

"Wait a minute Corona." said Edwin getting out of the bed and walking out into hallway and looking over the balcony. "Paris is here; I'll call you later."

Edwin sees Paris and starts screaming and cursing at her as she walks through the front door. He runs from the balcony and down the stairs. "Well Paris I see you decided to come back home; you couldn't stay home you black.... YAAAAAAAY." Edwin screamed and falls to the bottom of the stairs into the foyer and landing in front of the grandfather clock.

Paris is standing at the front door with her mouth open in shock. She runs over to Edwin lying at the bottom of the steps. "Edwin is you alright?"

"I think I broke my leg." said Edwin with his eyes fill with tears.

"Don't move Edwin, let me call the ambulance." said Paris reaching into her pocketbook and pulling out her cell phone and dials 911 and then she calls Anthony and tells him that Edwin fell down the stairs; but not to worry he is alright the ambulance is coming to take Edwin to the emergency room.

Two hours later Paris drives up to the house. Anthony drives up in his car and gets out and walks over to Paris's car to help Edwin get out of the car.

"I can't believe I broke my leg and now I have to be in this cast for six weeks." whine Edwin as he hopped up the driveway on his crutches as he goes into the house.

"I think you should stay downstairs" said Paris. "That way it will be easier for you to get around."

"And where am I supposed to sleep?" ask Edwin.

"Well it's up to you Edwin." said Paris helping Edwin into the family room.

"Yeah Dad; you matter as well sleep down here." said Anthony as he helped his father to sit down in the recliner. "That way if you need something you can still get up and get it."

"I don't want to sleep down here!" yelled Edwin

"Well I am afraid you don't have any choice." said Paris smacking her lips. "So let's not get stupid about this; you will pull out the bed in the coach or sleep on the recliner."

Paris and Anthony had pizza and salad for dinner and Edwin ate a ham and cheese sandwich because he couldn't make up his mind what he wanted to eat. The weeks went by fast and Edwin was at Paris's mercy and so he stopped cursing and screaming at her. Anthony went off to California with five thousand dollars that Paris had to all but beat it out of Edwin.

"I have to buy a car." argued Edwin.

"Well, you wouldn't have to buy a car if you weren't driving around drunk and having sex with your torn up drawer's on." said Paris.

"I wasn't drunk and having sex in the car." Edwin tries to stand up but he fell back down in the chair.

"Yes you was drunk and having sex in the car!" exclaimed Paris.

"I don't know who told you that "said Edwin with eyes budging out of his eye sockets.

"No one told me." said Paris. "I know you have been cheating for a long time."

Edwin got mad and got up on his crutches and went to yelling and cussing.

"You better sit down before you hurt yourself again." said Paris, walking out of the kitchen. "And by the way I'm giving Anthony the five thousand dollars out of your savings account and I know you don't want to hurt your son feeling by stopping me."

Six weeks gone by and Paris had finished four paintings for Hidden Valley Haven Women's Shelter. She came home tired and found Edwin sitting in Steven's car in the driveway.

"Hi Steven" said Paris. Paris parked her car next to Steven's car and letting the car window down. "I am surprised to see you here."

"Yeah;" Said Steven, "I had taken your husband to the hospital to get the cast taken off his leg."

"Oh really; Edwin you didn't tell me you were getting the cast off today." said Paris surprised that Edwin didn't tell her.

"I wanted to surprise you." said Edwin.

"Well you certainly did that." Said Paris walking around to the passenger side of Steven's car where Edwin was sitting and she opens the car door. "Let me help out."

Steven jump out the car and runs over to the passenger side to help Edwin. Edwin pulls out a cane and Steven helps Edwin get out of the car. Paris steps back away from the as Steven help Edwin walk up the drive way and up the front steps of the house. Paris couldn't help but to admire and yet feel somewhat envious that as crazy as her husband is and his family; they had each other and that was whole lot more than she had. Paris became depressed just thinking about it; if it was her in Edwin's place she would have no one to help her.

"Thanks man" said Edwin standing inside the doorway. "I can make it from here."

"You sure man, you don't need me to tuck you in bed?" asked Steven joking as he stepped back from the doorway and down the steps."

"No that's okay Steven; that's my job" said Paris smiling. "Thanks Steven you have been a big help."

"I'm sorry I can't hang around; but I have to go to work. said Steven, running to his car.

"I understand. Thanks again for your help Steven. said Paris.

Edwin sat down in his man cave and picked up the remote control to turn on the television and went to surfing the channels.

"So Edwin, how do you feel now that you have the cast off your leg?" asked Paris standing in the doorway of the "man cave"

"I feel fine" said Edwin in a nasty tone.

"OKAY! So things are back to normal; now that you have the cast off." exclaimed Paris with her hand on her hip.

"What is that supposed to mean?" asked Edwin.

"It means just what I said, things are back to normal. So when do you start physical therapy?" asked Paris she walked away from the Edwin just in case he decided to become stupid and hit her and went into the kitchen.

"The doctor said I won't need physical therapy?" said Edwin in a nasty tone as he reared back in the recliner to put his legs up.

"That doesn't sound right" said Paris as walks back to the doorway of the man cave looking at Edwin.

"Well I am telling you the doctor said I don't need any physical therapy." screames Edwin and turning up the volume on the television.

There was no more conversation between Paris and Edwin except for when Paris made beans and franks for dinner.

"Why you had to make beans and franks?" yelled Edwin as he threw his fork down on the plate.

"Well Edwin before we moved in this house you claimed beans

and franks were among the delicacies of many great dishes; so I thought you would enjoy it." said Paris smiling.

It was the first time Paris and Edwin slept in the same bed together in 6 weeks; and Paris felt uncomfortable; like she was sleeping in the bed with a stranger. So she got up and went and slept in the guest room. The next morning Steven was at the house early in the morning. Paris was dressed and on her way out the door when she saw Steven walking up the driveway.

"Well Good Morning, Steven." said Paris I am surprised to see you here so bright and early in the morning.

"Good Morning Paris." said Steven with a smirk on his face that made Paris feel uneasy. "I'm taking your husband to buy a car today."

"Oh really," said Paris.

"Edwin didn't tell you?" Asked Steven

"No; I guess he wanted me to be surprise." said Paris walking pass Steven. "So tell me, where are you and Edwin going to shop for a car?"

"We are going to look around in New Jersey." said Steven as he walked up to the doorway.

"Well enjoy your day." said Paris; she got into her car and drove off feeling happy to be getting away Edwin and Steven.

"I only got two thousand dollars to get a car. complained Edwin.

"That will get you a hoop-dee" said Steven driving on the expressway. "How come you so broke?"

"Paris decided to give Anthony five thousand dollars of my money to help him go to college. I sure wish I had Paris as a mother; she take the shirt off her back for that boy." said Edwin.

"Yeah, he sure has it a lot better than we did growing up." said Steven.

"Yeah, I never forget that Easter Sunday; everybody had a new coat; even mom and dad had new coats and I had to wear that old coat with no buttons and mom didn't even sew any buttons on my coat. Remember how I had to fasten my coat with 3 big old safety pins? ask Edwin.

Yeah man, said Steven, "I never forget how you cried because you didn't have a new coat to wear to church. Oh by the way, that reminds me I spoke to Jennifer and she called to ask me how you were doing. She told me you are mad at her. Why are you mad at Jennifer?"

"That was a while ago man." said Edwin he turned his head and looked out the car window feeling disgusted over having to buy a cheap car.

"I think she said you were mad with her over" ......Said Steven pausing and clearing his throat as if he was trying to remember something. "Ah ... safety pin that fell out of your drawers that night you had accident and totaled your car?"

"Look man that's not funny." said Edwin.

"So tell me how Paris has been sleeping lately."

"Hey man, you always are looking for a way to put me down." said Edwin.

"How am I putting you down man?" asked Steven "I just asked you a simple question about your how your wife is sleeping."

"Don't talk to me.....just don't talk to me." screamed Edwin.

"Okay I won't talk to you." "I just don't think it's a good idea that you and Corona are trying to kill Paris in her sleep."

Chapter 17

It was Friday afternoon and Paris stood in front of her painting staring; as if she had fallen into the painting of children swinging on a rainbow and dancing through a meadow of flowers.

"So this will be your fifth painting Ms. Paris how are coming along with it." asked Ms. Becky, standing next to Paris. Paris was starring at the painting and she was lost in her own thoughts.

"We just about have everything ready for the festival in two weeks, naked clowns and all." said Ms. Becky looking at Paris and wondering if Paris heard her.

"Oh, I'm sorry Ms. Becky; I didn't see you standing here." said Paris still staring at her painting.

"Yeah, I see you are a thousand miles away. You seem to have been distracted the over the last couple of days you been here; so tell me what is going on with you?"

Paris told Ms. Becky about Edwin being in a car accident and how the same day Edwin came home from the hospital he fell down the stairs and broke his leg.

"To tell you the truth." said Paris as she walks to the doorway; she stops and picks up her pocketbook off the chair next to the entrance of the room. "I think....no I don't think I know he is cheating on me." Paris started to walk down the stairs; then she stops and looks back at Ms. Becky and stare as though she was in a daze. "I just don't know how to leave him" Paris turned back around and continue to walking down the stairs and she got in her car and she looked back and saw Ms. Becky and Ms. Sarah standing in the doorway of the shelter looking at her. Paris drove back to town with tears in her eyes. Paris cried and she prayed "My God please help me to escape out of this snare of insanity that surrounds me."

When Paris arrived at home she found Edwin yelling and bragging on the phone about his new car to his brother and then he went into making animal noises as usual; and Paris found more time to spend at the shelter and when she wasn't at the shelter or at work; she spent time at church.

"How are you Sister Benson?" asked Brother Lentil. Brother Lintel was one of Paris's least favorite people at church because all he did was talk about how fantastic and smart his son is; he had a nice son; but the boy didn't stand a chance of anyone getting to know him or yet alone liking him because his father was always bragging about him.

"I'm fine, thank you" said Paris. She wouldn't dare ask him how he was doing because she didn't want to hear about little Elroy.

"How is Brother Benson doing?" ask Brother Lentil blocking the exit door as Paris tried to leave. "I hear he was in a car accident and broke his leg."

"It wasn't in the car accident when he broke his leg." said Paris waiting for brother Lentil to move out of her way. Brother Lentil had a puzzled look on his face as if he was in deep thought.

"How did he break his leg?" Brother Lintel finally asked.

"He broke his legs coming down the steps in the house." said Paris.

"That's what happens when the carpet gets dirt, it greasy; it will send you flying every time. Well I guess I better be getting on home. said Brother Lentil as he turned to walk out the door.

"He broke his leg coming down the steps screaming and cursing at me." said Paris, walking behind Brother Lintel.

"Why was he screaming at you?" asked Brother Lentil as he stops and turns around to look at Paris. "What did you say to him to set him off?"

"What do you mean Brother Lentil; by asking me what did I say to him to set him off?" ask Paris stopping behind Brother Lentil.

"What I mean Paris is that I can't imagine Brother Benson cursing at you; he is such a fine and upstanding brother; you must have said or did something to cause him to treat you like that."

"Brother Lentil isn't I a fine and upstanding sister; are you calling me a liar? ask Paris speaking slowly and softly.

"Oh no; said Brother Lentil it's just that..............."

"Let me tell you something Brother Lentil; I can't imagine your fine upstanding brother cursing me out and hitting me every time his mother calls or ends up in a mental institution and whenever his sick, demented, whorish sister gets into trouble, your fine upstanding brother takes it out on me; and yet you stand here and insult me and tell me that I am the reason why he mistreats me, abuses me!" Paris was so angry at Brother Lentil all she wanted to do was slap him around a few of times.

"Well Sunday when he comes to church, I would like to speak with both of you to see if I can offer you some counseling from the bible. I got to run; Elroy is waiting for me to take him to his art class; I tell you Sister Paris that is one talented, fine young man I have." Said Brother Lintel walking out the door; he didn't even bother to hold the door for Paris. When Paris step outside Brother Lintel was already in his car and pulling out of the church parking lot.

"Why....why did I even bother tell Brother Lintel? They are all prejudice against women." Paris thought to herself. Paris came home in through the garage door and into the kitchen entrance where she saw Edwin sitting at the kitchen table.

"Hey Paris, I was just about to call you; do you want to go for a spin in my new car?" asked Edwin.

"I was wondering when you was going to get around to asking me." said Paris as she turns around to walk back outside. "Come on lets go."

Edwin got up from the kitchen table limping on his cane and they both left through the front door where Edwin's car was parked in the drive way.

"I figure we can go to Ruby's for dinner." said Edwin, backing the car out of the driveway.

When they got to the restaurant Paris ordered the salad bar and ribs and Edwin order a steak and baked potato and his usual Gin and Coke. Edwin talked about where all the places they could visit and they could even go a visit Anthony so he could see his new car.

"What cha looking at Paris?" asked Edwin? Turning around and looking behind him.

"What do you mean what am I looking at?" asked Paris putting her fork down and wiping her mouth and hands with her napkin.

"I see you looking at that man over there?" said Edwin.

"You know Edwin;" said Paris as she leans across the table and whispers to Edwin so the couples sitting at the nearby tables can't hear her. "I am tired of you taking the "O" out of my joy. I am tired of going places with you, and you accusing me of looking at men. Furthermore, I am tired of your insecurities. I am tired of you're sick, twisted, and demented, asinine mentality. I am going to sit here and enjoy my meal and if you don't like it you can kiss my twist and you know where you can go."

"I know you be looking at men!" hollered Edwin.

"Go ahead and get loud and rowdy in here so everybody can see the fool that you are and I will have the manager call the police on you for disturbing the peace and have thrown out of here!" said Paris smiling as she sat back in her seat and continue eating.

Edwin looked around and saw the couple at the next table looking at him and he got quiet. They finished their meal without any more conversation and that was fine with Paris. On the drive back home Edwin talked to Corona on his cell phone and her son Butch got into trouble with the law because as Corona put it; a gang jumped on Butch and the police arrested him for fighting in a gang; and of course Butch was innocent. Edwin told Paris about Butch getting arrested. Paris knew Corona was lying and Edwin was satisfied in believing the lie. So Paris felt why bother discussing it.

For the next few weeks things were quiet except for the nightmares. Paris woke up kicking, swinging, and gasping for air. After she was able to breathe normal again she looked over at Edwin. Edwin wasn't in the bed. The bedroom door was left wide open. Edwin always closed the door when he leaves out the bedroom when Paris was sleeping.

"Could he have been smothering me and ran out the room when I woke up? That's not possible he can barely walk; yet alone run. He couldn't be smothering me and running with his cane." Paris thought to herself as she got up and went down stairs and saw Edwin sitting in his recliner in the family room watching TV.

"Hey Edwin, you couldn't sleep either?" asked Paris as she entered into the family room and she stares at Edwin watching television.

"My leg hurt." said Edwin rubbing his leg

"Did you take anything for it?" ask Paris still staring at Edwin trying figure out if he can really walk without his cane.

"No; I don't want to get addicted to pain killers." said Edwin

"What on earth are you watching?" ask Paris frowning.

"I'm watching Friday the 13th." said Edwin as he turned up the volume on the television to drown out their conversation.

"I am going back to bed." said Paris standing up. "You know you should really get therapy for your leg. I would hate to see your leg get worst." said Paris as she was walked out of the family room.

"I'll be alright." said Edwin.

Paris went back to bed but she just couldn't go back to sleep right away; because now she was starting to think that Edwin was smothering her and running, but that could not be possible. He can't run. Paris prayed for protection and prayed for answers and that she wasn't losing her mind and she cried herself to sleep.

Chapter 18

Saturday morning Paris was up early and she was racing around the house getting all her things ready to go to the shelter. This was the last weekend before the Domestic Violence Awareness Fair and Paris wanted to be at the shelter early just to help out. Within eight weeks Paris had did eight paintings and she was hoping that they would all sell to help with funding for the women's shelter. She ran upstairs to get her jacket out of the bedroom closet and then knocked on the bathroom door and opened it because she knew Edwin was in the shower.

"Edwin," said Paris; "I am leaving now; I'll see you later."

"Okay Paris, I'll see you later." Edwin yelled back.

Paris was wondering why Edwin was up so early on a Saturday morning; but she knew better than to ask. The house phone rang just as Paris came down the stairs. Paris ran into the kitchen and picked up the phone.

"Hello" answer Paris

"Hi Paris, how are you?" This is Cousin Mabel

"Oh hi Mabel "said Paris. Out of all of Inez's cousins; Mable was the only cousin that Inez liked.

"How are you Mable, we haven't heard from you in a long time?"

"May I speak to Edwin?" said Mable.

"Well Edwin is in the shower, you can call him back later on his cell phone. Do you have his cell number?" Paris felt somewhat insulted that Mable didn't seem to want to talk to her; but it was okay because she was in hurry.

"I was calling to tell Edwin that his mother is coming out of the hospital today on a day pass and she is planning on killing one of her grand children."

"What?!" said Paris falling back in to the kitchen chair.

"Yes that right, said Mable." I just spoke to Inez a few minutes ago and she said she is going to kill one of her grandchildren."

"Okay now" said Paris trying to gather her thoughts. "Are you sure about this; I mean did she actually say she was going to kill one of the grand children?"

"Yes, I clearly heard her say it." said Mable sounding like she was becoming impatient with Paris.

"Mable" said Paris speaking slowly. "Did you call and tell her doctor?"

"No. I figure I should tell Edwin being that he is going to pick his mother up from the hospital today." said Mable sounding upset like she was about to cry.

Paris wanted to scream and yell at Mable for not calling the doctor; but she had to compose herself and say a quick pray. "Okay, Mable; do you know what grandchild she wants to kill."

"No; I didn't ask her."

"Okay what time is she being release on her day pass?" ask Paris trying to keep her composure.

"Inez said she is coming out at noon time." said Mable.

Thank you for calling and telling us Mable I will let Edwin know.

Paris hung up the receiver on the phone and took a deep breath and then picked the receiver back up and dialed 411.

"Operator how may I help you?"

"Yes, may I have the phone number to Bellevue Hospital Psychiatric Ward?" ask Paris.

"Please hold." said operator and then a recording came on stating the phone number; but Paris didn't have a pen or paper nearby and could not remember the number. She hung up and called the operator again.

Operator, how may I help you?

"Would please give me the number to Bellevue Hospital Psychiatric ward and connect me to the hospital?"

"Yes the number is 212 555-1256; I am now connecting your call. May you have a nice day".

"Thank you operator" said Paris as she open the sliding door in the kitchen and steps outside onto the patio and carrying the house phone and closing the sliding door behind her.

"Hello Psychiatric Ward. Nurse Brown speaking; how can I help you?"

"Hello I need to speak with the head nurse please; this is in reference to Inez Benson who is a patient in your psychiatric ward?"

"Just one minute please." The nurse put Paris on hold and elevator music came on. A minute later a voice came on the phone.

"Hello this is Nurse Mack; how may I help you?"

"My name is Paris Benson am I speaking with the head nurse?"

"Yes you are how I may help you."

"My mother-in-law is an in-patient there. Her name is Inez Benson and she spoke with her cousin this morning and Inez told her cousin that she plans on killing one of her grandchildren and I really need to speak with Inez's doctor."

"Hold on I will get Dr Daniels for you."

A couple of minutes had gone by and Dr. Daniels came on the phone and Paris explained to him about the conversation she had with cousin Mable and her concerns about Inez coming out on a day pass.

"Thank you for informing me Ms. Benson. Let me assure you that Inez will not be given a day pass. Thank you again and feel free to call anytime." said Dr. Daniels.

"Thank you so much." said Paris. She hung up the phone and open the patio door and step into the house; she put the phone down on the snack bar and turn around and saw Edwin standing there looking at her."

"So." said Paris. "Where are you off to?"

"I'm going to pick up my mother from the hospital." said Edwin.

"Oh really" said Paris walking by Edwin "Well tell her I said hello and enjoy your day."

Paris turned around and walked out the patio door across the patio, through the grass, and around the house and out to the driveway and got in her car and took off.

Paris stopped at the coffee shop and picked up a cup of coffee. She needed something to clear her thoughts; she knew Inez wasn't going to kill Anthony; thank God he was away at school. Steven and Corona both had children; so what grandchild was she planning to kill? Paris had a long drive a head of her and she needed to talk to someone about all this crazy stuff. She had no one; all she could do is pray. Then she decided to call Edwin; after all Inez is his mother and once he arrives at the hospital Edwin would find out that she called and spoke with the doctor and if he starts yelling at her she would just hang up. She took out her cell phone and decided to call the house phone just to see if Edwin was still at home.

"Hello" said Edwin sounding like he was in a good mood.

"Hi Edwin," this is Paris. "I'm sorry for running out the house without telling you; but your mother isn't coming out of the hospital today on a day-pass."

"Oh yeah, I know I was going to pick her up but she called and said they cancelled her day- pass." Said Edwin sounding like he was happy about not having to spend the day with Inez.

"Well did you speak with your Cousin Mable?"

"No....I didn't. I haven't heard from her in a long time. Did she call?"

"Well" said Paris taking a deep breath. "Mable said that your mother plans on killing one of her grandchildren." said Paris.

"Oh yeah" said Edwin "she is always saying that."

"No...no....no what do you mean she is always saying that?" Scream Paris spilling coffee on her pants.

"What's wrong?" asked Edwin

"I just spilled hot coffee on my pants."

"Well you better be careful; where are you at anyway?" asked Edwin.

"I am at the coffee shop." said Paris; she was in shock that Edwin was so unconcerned about his mother's threats to kill one of her grandchildren. Paris tried to be calm and as she cleaned the coffee off her pants with a napkin.

"What grandchild is she talking about killing?" asked Paris.

"She is talking about killing Butch; she said that Butch gets on her last nerve." said Edwin in his nonchalant voice.

"Ah Edwin, you seemed to be okay with your mother threatening to kill one of the children; how long has she been making plans to commit murder?"

"Paris you are worried about nothing; it just that Butch get's on her nerves and she just saying she wants to kill him to let off steam." said Edwin laughing as he sat down at the kitchen table.

A cold chill ran down Paris's spine and heart started to race "Did you tell your mother where Anthony is?" asked Paris as she got out of the car and looked around the parking lot.

"No I didn't." said Edwin besides she said she was going to kill Butch not Anthony.

There was a long pause. Paris got back in her car. "I don't care what grandchild she is talking about killing; in fact I am just upset she is talking about killing somebody... anybody!" yelled Paris.

"You know, Paris you just blowing this all out of proportion." Said Edwin laughing at Paris and thinking how she is just a problematic person.

"I have to hang up I am in traffic now and you know I don't talk on the phone and drive." said Paris.

Paris got back out of the car and went back into the coffee shop and got another cup of coffee. On the drive to Hidden Valley Haven for Women Paris prayed that God would give her the courage to escape from her deranged and dysfunctional family. The insanity was starting to drive her crazy. In fact she felt that maybe she was just as crazy as they were for even staying in this marriage.

Once Paris arrived at the shelter she saw some of the women sewing and knitting and others were in the kitchen baking. Paris had brought in bags of sugar, flour and eggs to help with baking the cakes and cookies. By four-thirty that evening Paris was saying her goodbyes to the ladies and to the children and just as she was about to walk out the door Ms. Becky stopped her.

"So Ms Paris; how are you feeling?"

"To tell you the truth Ms. Becky; I feel like I am about to lose my mind!" exclaimed Paris.

"Come," said Ms. Becky let's go into my office. "Ms. Becky turned and called out to Ms. Sarah to bring in a pot of hot tea."

Paris told Ms. Becky about the Inez being in the mental institution and how she had plan on coming out to kill one of her grandchildren; Paris broke down in tears and told Ms. Becky about the nightmares of being smothered and how the nightmares was happening more frequently now that Anthony was away at school.

"Here have some more tea Ms. Paris" said Ms. Becky and passing Paris a box of tissues.

"So why don't you leave?" asked Ms. Becky

"I can't leave; because I don't know how to leave. I don't have anywhere to go; I have no family. I will be homeless. And besides I don't have any grounds for divorce." said Paris crying and wiping the tears away from her eyes.

"What do you mean?" asked Ms Becky.

"Well, as a Christian the only grounds for divorce is adultery. said Paris setting her cup and saucer down on the coffee table.

"So you don't think your husband is having an affair?" asked Ms. Becky.

"Oh yeah, he is having an affair; I just can't prove it. If I can prove it; then I would have grounds for a divorce and believe me Ms. Becky I would divorce him in a blink of an eye." said Paris.

"You can always hire a detective." suggested Ms. Becky.

"I don't have that kind of money." said Paris.

"Well," said Ms. Becky. "You need to get out of there. Eventually, he is going to kill you or you are going to snap and kill him."

"Can I come and stay here Ms. Becky?" asked Paris.

"No. said Ms Becky; these women are much worse off than you are; they come in beaten up and some have severe mental health problems." "So this wouldn't be a good place for you."

"Don't you have relatives or friends you can stay with?" asked Ms. Becky.

"No; I don't have any friends; I have been so busy taking care of my family I never taken the time to make friends." And I have no relatives that I know of." said Paris.

"I want you to know Paris you are in a dangerous situation and you need to tell everybody; like the elders in your church, any friends and associates that you may have. Tell your doctors and tell Mr. Bonds for your own protection that your husband is smothering you while you are sleeping."

"Like somebody is going to believe me or somebody is going to care; and when I tell them that I think Edwin is smothering me they are just going to think I'm crazy." said Paris. Standing up and putting her on her jacket.

"You need to make it everybody's business for your own protection; the more people that know Paris, the safer you will be until you can figure out how you going to leave." Said Ms. Becky; standing up and walking Paris out to her car.

"Thanks for taking the time to talk with me Ms. Becky." said Paris as she got in her car and drove away.

Chapter 19

"I sure did miss you baby." said Edwin lying in bed holding Jennifer in his arms.

"So did your wife come home yet?" ask Jennifer.

"No" said Edwin as he pushed Jennifer off his chest and sat up in bed.

"I'm sorry I asked." said Jennifer.

"I'm not upset with you; it just that every time I think about Paris I get upset."

"Rightly so; you should be upset; being married to a nut case for over 20 years." said Jennifer now sitting up in bed.

Edwin got up from the bed and start putting on his clothes.

"Why are you leaving so soon?" asked Jennifer.

"We are leaving." said Edwin putting on his pants.

"I'm sorry I asked about your wife Edwin" said Jennifer getting out of the bed. "So if you don't mind me asking why didn't she come home?"

"They wouldn't let her come home because she was talking about killing Corona's son." said Edwin.

"Wow that is horrible." Jennifer hurried up and put on her blouse and skirt.

"So are they going to lock her up for good?"

"No." said Edwin. She will be home in two weeks.

"Wow, in 2 weeks; well I sure hope she doesn't find out about me; she sounds like a real basket case just waiting to make a scene and why are you so in a hurrying to go home?".

"I got things to do and do me a favor and drop the questions. said Edwin picking up his wallet from the night stand. He opens his wallet and takes out ten dollars and places it on the night stand. I have to go; are you ready?" ask Edwin

Edwin and Jennifer stepped off the elevator and proceeded to walk across the hotel lobby

"Oh No!" yelled Edwin.

"What's wrong?" asked Jennifer frowning.

"I forgot my cane; I left my cane upstairs." Edwin turned around and rushed back to the elevator but the elevator doors had close; so Edwin ran up the stairs to the 2nd floor. He went in the room and he couldn't find the cane. He looked in the bathroom and there was no cane. He looked in the closet and there was no cane. He looked in every corner of the room, no cane. He looked under the bed and there was no cane. Jennifer stood in the doorway watching Edwin running around the room like a mad man looking for his cane.

"Edwin honey," said Jennifer. "You didn't come into the hotel with a cane."

"I didn't walk in here with a cane?" ask Edwin, turning around in the room looking for his cane.

"No sweetie, you didn't." said Jennifer; standing in the doorway with her arms folded across her chest and chewing gum. "I don't see why you need a cane; you are walking perfectly fine."

Edwin walks over to the door and grabs Jennifer by her hand and rushes down the hall to the elevator. Edwin and Jennifer stopped at the front desk; so Edwin could pay for the room.

"Excuse me Miss" said Edwin looking wild man. "Did anyone turn in a cane?"

"No Sir." answer the Clerk.

"Well how long have you been here?" asked Edwin

"I have been here since you checked in this afternoon and no one has turned in a cane." said the Clerk as she backed away from the desk.

"You said you were here all afternoon when I checked in; did you see me with a cane?"

"Sir, I see many people pass through this lobby and I can't say for certain if I saw you with a cane. What kind of cane was it?" asked the Clerk

"What do you mean what kind of cane was it?!" yell Edwin "What do you think I was walking with a candy cane?"

"Hey Edwin, don't be rude; she is only trying to help." said Jennifer.

"My cane has to be around here somewhere" said Edwin. He walks around the hotel lobby several times looking behind and on the side of the coaches, chairs, tables, and plants. Jennifer stood watching Edwin roam around the hotel lobby like a wild animal looking for his prey. Then Edwin circled his way back over to the desk where the clerk stood writing.

"Excuse me." said Edwin banging on the desk to get the clerk's attention.

"Yes Sir how may I help you?" asked the clerk; looking at Edwin like he had lost his mind.

"Do you have a lost and found?"

"Oh come on Edwin are you serious?" ask Jennifer standing behind him.

"Just shut up Jennifer!" yell Edwin.

"Sir, everything that is lost is dropped off at the front desk." said the clerk as she backs away again from the desk. "May I suggest Sir that you write your name and telephone number down where you can be reached and if someone should turn in the cane we will certainly call you."

Edwin scribbles his name and phone number on a piece of paper and storms out of the hotel lobby waving to the security guard for his car to be brought to the front of the hotel.

"Maybe you left the cane in your car." suggested Jennifer walking behind Edwin.

"Yeah maybe you are right." said Edwin; when his car arrived; he tipped the man five dollars and opened car door and looked in the front seats and looked in the back seats and he looked in the trunk but there was no cane to be found.

"My cane is not here!" yells Edwin.

"Well", Said Jennifer. "I think I will just get a cab and go back to my sister's house from here."

"Oh no, you are not going anywhere!" Yell Edwin grabbing hold of Jennifer's arm and pulling her to the passenger's side of the car. "You got me into this mess and you staying with me until I find my cane. Edwin forces Jennifer in the car and slams the door and then walked back to the driver side of the car, got in and he took off screeching down the street.

"Edwin explain to me what are you talking about. What mess did I get you into?""

Edwin just ignored Jennifer as he merged onto the highway.

"You better slow down." said Jennifer. "You know you driving "while-black" in New Jersey and where are we going anyway?" asked Jennifer.

"I am back tracking to everywhere we went this afternoon." said Edwin.

Edwin drove an hour back to a gas station he stopped at before he picked Jennifer up from her sister's house.

"What are we doing over here?" asked Jennifer.

"I stopped here to get gas." said Edwin getting out of the car and walking into the 711 store, he saw the woman behind the casher register ringing up lotto tickets for a customer.

"Excuse me, Miss. I think I lost my cane in here earlier today." said Edwin as he walks behind the customer standing in front of the counter.

"No sir;" said the woman turning her attention back to the customer standing at the counter. "That will be forty dollars sir."

"I will take a pack of Newport cigarettes and $25.00 on pump number five." said the customer handing the clerk a credit card.

Edwin paces back and forth behind the customer and when the customer finished his transactions Edwin ran up to the counter. "Are you sure you didn't see my cane?"

"No Sir, I didn't see a cane." said the woman, stepping back from the register to look down on the floor. Oh wait a minute Sir, here is a cane. She bends down and picks up the cane; but before the woman could show Edwin the cane a short stocky white man about five feet tall came running out from the back room.

That's my cane." said the man rushing pass Edwin to the counter.

"Oh Mr. Solomon, said the woman. "I'm sorry; I just saw the cane on the floor; I didn't even realize you were still here."

"Give me my cane." Said Mr. Solomon.

Edwin was furious and he slammed his fist down on the counter. "Do I look like I walk around on a midget cane?" yells Edwin turning around and he swings open the door and leaves the store.

"What's wrong?" ask Jennifer when Edwin got back in his car slamming the door and he took off speeding down the street.

"Nothing is wrong; they just tried to give me a midget cane." said Edwin.

"I didn't know 711 sold canes." said Jennifer.

"I didn't say they tried to sell me one, I said they tried to give me one." said Edwin as he merged back onto the highway.

"Why would they try to give you a midget cane or was it a cane for midget?" asked Jennifer laughing.

"Shut up Jennifer just shut up!" screams Edwin.

"I'm sorry okay; it's just that I never seen a midget on a cane." said Jennifer giggling.

Edwin had driven back near the hotel. "What are we doing back here?" asked Jennifer looking confused.

"I told you before I am backing tracking; now just shut up." said Edwin getting out of the car and going into the drugstore and Edwin questioned the floor clerk, cashier clerk, and the pharmacy clerk and when everyone said they didn't see his cane; he proceeded to race through each isle in drug store looking for his cane.

"Would you like to purchase a new cane?" Ask the sales clerk.

"No, I have a designer cane; nothing like the junk you sell here!" said Edwin storming out of the drug store and gets back into his car where he found Jennifer texting on her cell phone.

"Well Edwin, did you find your cane?" asked Jennifer.

"Did you see me get in the car with a cane?" ask Edwin; turning on the engine. Edwin then gets back out of his car and he looks in the trunk and then looks in the back seats of the car; but there was no cane. Edwin gets back in the car and pull out from the drug stores' parking lot and driving slowly down the street back toward the hotel.

"I know we are not going back to the hotel!" said Jennifer.

"No, said Edwin "I am just trying to remember where I could have gone with my cane."

"What is the story with you and this cane; I mean did you inherited or something?" said Jennifer.

"No" said Edwin. "It just has to be the same exact cane."

"Why?" ask Jennifer.

"What do you mean why?" ask Edwin.

"I mean why do you need it to be the same exact cane; I mean does it have some sort of special mechanism in it or something?" ask Jennifer frowning and looking confused.

"No Jennifer dear; it's just that I am depended on it when I go for physical therapy." Said Edwin in a calm voice and turning up the volume on the radio.

"You need to go for some mental health therapy too." laughs Jennifer.

Edwin pulled the car over and grabs Jennifer by her neck. "Let me tell you something Jennifer darling; don't you ever tell me I need therapy again because if you do I will punch your lights out. Now I am telling you for the last time. Shut up!" Said Edwin turning the car around heading for the highway an hour later Edwin pulls in the bar's parking lot.

"Oh goody" said Jennifer getting out of the car. "I'm thirsty."

"We are not staying!" said Edwin getting out of the car and slamming the door and quickly walks over to the club.

"Well I have to use the bathroom." said Jennifer walking ahead of Edwin and going into the club.

Edwin's cell phone rings, he pulls his cell phone out of his pants pocket and sees its Corona calling. "Hey Corona, what's up?

"Hey Edwin, I need to borrow a hundred dollars because I have to pay my phone bill." said Corona.

"I don't have time to talk to you now." said Edwin standing outside the club.

"What's going on with you?" ask Corona,

"I lost my cane." said Edwin.

"You lost your cane, how on earth did you managed to lose your cane Edwin?" ask Corona.

"I don't know." said Edwin pacing back and forth in front of the club."

"Well you can't go home without a cane." said Corona

"Yeah, I know cause if I do; then Paris will know that I have been smothering her." said Edwin.

"Can't you buy another cane" asked Corona.

"Corona, if I go home with different cane Paris is going to have a hundred questions." said Edwin still pacing back and forth.

"Yeah, you right about that and no one who is depended on a cane put it down and lose it. Anyway, can you give me a hundred dollars for my phone bill?" asked Corona.

"I got to go, I talk to you tomorrow." said Edwin clicking off his cell phone and walked into the club. Edwin stopped at the bar and began banging on the bar counter. "Can I get some service over here" yelled Edwin.

Just one minute Sir; I'll be right with you. Said the woman behind the bar pouring a drinks for customers.

"I need to ask you a question." yells Edwin.

"Just a minute Sir, I will be right with you." Said the woman.

"I just want to know if you saw my cane I left in here earlier today." said Edwin.

The woman came over and looks at Edwin like he was crazy. "No Sir; I didn't see your cane; would you like a drink?"

"No, I want my cane." Shouted Edwin leaning over the counter yelling at the woman

The bouncer came over and told Edwin to hold it down. Edwin only got louder and tries pushing the bouncer away from him and the bouncer punched Edwin in the stomach. Jennifer came out of the ladies room saw the bouncer throwing Edwin out of the club. Jennifer ran out the club and saw Edwin getting up off the ground, bending over holding his stomach and grasping for air. After a few minutes he stood up and starts dusting him off and starts limping back to the car.

"Are you alright"? Ask Jennifer.

"Yeah, I think I sprain my left ankle. said Edwin.

Jennifer puts Edwin's arm around her neck and puts her arm around his waist and helps him back to the car.

"Do you think you can drive?" ask Jennifer.

"Yeah it's my left ankle" said Edwin getting into the car.

Jennifer walked around to the passenger's side of the car and opens the door and get in.

"Are you sure you left your house with your cane?" ask Jennifer.

"Yeah Jennifer, I told you a hundred times; I had my cane when I left home" said Edwin.

"Well let me look in the trunk?" asked Jennifer.

"I have already looked in the trunk twice and it wasn't there." said Edwin sounding frustrated.

"Well a fresh pair eye can't hurt." said Jennifer as she got out of the car.

Jennifer walks to the back of the car and knocks on the trunk for Edwin to unlock it. She opens the trunk and all she see is a spare tire and a jack; she slams the trunk close and then she goes to the back passenger side of the car and opens the door and there is nothing on the seat; then she bends over and feels under the seats and she feels something hard; round, long and smooth and pulls it out from under the car seat and see that it's Edwin's royal cane that he been acting fool over for the last couple of hours. Jennifer takes the cane out the car and opens the front passenger door where she had been sitting and puts the cane in the seat next to Edwin and slams the car door shut and starts walking across the parking lot toward the club.

"Hey Jennifer," yells Edwin. "Where are you going?"

Jennifer stops and turns around with her hand on hip. "I am going back in the club and get myself a drink and then I am calling a cab and going back to my sister's house."

"Wait; I'll join you." yells Edwin; getting out of the car and limping toward Jennifer.

"Oh, no you don't. You acted like a fool all night; take you stupid behind home and leave me alone!"

"Why you going to be like that baby?" ask Edwin with his arms stretched out.

"Go home Edwin because if you don't I will scream so loud I will have the swat team out here on your crazy behind." shouts Jennifer; shaking her finger in Edwin's face.

The bouncer came out of the bar and saw Jennifer and Edwin arguing in the parking lot.

"Excuse me, Miss. Is this guy bothering you?"

"Yes he is!" said Jennifer, with her hand on her hip and nodding.

"You better get to moving mister before I have to splatter your guts all over this parking lot."

"Yeah, yeah alright" said Edwin waving his hands and walking back to his car.

"You are not right Jennifer!" screamed Edwin as he got into his car and drove off into traffic screaming and cussing.

When Edwin came home he found Paris sitting in the living room reading.

"Hi Paris" said Edwin limping through the front door with his cane into the foyer.

"Oh Edwin," said Paris getting up off the sofa and walking into foyer to greet Edwin.

"How are you feeling; you were gone all day where were you?"

I was just about to call you. I went to see my mother and spent some time with her." said Edwin limping down the foyer.

Your mother called this afternoon; and she was looking for you to come for a visit. said Paris.

"I just left my mother." said Edwin.

"Then why did she call, and say she was waiting for you to visit if you had already been at the hospital?" asked Paris.

"I don't know why she called, why you would ask me a question like that; she is in the nut house!" said Edwin limping on his cane pass Paris down the foyer and through the kitchen to his man-cave."

Paris knew Edwin was lying and she follows Edwin to his man cave; "so how have your leg been doing since they have taken the cast off Edwin?"

"It hurts." said Edwin

"You seem to be limping worst than you had been; if you went for physical therapy it would help you to get back up on your feet so you can go back to work. Said Paris looking at Edwin wondering what he has been up to.

"The doctor said I don't need physical therapy" shouted Edwin sitting in his recliner and turning on the television with the remote control.

"That doesn't make sense Edwin." said Paris; walking into the room and sitting down on the coach next to Edwin sitting in his recliner.

"I don't want to talk about it" said Edwin.

"You don't want to talk about it; you look like you are getting worst?" said Paris frowning.

"Just what I said" answered Edwin "I don't want to talk about it."

Paris left the room and went back into the living room where she sat praying for a release. "Oh my God please show me a way out."

Chapter 20

Sunday morning came around real fast and Paris sat down stairs at the kitchen table waiting for Edwin to go to church with her and trying to piece together the nightmare she had of being smoother again. I have to stop taking those sleeping pills." Paris said to herself. Those pills must be causing me to have these nightmares. Being smothered seemed so real but there was Edwin asleep next to her. Edwin finally came downstairs limping with his cane. Paris got up from the kitchen table pick up her bible and her pocketbook and walks down the foyer were Edwin was leaning on the wall and holding on his cane for support.

"Well, I am ready to go." said Edwin.

"Okay." said Paris as she held the front door open and watched Edwin limp down the driveway to his car.

"Are you sure you going to be able to drive" ask Paris.

"Yeah, I go through this every day." said Edwin opening the car door and getting in behind the wheel.

When they got to the church they were late as usual and Edwin of course had to make his grand entrance and refused to sit in the back. Paris could barely sit through the services. It was the nightmares of being smother that she could not get out of mind. She got up and went to the bathroom and went into one of the stalls so no one would see her crying. Paris felt like she was losing her mind; after she cried for a good five minutes she came out of the stall. *"I sure wished I had driven my car so I could just walk out of here. I can't stand sitting next to Edwin "the great pretender" as though everything is fine."* Paris thought to herself as she freshens up her make-up. After the service Brother Lintel walked up to Edwin and Paris and greeted them.

"It's nice to see you both here at the services today Brother Benson." said Brother Lintel shaking Edwin's hand.

"Thank you; it's really nice being here." Said Edwin lying; knowing the only reason he was there was because Inez told him to always go to church.

Paris stood next Edwin but Brother Lintel never acknowledges Paris at all.

"Let go back in my office so we chat for a few minutes." said Brother Lintel.

"Can I come along too, or should I just wait in the car? ask Paris.

Brother Lintel turned around "Of course, it wouldn't be a party without you Sister Paris.

Paris didn't find Brother Lintel funny at all; she follows Edwin and Brother Lintel to his office.

Brother Lintel sits behind his desk and he places his bible in front of him and Edwin and Paris sits in the two chairs directly in front the desk.

Paris told me the other day when she was here at church that you all are having some marital problems Brother Edwin; do you mind telling me what's going on?

"Paris is never happy." said Edwin. I provide a roof over her head and food on the table and all she does is complain; in fact, she is the reason I fell down the stairs and broke my leg!

"What; you are lying!" yells Paris; sitting on the edge of her chair looking at Edwin.

"Just a minute Sister Paris, let Brother Benson finish what he has to say and then you can speak." said Brother Lentil.

"She had me so upset; because the day I came home from the hospital I beg Paris to stay home with me; but oh no, she just had to go to work." said Edwin sitting on the edge of his seat looking like a wild man with his eyes budging out. "And you know what else she has been doing Brother Lintel.?"

"No, I have no idea; do tell. said Brother Lentil looking at Paris with a look of disappointment shaking his head.

"Just so you know my poor mother is in New York in the hospital and I have been running back and forth with my broken leg meanwhile Paris has taken up with some women's movement group against men." said Edwin trying hard to look sad.

Paris sat there with her mouth wide open and tears started to flow from her eyes.

"Here are some tissues Sister Paris "said Brother Lintel.

Paris snatches the tissue box from Brother Lintel and pulls out a tissue and wipes her eyes and her nose and sat the tissue box on the desk.

"Brother Lintel, Edwin is sitting here telling you a bold face lie!" said Paris.

"Oh I am lying about Mommy being in the hospital Paris?" shouted Edwin.

"No you are not lying about your crazy demonic mother being in the hospital; but you did not fall down the stairs because of me. You were cursing and screaming at me for no reason and you missed a step and fell. And furthermore, I have not taken up with some woman's movement against men!" said Paris standing up crying and yelling at Edwin.

"Okay, calm down Sister Paris and have a seat." Said Brother

Lintel with his hand folded on his desk. "You know the bible says a wife should have deep respect for her husband and she should be in subjection to him because he is the head of the household."

"I'm the one that came to you Brother Lintel; to tell you that we are having marital problems and you have not even heard my side and sit there and tell me that I need to have deep respect and be in subjection to a man that smothers me in the middle of the night and runs." cries Paris.

"Well, Sister Paris I don't see how Brother Benson could possibly be running when he can hardly walk. So tell me Sister Paris have you been watching horror movies on television?" asked Brother Lintel with a smirk on his face.

"She is always watching those "Life Time" movies." Edwin interrupted.

"No Brother Lintel I do not be watching horror movies." Said Paris feeling betrayed and beaten down.

They sat in the church for 45 minutes listening to Brother Lintel tell Paris about how she needs to be a supportive wife and being bible whipped at the same time.

"Sister Paris" said Brother Lintel God hates divorce.

"Yes I know" said Paris. "I remember reading in the bible how the men were mistreating their wives and divorcing them to marry younger women and God was angry with them."

"And let me tell you Brother Lintel." interrupted Edwin "when we go to concerts she stands up and screams and dances in front of everyone."

"That is not befitting of a Christian wife to be acting like that Paris."

Paris took a deep breath pressing her lips together and looks down and then looks up at Brother Lintel.

"Tell me something Brother Lintel have you ever went to a ball game and jumped out of your seat and screamed for your favorite team?" asked Paris in a bitter soft tone and leaning on his desk.

"Yes I have." said Brother Lintel.

"Well; that is no different than what I do at a concert and there is nothing wrong with dancing. I grew up dancing. And you know why I dance Brother Lintel?" asked Paris steaming mad.

"No Sister Paris, why don't you tell me why you dance." Said Brother Lintel; leaning back in his black leather swivel chair.

Paris leans across and looks at Brother Lintel in his eyes as she spoke slowly and whisper. "Because I like to dance!"

"What, what...what did she say?" asked Edwin.

"I said I liked to dance Edwin." Shouted Paris; staring at Edwin with hate in her eyes as she sat back in the chair.

There was a silence that filled the room. Paris never felt so abused and hurt in her life. Finally Paris asked Brother Lintel how his son Elroy was doing in his art classes. That got Brother Lintel off of Paris's case and he went into his Elroy stories and then Edwin was ready to leave. And nothing was resolved and Paris and Edwin argue all the way back home and the argument continue on into the late evening and then the house phone rang and Paris answered the phone and it was Corona crying.

"Hello.....Corona is that you?" asked Paris

"I am so upset" said Corona crying. I ....I made a terrible mistake.

Paris started to wonder why Corona was calling on the house phone and not calling Edwin on his cell phone. "So what kind of mistake did you make?"

"I am pregnant with Sam's baby." cries Corona,

"Who's Sam, Corona?" asked Paris.

"You know Sam...Samuel Benson." said Corona.

"Samuel Benson, Corona?" ssked Paris in shock; as she sat down on the bar stool in front of the snack bar. "You are pregnant by your father's nephew, your first cousin?"

Edwin rushed over and snatched the receiver from Paris. "Hey Corona what is going on?"

"I want to talk to Paris." said Corona.

Edwin was just as much in shock as Paris was and he handed the phone back to Paris.

"Yeah Corona, how did you managed to get pregnant by Sam?" asked Paris feeling like maybe she shouldn't ask..

"I called Sam and asked him to borrow five hundred dollars he told me come over because he had the money." cries Corona

"When did Sam ever have five hundred dollars?" asked Paris; "Oh never mind finish telling me what happen."

"Well." said Corona still crying. "He said he had the money and to come over and I went over to his house and we went to drinking and smoking some weed and then Sam said he would only give me the money if I go to bed with him."

"And what did you need this money for?" Asked Paris

"I was late paying my rent." cried Corona.

"Why didn't you just tell him you would pay him back?" Asked Paris

He wanted me to pay him back the following week and I told I wasn't going to be able to because I had other bills to pay. said Corona still crying.

Paris knows that Corona lives in the projects and her rent wasn't any more than $350 dollars a month and that included electric and gas.

"So Corona, you just went to bed with Sam for money?" ask

Paris shaking her head in disbelief. "Okay so why are you calling me to tell me this; I mean what do you expect me to do about it?"

"Well I am 5 weeks pregnant and I was wondering should I get an abortion?"

"Corona, you have had four abortions already and I just want to enlighten you that abortions are not a form of birth control. You are a Christian and you supposedly go to church every week and you are calling me to ask should you have an abortion after you purposely went and had sex with your cousin Sam." Said Paris; shaking her head and looking over at Edwin. "To be perfectly honest with you Corona, I can't wrap my brain around this situation. I'm sorry but I have to go." Paris turns around and passes the phone to Edwin.

"Here Edwin talk you to your sister." Paris turns around and looks at the clock and it now nine o'clock. Paris boiled some water and made a cup tea and added some brandy and went up stairs and went into the guest room laid down and turn on the television and watched "The Land of the Giants" until she fell asleep.

Two weeks went by since Paris and Edwin went to speak with Brother Lintel and within those two weeks Corona went to Harlem Hospital and had another abortion.

Corona called and told Paris that the doctors told her that another abortion could kill her; so she can't have anymore. Paris didn't even bothered to respond and just wondered why Corona bothered to tell her.

Saturday and Sunday Paris was busy with the festival for Hidden Valley Haven for Women. The weather was a beautiful fall day; it was actually jacket type of weather. Some of the women in the shelter had formed a band and they played country music and sang folk songs. Other women from the shelter had created games with prizes for the children The mayor of Hidden Valley showed up and spent a good 45 minutes giving a speech about all his plans to help Hidden Valley grow; but he didn't mention one word about helping abused women. The festival lasted from 11am to 6 pm and when it ended on Sunday all of Paris' paintings sold except for two which Paris was surprised that any of them sold because she didn't have a lot of time to work on her paintings. Paris helped Ms. Becky and Ms. Sarah load boxes in the trunk of Ms. Becky's car.

"Thank you so much for your help Ms. Paris" said Ms. Becky smiling. "We were able to raise ten thousand dollars in two days; and that's not bad for this little town".

"Yeah." said Paris it was a very nice turn out and I'm sorry it's all over with. I really enjoyed working you all."

"So Ms. Paris have you figure out how to get out of your situation?" asked Ms Becky, as she stepped back and closed the door on truck of her car.

"To be quite honest no, I haven't. You know it's like being caught up in a snare of a nightmare and wishing you could just wake up; but you can't." said Paris.

"Why don't you come back to the house and let's talk." suggested Ms. Becky.

"Another time." said Paris. I had such a wonderful day and I just want to spend the rest of the day feeling good and not thinking about my problems."

Paris, Ms. Becky and Ms. Sarah said their goodbyes and Paris took the scenic route back home and just enjoying the drive and looking at the Fall leaves on the trees that turned orange, yellow and red and watching the doers crossing the roads but she couldn't help but to think about the question Ms Becky asked her about getting out of her situation. Paris followed Ms. Becky's suggestion about telling everybody about her bad situation at home; but she didn't see how that helped her.

Paris remembered how she went to the church on a Monday afternoon to do some volunteer work and over heard a group of her so-called Christian sisters talking about how stupid she is to put up with Edwin and how they would leave.

"Well she can't divorce him unless it is on ground of adultery; she just can't walk out." Said Karen.

"Oh she must have done something wrong for a fine man like Edwin Benson to carry on like that; I mean there are two sides to every story." Exclaimed Patricia; scratching her head."

How could he smother her and she doesn't know it?" asked Belinda.

"I say she nuts! I would take out my cast iron frying pan and go up side my husband head if he would try that on me." Said Cynthia.

"Well, you know Paris, she thinks she is a white woman. And you know how white women are always getting the beat down by men." Said Jackie. And all the women agreed and laughed about Paris being a dumb blond underneath all her black skin.

"Yeah, well she living in that big fine house they built; with the swimming pool in the back yard, and chandeliers hanging all over the house and they got 3 fire places, 5 bedrooms with a bathroom in each bedroom. It's no way I would get up and leave." said another woman.

"Well I never seen her with a black eye she probably just crazy and got a man on the side and just trying to get rid of Edwin." said Angel.

"Well said Beverly, it wouldn't be me I am not that stupid to let a man run over me."

Paris stood in the doorway of the church and listen to the bitter gossip trying to hold back the tears; she couldn't believe what she was hearing.

One of the women turned around to leave the church and saw

Paris standing in the doorway. "Oh Paris we didn't see you standing there."

Paris was hurt and furious and tears started to stream down her face and she walked into the church and stood before the women.

"You all are worst than Edwin. At least I know his problem is having to deal with a mentally ill mother; but you all are just low down under handed and evil women and you call yourselves Christians!" You sit up and talk about me and call me stupid; you talk about what you would do if you were me; well you are not me and you wouldn't know what you would do if you were me. You all are just as ignorant and hateful as the day is long talking about only white women get abuse. You all sound like a bunch of ignorant fools!" said Paris; wiping the tears away from her face. The women stood with the look of shock and shame on their faces as Paris spoke in a low and bitter tone; walking back and forth in front of them like a drill sergeant in the army and pointing her finger.

"Well let me educate you on domestic violence. Anyone can become a victim of abuse. Women, men and children regardless of race, creed or nationality; and it don't matter whether a person is educated, wealthy or poor. And just so you know why I am in this situation... It's because I married a man whose mother suffers with mental illness which I didn't know about until after my son was born. Paris stops and opens up her pocketbook and took out a tissue and wipes her face. And let me tell you so-called christians something mental illness is not easy for families to deal with especially when we have to be criticized by ignorant people like yourselves. I stayed in the relationship with my husband because I love my family and I love my God and I have to make sure I am doing the right thing and giving my best before I just jump and walk away." cried Paris. "and unlike many of you that have family; I don't..... I don't have anyone." cried Paris wiping her tears away; "I have no one to talk to in order to help me make heads or tails of what I am going through. You don't know what it is to wake up in fear; to live in fear, because you don't understand what is going on and not knowing which way to turn. I call myself helping my husband with his mother who suffers with mental illness and I end up in a very bad situation. And all you can do is call me stupid, gossip, and laugh and pass judgment on me!"

The church sisters gather around Paris to comfort her and she backs away from them. "We are so sorry Paris; we didn't mean to hurt you. Said one of the women and the others try to echo words of comfort. One of the women walked up to hug Paris but Paris backs further away from the group of women.

Paris cries with tears streaming down her face. "Not one of you calls and asked me how am I doing or ask is there anything you could do to help me; or give me a word of encouragement or perhaps offer me some advice. I bet none of you even pray for me."

"Oh Paris, we are so-so sorry; we just didn't know." said Jackie.

"Oh really, but you knew enough to stand here and laugh at my situation and to call me stupid and pass judgment on me." said Paris.

Can I give you a hug Paris? asked another woman.

"No; why would I want a hug from you! You think my life is pure entertainment; something for you to laugh and joke about. Well, let this coming from me echo within your minds for the rest of your life. YOU CAN ALL DROP DEAD! yelled Paris as she stormed out the church and she bumps into Brother Lentil on her way out.

"Sister Paris is you alright?

Paris turns around walks back and looks Brother Lentil in his eyes and stares for a few seconds. "Why would you even ask." ask Paris. "All you care about is your son. I feel sorry for your wife because she thinks

she has a husband when all she has is a shell of a man; a hologram!"
Paris then turns and walks out the door.

"She just a bad seed, an apostate, that's how they all act.
exclaimed Brother Lentil and the women agreed with him.

The festival for Hidden Valley Haven for Women is just what Paris needed to lift her spirits. When Paris arrived home she met Edwin at the garage door putting a suit case in the trunk of his car.

"Hi Edwin" said Paris "Where are you off to?"

"Hey Paris; I was just about to call you. I got a call from my boss and he wants me to meet him in Detroit to close a deal on some property for timeshare."

Paris could care less where Edwin was going but she had to pretend that she was concern and upset he was leaving.

"Oh Edwin." said Paris giving Edwin a hug. "Why didn't he wait until tomorrow to tell you; instead of having you leave on a Sunday evening?"

"Well, he wants me there first thing in the morning." said Edwin, closing the trunk of his car.

Paris was thrill but she try not to show it but she knew Edwin could see the look of joy in her eyes.

How long are you going to be gone?" asked Paris, trying to sound sad walking into the garage to go into the house.

"I will be back on Wednesday morning." said Edwin.

"Oh okay;" said Paris; she turns around and walks back and giving Edwin a slight hug. "You have a safe trip and give me a call to let me know you arrived safe and sound."

"Okay." said Edwin getting into his car and pulling out of the garage and he stops long enough to tell Paris to take care of herself. Paris went into the house and lit up the kitchen with her smile. Edwin was gone and that made her day.

Chapter 21

Edwin almost missed the flight going to Detroit when he boarded the airplane. He saw Jennifer sitting in her seat mad with her head phones on.

"Hey baby." said Edwin; sitting down next to Jennifer and kissing her on her cheek. "I'm sorry I am late; I got tied up in traffic and I had to take care of some last minute business for Paris."

"You are always late." said Jennifer as she taking off her head phones. "And furthermore, I am sick and tired of hearing about your crazy wife. The least you could do is be on time. We should have left yesterday; you know today is my birthday."

"Don't worry baby, we will be in Detroit in time for your birthday party." said Edwin.

"Yeah right, for your sake I hope so." said Jennifer.

"Well the party isn't starting until nine o'clock we have plenty of time to get there." said Edwin

"I don't see how you figure that Edwin when it is now six thirty." said Jennifer looking out the window as the airplane starts to take off. "And by the way, what is so important that you have to get back home this week?"

"You do know that I have a job Jennifer?"

"You could have gotten permission to work out of the Detroit office." said Jennifer.

"Paris is coming home on Wednesday from the hospital and I

have to be back in time to pick her up." said Edwin; reclining in his seat.

"I just don't understand you Edwin; why don't you lock her up and throw away the key?" asked Jennifer annoyed with Edwin.

"I don't appreciate you talking about my wife like that." said Edwin in a low tone. "I don't want to discuss her; now leave me alone I'm tired."

"What did you do today that makes you so tired?"

I had to wash Paris' clothes and clean up the house for her to come home and I told you I don't want to talk about it." said Edwin folding his arms across his chest and closed his eyes.

Jennifer puts her head phones back on and pulls out a magazine. An hour and fifteen minutes later Edwin and Jennifer is standing in the Detroit airport. After waiting twenty minutes for Jennifer's brother to pick them up; she decides to call her brother.

Hey Carl where are you? asked Jennifer pacing back and forth.

I am here at the airport. said Carl.

Well, we are at gate 20. said Jennifer where are you at?

"I'll be there in a few minutes. Make sure you are standing outside. said Carl.

"Okay." said Jennifer she clicks off her cell phone.

Five minutes later Carl pulls up in a truck in front of Jennifer and Edwin. He gets out of the truck and takes Jennifer and Edwin luggage and throws it in the back of the truck. Jennifer introduces Edwin to Carl and they chat about the weather and sports for about an hour before arriving at Carl's home.

"Look Jennifer this is supposed to be a surprised birthday party; so I am going to go in the house and let everyone know you are here and when everyone yells surprise you are going to act like you didn't know anything about it." said Carl.

"Well if this is supposed to be a surprise birthday party; why on earth did you tell me about it Carl? asked Jennifer looking at Carl with her head tilted to the side from the back seat.

"It was the only way I could get you here in time for the party Jennifer. Okay!" said Carl annoyed and opening up the door and getting out of the truck. Carl went into the house and a few minutes later he came out of the house running back to the truck.

"Okay Jennifer I am going to go up to the house and open the door and you walk in first and don't forget look surprise." said Carl.

Carl and Edwin followed behind Jennifer carrying the suitcases walking up to the house, Jennifer pause for a moment and took a deep breath.

"Don't forget Jennifer, look and act surprise!" Whisper Carl.

Jennifer slowly turned the door knob and then pushes the door open and step in the house with Carl and Edwin following behind her.

"Everyone jumped from their hiding places screamed surprised and threw confetti. Jennifer let out a fake screeching sound and turn and look at Carl and then at Edwin.

"Oh Wow, I can't believe this!" said Jennifer pretending to be out of breath. "So this is what you guys were planning behind my back; no wonder Edwin you were in such a hurry to get me here. Everyone laughed and cheered; but the party ended early because Edwin got drunk and went to accusing one of the guest about looking at Jennifer.

"Carl I want to go me home; I am exhausted."

"Jennifer, I thought you were going to spend the night?" ask Carl as he wondered why he even bothered with Jennifer; being that she is nothing but a spoiled brat.

"I want to go home; so I can be in my own bed." said Jennifer.

"Hey man, grab your suitcase." said Carl as he stood up from the sofa and picked up Jennifer's suitcase and walked toward the door.

"Okay; just a second." said Edwin as he stood up and staggering across the living room.

"Man, just sit down." said Carl shaking his head and he picked up Edwin suitcase and went out to the truck. "I'll load the suitcases on the truck."

Jennifer left out the house and Edwin staggering behind. Jennifer helped Edwin into the back seat as he sang happy birthday. Edwin woke up in the middle of the night and didn't know where he was. He looked over and saw Jennifer sleeping and then look on his wrist to see the time and but he didn't have on his watch. He sat up and turned on the lamp next to the bed and the light woke Jennifer up.

"What are you doing?" asked Jennifer she rolls over and faced Edwin frowning from the light shinning in her face.

"I am looking for my watch." said Edwin. Getting out of the bed and looking through his pants pockets."

"You can find it later; now go back to bed!"

"I'm calling home to see if Paris sees my watch." said Edwin pacing back and forth.

"You are calling Paris!" Jennifer sat up in the bed wide awake looking at Edwin like he has lost his mind. "How are you calling Paris at home Edwin?"

"What do you mean how am I calling Paris; I am picking up my phone and calling her."

Jennifer sat further up in the bed and watched Edwin take his cell phone out of his jacket pocket and pressed the speed dial button. He turns around and looks at Jennifer then he clicked off the phone.

"Man oh man, I must be really losing it; I forgot Paris is in the hospital. I had way too much to drink." said Edwin sitting down at the foot of the bed with his hand on his forehead.

"Yeah, you certainly did." said Jennifer wondering if Edwin has lost his mind.

"What's your brother's number?" ask Edwin turning around and looking at Jennifer.

"I know you are not talking about calling my brother at three o'clock in the morning!" Exclaim Jennifer lying back down in the bed.

"I spent a thousand dollars for that watch and I want my watch back." yell Edwin.

"Get in the bed and we will call Carl later."

"Your problem Jennifer is that you only think about yourself and nobody else. If you were the one that lost your watch, you would be over at your brother's house right now looking for it." Exclaim Edwin as he crawled into bed.

Jennifer sat up in the bed and she was so angry with Edwin for interrupting her beauty sleep. "First of all I wouldn't have lost my watch Edwin because I would not have been at that party drunk and acting a fool, talking all loud. Telling everybody about your big house and all these places you and your family has visited. Talking about your money that you don't have and that cheap car you just brought. And let's not forget you falling down and throwing up all over my brother's bathroom. I have never been so embarrassed in all my life. Oh yeah, let's not forget the argument you had with my brother's neighbor claiming he was flirting with me right in front of the man's wife. You need to shut up and go to bed before I put your ignorant behind out in the street."

"You know something Jennifer you are not right; Said Edwin watching Jennifer turn over to go to sleep. "That's okay you want to be like that. I am calling your brother as soon as the sun comes up and my watch better be there."

"Just turn off the light Edwin."

Chapter 22

Ten o'clock Paris was at work going over inventory with Mr. Bonds when Edwin called.

"Hey Paris, how are you?"

"Oh hi Edwin, I am surprised to hear from you so early in the morning. How was your trip?"

"It was fine. I think I lost my watch. Could you look around the house and see if I left it at home."

"Sure no problem; I will look as soon as I get home. said Paris rolling her eyes; she knew Edwin had been drunk again and this time he lost his watch.

"When can you call me back?" ask Edwin.

"I don't know Edwin I have errands to run before I go home."

"Yeah okay Paris, call me as soon as you find it." said Edwin clicking off his phone.

"Is everything alright?" ask Mr. Bonds.

"Yeah, everything just peachy." said Paris trying to sound convincing. "I have to make another phone call, I will be right back."

"Take your time because we are going to be here working late on this inventory." said Mr. Bonds.

Paris shook her head and rolled her eyes as she put on her jacket. The thought of working late made her feel tired; it was not on her agenda. She went outside and the brisk cold winds that pierce though her body felt so refreshing; it was just what she needed to air out her thoughts. She took out her cell phone from her jacket and called her doctor.

"Good Morning Dr. Levy's office how may I help you?" answered the Receptionist

"Good Morning my name is Paris Benson and I would like to set an appointment with Dr. Levy for tomorrow."

"Hold on please while I check his schedule."

The receptionist put Paris on hold and music came on. It was George Benson playing "How can you stop the rain from falling." Paris sat down on the bench in front of the office building and just enjoying the music which was interrupted by the receptionist.

"Hello Ms. Benson.......Ms. Benson are you there?" asked the Receptionist.

"Yes, I am." said Paris feeling somewhat disappointed that the receptionist interrupted the music.

"I'm sorry I kept you holding; but Dr Levy only has one available opening and that is at 8 am Thursday morning."

"That will be fine; I will be there at eight." said Paris clicking off her cell phone and walks back in the office. Paris and Mr. Bonds worked until seven o'clock in the evening and Mr. Bonds insisted on ordering Chinese food so they could finish the inventory; Paris didn't get home until nine o'clock and all she could do was make her some tea and take a bath and go to bed. She forgot all about looking for Edwin's watch until he called.

"Hey Paris did you find my watch?" Ask Edwin.

Paris took a deep breath and prayed for forgiveness because she knew she was going to lie.

"Edwin I looked all over the house and I couldn't find your watch anywhere. said Paris trying to sound convincing. "I was just about to call but I decided to search for it again before calling you."

"Thanks Paris for trying." Said Edwin sounding like he was about to cry.

"Well" said Paris. "You must have been hanging out with some really uncouth people for someone to have stolen your watch."

"Yeah, I know Paris I just feel so bad I lost my watch." said Edwin.

"You are hanging with the wrong crowd Edwin. No matter how drunk you have gotten in the past our friends would have never stole anything from us." Paris couldn't help but to feel sorry for Edwin. Paris loved Edwin and she knew he needed help but Edwin was so caught up in a snare of confusion and the insanity of his family; that it was nothing she could do to help Edwin and Edwin refused professional help.

"Yeah I know; I messed up Paris." said Edwin feeling sorry for him. "I should have just stayed home."

"I'll talk with you tomorrow; I have to take this call." said Paris clicking the button on her cell phone to speak with Virginia.

"Hello." said Paris.

"Hey Girly, how are you doing?" asked Virginia

"Oh I'm alright, just tired from working. Said Paris.

Paris hadn't seen Virginia since the barbeque and forgot she even existed with all the crazy stuff that had been going on in her life.

"So I have been down in Georgia visiting family and we have planned to move to Georgia to be with family and beside my husband job has moved to Atlanta." said Virginia

"Wow that is so awesome. I am so happy for you; but I am going to miss you and you just got here and now you are moving." said Paris.

"I know and as strange as Hidden Valley maybe I'm going to miss the beauty of it; but I am happy about moving back home to be near my family." said Virginia.

"Family." said Paris smiling. That is a wonderful thing to have. Hey what are you doing tomorrow night?

"I will be packing and that is about it." Said Virginia

"Well, Edwin is out of town and Anthony is away at school. Why don't you come over for dinner and I will throw on some turkey wings and some collard greens and cornbread."

"Well you know me; I am always down for a free meal." said Virginia laughing.

Tuesday night Virginia and Paris talked for hours about everything under the sun as they ate their dinner. Paris was so happy she invited Virginia over and couldn't understand why she had taken more time out to spend with Virginia.

"Paris I heard what happened at the church a couple of weeks ago." said Virginia, as she sat across the kitchen table from Paris.

"I have just really been going through a bad time." said Paris. "It's these nightmares I have been having. I feel like I am about to lose my mind. I can't figure out what's real and what's not real."

"What kind of nightmares are you having? "asked Virginia chewing on a turkey wing.

"I'm not sure if they are nightmares?" stated Paris.

"I dream that I am being smothered but I never see who or what is doing it."

"Wow that is deep; did you go and see a doctor about it?" ask Virginia.

"I have an appointment on Thursday morning right here in the medical court."

"Have you talked to your husband about it?" ask Virginia.

"I believe I mention it to him; but I not sure if I did or not." Said

Paris, I am so confused I can't remember. "Sometimes I think it's him smothering me; but he can't run because he can barely walk."

"Well it's good you are going to the doctor on Thursday Paris. The doctor will probably give you something to help you sleep." said Virginia

"I don't need anything to help me sleep I need something to help me get focus and pull my head together so I can think straight again." said Paris.

Well, I tell you Paris it would help if you would go back to church and do a lot of praying; because girlfriend, whatever you going through you are going to need God to get you out of it. said Virginia.

Paris and Virginia talked until about nine o'clock and Paris agreed to go back to church and then they said their goodbyes.

Chapter 23

"Hey Paris, I'm home." yells Edwin as he enters the house through the garage door limping on his cane and carrying his luggage. Paris where are you? Edwin yelled again turning on the kitchen light; looking around in the kitchen and then in his man-cave and then walking down the foyer and he looked in the dining room and in the living room. There was no Paris. Edwin looks at his watch it was nine o'clock at night. Where could she be; maybe she upstairs asleep? Edwin thought to himself as he went upstairs and turns on the hallway lights at the top of the stairs and checked in the master bedroom, guest bedroom, the office room and Anthony's room. And then he went back into the master bedroom and turns on the light and look in the night stand and then he look through the dresser drawers. "Somebody at that party stole my watch!" exclaimed Edwin as he turns around and exiting the bedroom. Edwin ran back downstairs holding his cane in his hand and open the door to the basement. The basement lights is off and now Edwin is really worry and wondering where Paris is.

Edwin's cell phone rings and he answers it without checking to see who is calling.

"Hey Edwin, you made it back home yet?" ask Corona

"Yeah, Corona I just got in a few minutes ago." said Edwin as he walked into his man cave and turning on the lights and sat down in his recliner. "So how is mommy doing now that she is back in her apartment?"

"She is doing fine; she was so happy you brought her home from the hospital. Did you tell Paris that mommy home now?"

"Paris is not home." said Edwin as he looked at his watch wondering where she could be.

"What do you mean she not home?" ask Corona yelling in disbelief. "She is always home!"

"I know. I can't imagine where she is at. It's almost nine thirty and she not here."

"Well did you call her cell phone?" ask Corona.

"I was about to call her when you call" said Edwin.

"Maybe she ran off with another man." said Corona laughed and snorted.

"I wish" laugh Edwin. "Besides no man would want her anyway; she is all old and ran down, stink and ugly."

"Paris isn't stinking; she just stank. said Corona

Edwin and Corona continued to laugh and make jokes about Paris and Edwin starts barking and calls Paris a dog.

"So, when are you going to tell her that you are moving mommy in?" asked Corona trying to catch her breath from laughing.

"I don't know but I am going to have to pick the right time; you know how she gets with panties all stuck up her butt and thinks she better than everybody." said Edwin turning the television on.

"Well, if you would just go ahead and kill her you wouldn't have to tell her anything and then mommy could just move in." said Corona sucking her teeth. "Why don't you just kill her and get it over with?

"You know the last time I thought I had really smothered her to death. Then I heard her walking downstairs in the middle of the night. She scared the daylights out of me." Said Edwin

"Well" said Corona laughing "You needs to do it one more time and do it right this time."

"You know Corona, you have so much to say but you should come over and spend the night and help me kill her....wait a minute Corona, I think I just heard her drive up. I talk to you later. Said Edwin; clicking off his cell phone and he gets up and walked halfway down the foyer and then turns back and runs to the family room and picks up his cane then turns around and starts limping down the foyer and Paris walks in the house.

"Hey Paris, where have you been all night?" asked Edwin kissing on the forehead.

"I was at church" said Paris sitting her pocketbook down on the bench in the foyer.

"You went to church; I thought you weren't going back?"

"Well, I thought I wasn't either; but I need God in my life, so I went back and did a whole lot of apologizing to God and to some folks that needed an apology. So Edwin how was your trip? asked Paris as she walked down the foyer passing by Edwin.

"It all went well and I managed to get back into New York City in time to bring my mother home from the hospital." said Edwin.

Oh she came home today; so is she in her apartment or is she staying with Corona? Asked Paris as she walked into the bathroom and wash her hands with Edwin following behind her.

"No she is back in her apartment." said Edwin, as he standing in the bathroom doorway.

"Okay; so she is back on her meds and is functioning okay?"

"Yeah, she should be okay." said Edwin.

Paris came out of the bathroom and went into the kitchen and dried her hands off with a paper towel. "I just don't know what it is that when I come home from church I am always starving. Did you have anything to eat Edwin?" asked Paris, opening the refrigerator door.

"Yeah I had dinner with mommy." said Edwin following Paris into the kitchen.

"Hum is too late to be eating pasta, I will just have these leftover turkey wings said Paris as she took it out of the refrigerator. Then Paris started to fill sick and she went over to the kitchen table and sat down.

"What's wrong, are you alright?" ask Edwin.

"I can't breathe and my heart is pounding." said Paris gasping for air and coughing. "I can't breathe."

Edwin limped over to Paris. "You want to go to the hospital?"

"Yeah, I better go to the hospital." said Paris.

Edwin hurried Paris out to the car and took her to the hospital. In the emergency room Paris was taken into an exam room right away and the nurse checked Paris' blood pressure and her pulse and then her temperature and the nurse hurried out of the room and came back with a doctor. Let's get an IV in her right away. Tears started to stream down Paris face; she knew she was sick and might die. And there was no one there to tell her she was going to be alright and not to worry; no one to tell her that they loved her.

"I am having problems finding a vain." said the nurse.

"We got to get an IV in her right away." said the doctor.

The nurse stuck Paris the second time in her arm and missing her vain again.

"I can't get the IV in your arm we going to have to put it in your neck." said the nurse looking down at Paris.

"Don't you touch me; you missed my vain because you don't

know what you are doing." yell Paris with tears streaming down her cheeks.

"Ms. Benson, the doctor interrupted; we have to get an IV in you; because your vitals are low"

"Then you put the IV in my arm." said Paris; starring at the doctor.

The doctor asked the nurse to give him another IV within seconds the IV was in Paris's arm and the doctor had Paris moved to the second floor and he ordered blood work for test to be done..

"Did I have a heart attacked" Paris asked the Doctor Hanover?

"No, however you might have had a mini stroke but we won't know for certain until we run more test."

"Don't tell me that doctor; I can't deal with this." Said Paris as tears filled up in her eyes.

"Don't worry Ms. Benson; we don't know anything until we get the labs test done. Did you come to the ER along? Asked Dr. Hanover making notes on Paris's chart

"No; my husband is in the waiting room."

"Okay I will let him know that you will be staying in the hospital for a few days." Said Dr. Hanover as he exited the room and went to see Edwin in the waiting room.

"I have to go Corona I see the doctor coming; I call you later." Said Edwin clicking off his cell phone and stood up as the doctor approached him.

Hi I am Dr. Hanover are you Mr. Benson; Paris' husband?

Yes, I am. How is she doing? Ask Edwin shaking Dr. Hanover's hand.

"She is doing okay now; however when she came in the emergency room her vital signs were low; but we were able to stabilize her and she will be fine as soon as we can get blood work done and find out why her vitals were so low. said Dr. Hanover.

"Will she be able to come home?" asked Edwin.

"No, I m sorry to say we are going to keep her in the hospital for a few days for observation and to run some test on her; she appears to have had a mini stroke but we won't know for certain until we take some more test; if you should have any questions feel free to call me at this number." Said Dr. Hanover he handed Edwin his business card.

"Thank you doctor; is it possible that I can see her before I leave?

"You can see her for a minutes; she is on the second floor." said Dr. Hanover.

When the doctor walked away; Edwin took out his cell phone and calls Corona.

"Hey Corona, What are you eating?" asked Edwin

"An apple." said Corona chewing.

"Well could you not chew in my ear?" ask Edwin.

"Okay....okay I'm sorry. So what's up?" ask Corona

"They think she had a mini stroke but they are not for sure what is wrong with her."

"What do you mean they are not for sure?" Ask Corona.

"The doctor has to run more test on her so they are keeping her in the hospital for a few day. Do you know she almost died; the doctor said her vitals were low when she came in the hospital?" asked Edwin like he was expecting to receive sympathy from Corona.

"Wow, that's too bad that she didn't die; now you have to continue on with your plan to kill her; but it should be easier now to get rid of her that she has a medical history of being ill." said Corona.

"It's not going to be that easy Corona, Paris has been going around telling folks that I have been smothering her and running."

"Edwin why don't you try and kill her while she is in the hospital?" Corona politely asked while laughing.

'Mr. Benson ....Mr. Benson" the receptionist call Edwin to come the information desk.

"I got to go I talk to you later." Said Edwin clicked off his phone and limped over to the desk.

"Yes you call me?" ask Edwin as he approached the desk.

"The doctor asks me to inform you that you can see your wife in room 202. Go straight down this corridor. You will see a bank of elevators on the right and you can take the elevator up to the second floor and once you are there follow the white strip on the floor and it will take you to the nurse's station and they will show you to your wife's room." Said the clerk; looking at Edwin up and down over the top of her eyeglasses.

"Thank you" said Edwin as he took the visitor's pass with the room number on it from the clerk.

Edwin entered the room and saw Paris lying in the bed watching television.

"How are you feeling Paris?" ask Edwin walking over to Paris lying in the bed.

"I am okay; I just hate I have to laid up here with this IV in my arm."

"I am so sorry you are sick Paris." said Edwin now holding Paris' hand. "The doctor said he think you had a mini stroke."

"Yeah I know and that is why he is keeping me in here."

"You will be alright. The doctor said he is not for sure you had a stroke. Said Edwin

Paris started to cry and Edwin gave her a hug. "Well to tell you the truth Edwin, I really don't think the doctor knows what he is talking about."

"Well is it anything I can get you from the house?" Asked Edwin

"Yes, I need clean underwear and clothes and my toothbrush and my bible." Said Paris; she couldn't help but to wonder if Edwin would actually bring her the things she asked for.

"Okay I will bring it in the morning." Edwin gave Paris a long hug and kissed her on the cheek. "You are going to be alright Paris."

When Edwin left the room all Paris could do was cry and pray that she would live to get away from Edwin and his crazy family.

"Paris, Paris" a voice was calling her and Paris woke up and was confuse as to where she was until she saw a pretty black woman with short curly hair standing by her bedside with scrubs on speaking to her with a thick Jamaican accent. "Ms. Paris I am your night nurse. My name is Wanda and I am going to take your blood pressure and the doctor has order some blood work to be done."

"So where are you from?" ask Paris trying to prolong the dreaded procedure of drawing blood.

"I am from Jamaica" said the nurse. "Now open wide so I can take your temperature."

Paris opened her mouth and let the nurse put the thermometer under her tongue. After taking her blood pressure Paris told the nurse that she had only one opportunity to draw blood and if she misses her she is not going to allow her to stick her again.

The nurse missed Paris' vein and Paris had a temper tantrum and told her to find someone who can draw blood from spaghetti veins. After being in the hospital for 3 days Paris was ready to go home.

"When is the doctor coming to see me?" Paris asked the nurse.

"He should be around later this morning." said the nurse handing Paris her meds.

"Are you finished taking my vitals." Ask Paris.

"Yes; but you have to take your medication."

Paris took the pills and asked the nurse was she finished with her.

"Yes but I will be back before lunch." Said the nurse smiling as she left the room.

As soon as the nurse left the room Paris jumped up and went into the bathroom. When she finish washing up; she comb her hair and put on a little make up as soon as she finished someone knock on the bedroom door.

Paris ran out of the bathroom and sat in the chair and picked up a magazine as though she had been sitting there reading it.

"Come in." said Paris facing the door.

A tall slender middle aged white male with brown hair, wearing glasses and long white coat entered the room.

"Good Morning Ms. Benson;" said I am Dr. Hanover, how are you feeling this morning?"

"Yes I know I met you in the E.R. I am doing fine doctor and I am ready to go home." Said Paris smiling as she sat up straight in her chair.

"We have a few more tests we have to do before we let you go." said Dr. Hanover walking over to Paris.

"What kind of test" ask Paris frowning

"We are going to do another electrocardiogram it seems there was a defect in the first exam we did on you in the emergency room and we are going to do a MRI just to double check to make sure you didn't have a mini stroke." Said the Doctor smiling as he jotted down notes on his clipboard.

"Well what about that blood work that has been done on me?" Ask Paris.

"So far everything came back negative; if you don't mind I would like to listen to your heart."

Dr. Hanover listen to Paris heart, check her throat and took her blood pressure and told her that she would be going home by the end of the week.

Paris cell phone rang just as the Dr. Hanover left the room and it was Anthony.

"Hello" answered Paris.

"Hi Mom, Dad called and said that you were in the hospital are you alright?"

"Yes I am fine." said Paris.

"What happen?" Ask Anthony

"I got sick and your father brought me to the hospital." Said Paris

"What was going on with you that made you go to the emergency room?" ask Anthony

"I felt light headed and my heart was racing and I felt pressure under my foot so your father brought me to the hospital."

"Well, I'm coming back home."

"There is no reason for you to leave school." "They just are keeping me here to run test in order to collect some insurance money." said Paris trying to sound convincing. She changed the subject and talk to Anthony about school and his part time job. This made her feel so much better just to get her mind off of her health problems.

"Hey Paris; how are you? Virginia and Belinda from the church entered the room while Paris was on the phone.

"Hey Anthony, I have to call you back I have company from the church." said Paris looks up and smile at the ladies entering the room.

"Okay Mom; keep me posted. I'll call you later. I love you." Said Anthony

"Love you too." said Paris clicking off her phone.

"Well hello ladies; what a nice surprise."

"We heard you were in the hospital so we decided to drop by and see how you were doing?" Ask Virginia, as she bends over to give Paris a hug.

"I just think I needed some bed rest; but you know you can't really do that in the hospital with the all the test they do on you; and they are driving me crazy with all the blood work." Said Paris scratching her head and wondering how the ladies found out she was in the hospital.

"So how long are they keeping you?" Ask Virginia

"They said to the end of the week; so Virginia, are you all packed and ready to move?" Ask Paris.

"Yeah, I just have a couple of more things to pack and then we leaving by the end of next week." said Virginia, smiling and looking around the room as if she was looking for something.

"Has Edwin been over to see you?" ask Belinda

"Well I only been in here since Sunday or was it Wednesday. I can't remember but I only been here two days, I think and Edwin had to go out of town on business for a day". Said Paris frowning and trying to remember when Edwin came to see her.

"I hope you don't mind me asking but how are things going for you at home?" asked Belinda sitting down in a chair next to the bed.

"Maybe this isn't the time to talk about it." Said Virginia

"No, said Paris I need to talk about it; because I am really trying to work things out; but yet I want to leave. I am just tired of dealing with the abuse and the insanity."

"Well you know you can't get a divorce unless it is on grounds of adultery and you know God hates divorce." said Belinda.

"Yes, I know Belinda, but God hates abuse too. So am I supposed to stay in an abusive marriage because God hates divorce; that doesn't make sense to me?"

"I know one thing; I wouldn't want to leave that big house." said Belinda

"A house and material things aren't everything Belinda my life, my sanity and my spirituality is more important, than living in a big house." said Paris shaking her head and feel annoyed with Belinda.

"Well, said Virginia you don't have to divorce him; you can just leave."

"I just don't know how I will survive; I mean I only work part time and I bring home only little over fifteen hundred dollars a month. How can I survive on that?" asked Paris.

"Well if you had grounds for a divorce then you could make him pay alimony and sell that big fine house and you will have the money to start over with." said Belinda thinking how stupid can one be.

"Easier said than done Belinda; first I would have to come up with proof. You just don't understand. I think my life is in danger but I am not certain. Here I am married to a man for almost 30 years and we raised a son together and in church every week together; or we use to be any way and now I think this man is trying to kill me. I don't know if I am losing my mind or is this reality?" ask Paris.

"Oh I got to run; I have to pick up my twins from school. Call me sweetie if you need anything." Said Virginia; hugging Paris and running out the door with Belinda running behind her.

Chapter 24

Paris sat in the bed feeling alone not knowing what to do about her situation and trying to imagine what her life would be like with no family at all. Maybe she never had a family at all; not even when she was a child. Her mother words came back to her when she was a child "Don't love nobody if they don't love you." Paris couldn't figure out who or what her mother was talking about. Of course her mother loved her; she was a child; that's what Paris thought as a child. But the echoing voices of her neighbors and her aunts came back to her as she sat in the hospital room. She is adopted; she doesn't belong! Tears started to fill Paris' eyes and then her cell phone rang.

"Hi Paris, how are you doing?"

"Oh, hello Mr. Bonds. I'm okay." said Paris wiping the tears from her eyes.

"Your husband told me you were in the hospital; I couldn't believe it. I mean you seem so healthy and all." Said Mr. Bonds

"Well looks can be deceiving Mr. Bonds." Said Paris, rolling eyes and looking up at the ceiling; wondering why he bothered to call.

"Is it something serious?" ask Mr. Bonds.

"No, they are just running test they have no idea what is wrong with me." said Paris.

"Well, do you think you will be out the hospital by the end of this week?"

"Yeah I should be according to the doctor. said Paris feeling annoyed with Mr. Bonds' questions.

"Good because I have a special project we are going to be working on and we have to go to Albany, New York for a couple of days."

"What kind a project?" ask Paris.

"The Boys and Girls club are hosting an art show in Albany and we are going to help them put some of the artwork." Exclaim Mr. Bonds.

"Hey that sounds real exciting, how long will we be gone?" asked Paris she was excited and ready to go.

We will be in Albany from Friday to Sunday."

"That's sound like something I could really use." said Paris.

"You think you will be up for the challenge?" ask Mr. Bonds.

"You better believe I will! said Paris.

Paris was excited to be able to work on another art project; but she knew Edwin was not going to be agreeable; but she didn't care. This was the boost she needed.

Chapter 25

"You know Edwin; traveling back and forth from Detroit to Pennsylvania is really getting expensive." said Jennifer.

"Well you can drive you; it's only a six and half hours"

"Speaking of driving; what about my car you promised me?" asked Jennifer sitting up in the bed.

"I had to buy myself a car." said Edwin. "I know you remember the car accident that you caused."

"You need to quit lying Edwin; I am not responsible for you totaling your car." yelled Jennifer. "Oh really, well my watch was stolen." Edwin got out of bed and started putting his clothes on.

"Where are you going?" Ask Jennifer.

"No where I am just tired of lying up with you and you don't care anything about me; you let that man steal my watch." said Edwin.

You were drunk and acting a fool Edwin and far as I am concern you could have flush it down the toilet. yelled Jennifer.

Edwin's cell phone rang and Jennifer reaches over to the night stand and picks it up.

"Edwin it's your wife" said Jennifer passing the phone to Edwin.

Edwin races over and snatches the phone out of Jennifer's hand.

"Well aren't you going to answer it Edwin?" Ask Jennifer

"No. I will talk to her later." said Edwin reaching over and pulling Jennifer up out of the bed.

"Ouch you are hurting my arm." Yell Jennifer.

"Get dress; I am hungry and I want to go out to eat. said Edwin picking up his wallet off the dresser and putting in his pants pocket.

"Okay...okay don't rush me." said Jennifer walking across the room to put her clothes on.

"Edwin maybe you should have answer your wife's call. She might be calling to say she is on her way home. I wouldn't want her to walk in on us." said Jennifer.

"I told you she is not coming home to the end of the week! yells Edwin.

"Why didn't they release her last Wednesday?" Ask Jennifer.

"I told you they thought she might have had a mini stroke." said Edwin.

"Well I am leaving first thing in the morning." said Jennifer walking out of the bedroom and down the stairs.

"Shoot" said Edwin turning around and going back up the stairs. "I forgot my cane."

A few minutes later Edwin comes limping down the stairs with his cane and they went to the Hideout Bar and Grill for dinner. Edwin order his usual drink and Jennifer had a glass of wine. They sat at a table in the back of the restaurant with country music flowing in the background and without a word spoken; when the waiter came out Edwin order steak and a baked potato and Jennifer order the fishermen's boat.

"Why are you so quiet this evening?" Asked Edwin

"I was just wondering what is up with you and this cane?" Asked Jennifer

"I guess I'm just attached to it." Said Edwin shudder his shoulders.

"Yeah, I see that." said Jennifer she felt uneasy bring up the subject about the cane but she could not think of a better time to discuss it. "Do you still go for physical therapy?"

"Yep I still do. I was going three times a week but the therapist said I am doing so much better; but now I only need to go once a week." replied Edwin, cutting into his steak

"So your therapist thinks you should still be using a cane?" asked Jennifer taking a deep breath and sipping her wine.

"Why are you asking me all these questions; you got something against my cane?" asked Edwin, with his eyes bulging out of his eye sockets.

"I am just concern." said Jennifer. "I think you are just a little too dependent on the cane."

"What is your problem Jennifer you jealous of my cane?" ask Edwin.

"I am tired of you and nasty your attitude! yells Jennifer slamming her fork down on the table.

"What you trying to get loud with me?" ask Edwin.

No. said Jennifer in a soft voice; noticing the people at the nearby tables was looking at her and Edwin. "I want to go back to the house."

"I am not finish eating." said Edwin cutting into his steak.

"I would like to go back to the house so we can have this argument in private." whispered Jennifer. "And then we can have make-up sex."

Edwin turns around and snaps his fingers at the waiter. "Waiter, waiter, check please."

Edwin and Jennifer were back at the house within fifteen minutes.

"Wow that was fast; it took us thirty minutes to get to the restaurant; but only fifteen minutes to get back home." Said Jennifer quickly getting out of the car and walking up the driveway and and then turning around facing Edwin and starts walking backwards toward the house. "Hey honey, could you not park behind me so I could get out in the morning?"

"No problem; come into the house through the garage." yells Edwin driving into the garage. Jennifer runs down the driveway goes through the garage into the kitchen. Edwin sets the shopping bags down with food on the snack bar and then proceeds to the cabinet to get glasses.

"I am going upstairs." said Jennifer running down the foyer and then up the stairs.

"What are you going upstairs for?" yelled Edwin frowning.

"To put on something sexy, while we are eating." yells Jennifer.

"Okay. I will be waiting baby. said Edwin putting the food in the microwave.

Ten minutes later Edwin hears Jennifer running down the stairs and Edwin walks into the foyer and sees Jennifer running out the front door with her overnight bag and she gets into her car. Edwin runs out the house into the driveway behind Jennifer.

"Where are you going, what's wrong Jennifer?" Edwin screams and curses at Jennifer as she speeds off down the isolate road. Edwin goes back in the house and slams the front door cursing and yelling. He breaks down and sits on the steps in the foyer and cries. Edwin cries for about an hour and then his cell phone rings and he reaches into his shirt pocket and pulls out his cell phone.

Chapter 26

"Hello" said Edwin trying not to sound upset.

"Hi Edwin.....Edwin are you alright?" Ask Paris

"Oh yeah I'm okay." said Edwin standing up and walking up the steps and he goes in the bedroom and lies down on the bed.

"I was calling to tell you that I will be going out of town next week on a business trip." said Paris firmly and waiting for Edwin to object.

"Oh really," said Edwin sitting up on side of the bed. "Well who are you going with?"

"I am going with some of my co-workers." said Paris.

"Aren't you too sick to be going anywhere next week?" ask Edwin.

"Well actually it's not until next weekend." said Paris trying to sound convincing. "And I will be out the hospital way before next weekend."

"Are you sure you going to be alright; they were supposed to let you out before. Maybe you are sicker than they are telling you." said Edwin trying to sound concern.

"They only kept me so they could run test and so far all the test results has came back negative." Said Paris growing impatient with Edwin's annoying questions; Paris felt that Edwin just wanted her to be sick in the hospital suffering and then just drop dead.

Edwin stood up and starts pacing back and forth and he could hear is Corona telling him how he needs to hurry up and kill Paris and if she goes away that will delay him killing her. "I don't think you should go; you might go and get sick."

"I was in doubt about me going at first; but I decided to go anyways. So I will be coming home before the week is out. So tell me Edwin how things are going with you? asked Paris.

"I am doing okay; my leg still is giving me trouble; but other than that everything is okay, you didn't tell me what you plan to do up in Albany?" asked Edwin sitting down on the bed.

"We are going the Boys and Girls club to help them put together an art exhibit in order for them to raise monies for their center." Said Paris not really wanting to answer the question because she knows Edwin is really not interested.

"Oh so tell me Paris; you were going to leave town and forget about me?" Ask Edwin.

Paris didn't answer Edwin, knowing that he is about to start an argument; she began to get a headache and at this point she just wanted hang up on Edwin; but that would only escalate the argument.

"Is that right Paris; you just going to go off with your boss and forget about me and God? Ask Edwin standing back up and pacing back and forth.

"Well Edwin, it's like this..." said Paris taking a deep breath.

It's like what Paris?

"I am going and that is all it is to it". said Paris calmly sitting up in the chair; eating her dinner.

"Well, I am going with you!" said Edwin trying to figure out how to stop Paris from going and getting Corona up to the house to help him kill Paris.

"Why would you want to go Edwin; when you know you are not into the arts and don't you need to go to work?" Asked Paris.

"I'm coming because I'm not letting you go off with another man!" screams Edwin.

"Edwin, "I have to go."

"Why you got to go all of a sudden?" asked Edwin

"Because you are screaming at me and you are not taking into consideration I am in the hospital sick." explained Paris.

"I'm coming to the hospital to see you now." yells Edwin.

"You have not been to the hospital since I was admitted and why haven't you brought me my personal things like I asked you to?"

"I'm sorry Paris, I haven't been there. I been so busy; but I will be right there with your overnight bag." said Edwin.

"Yeah; Okay Edwin." said Paris clicking off her cell phone. She rang for the nurse and when the nurse didn't come; Paris got up and went to the nurse's station. There were two doctors standing behind the counter and a nurse was sitting with her back to Paris. Another nurse passes Paris by and picks up medication from the counter and walks away.

"Excuse me, could someone please help me?"

One of the doctors turn and walks away the other doctor was in a conversation on the phone.

"Excuse me." said Paris this time with tears flowing from her eyes. "Could someone please help me?"

The doctor on the phone turns and sees Paris and walks over to the nurse and gestures for her to go and see Paris. The nurse turns around and sees Paris standing there crying and comes from behind the nurse's station and put her arm around Paris's shoulders.

"What's the matter, honey?" Ask the nurse. Paris was crying so hard she couldn't answer the nurse.

"Is anything hurting you?" ask the nurse.

"No;" said Paris wiping her tears away. "I just don't wish to have any visitors that include my husband."

"Okay I will let the admission desk know right away; can I get you anything?" asked the Nurse.

"Yes; I would like a cup of tea and two aspirins; I have a headache."

"Let's get you back into bed and I will get you a cup of tea and I will see if the doctor will prescribe the aspirins for you." said the nurse holding Paris' arm and escorting her back to her room. Thirty minutes later Edwin rushes into the hospital and stops at the visitor desk.

"I'm here to see my wife Paris Benson and she is on the second floor." Said Edwin, waiting anxiously for the clerk to give him a visitor's pass to pick Paris up.

"Just one minute Sir. Said the little elderly white lady with silver grey hair and wearing glasses sitting at the visitor's desk. "You said your wife's name is Paris Benson."

"Yeah, that's right; B E N S O N is her name." said Edwin watching the clerk slowly typing.

"I'm sorry Sir; but your wife can't have visitors at this time." said the clerk shaking her head.

"What do you mean she can't have visitors; this is visiting hours isn't it; I just got off the phone talking to her."

"I'm sorry Sir; but your wife is not able to accept visitors at this time sir." repeated the clerk.

"Well I want to see her doctor." yells Edwin.

"I'm not sure if her doctor is on duty right now; but I can see if another doctor is available; just have a seat sir."

Edwin sat down and waited in the visitor's waiting room for twenty minutes and then he became irate. He got up and walked back to admission desk yelling.

"When am I going to speak with a doctor about my wife?"

"I am sorry sir; as you can see I was very busy with other visitors. I apologize and I will get someone for you right away." Said the clerk as she gets up from the desk and walked into a backroom. Fifteen minutes later the clerk return with a doctor and a security guard. The security guard cross the waiting room and stands at the exit and the clerk points Edwin out to the doctor.

Hello Mr. Benson, I am Dr. Sanders extending his hand out to Edwin's to shake hand.

"I'm sorry I am just upset over my wife and I wanted to see her; but I am not allowed upstairs; how is she doing? Ask Edwin not shaking the doctor's hand.

"I am not your wife's doctor; however she is doing fine; but she just needs to rest and she will be going home in a couple of days. said Dr. Sanders.

"I would really like to see her doctor; because I have been out of town all week on business and I only spoke to her a few minutes on the phone since I have been back." Said Edwin, trying to look sad and sound concerned.

"Well, she is resting now; why you don't go home and relax and call her later." suggested Dr. Sanders smiling.

"I hope you all haven't done something to my wife."

"I assure you Mr. Benson. "Your wife if fine; in fact when she wakes up we will ask her to give you a call." said Dr. Sanders.

"Okay; said Edwin, he turned around and walked to the exit and then he stopped and walked back to the visitor's desk and the security guard walks over and stands behind Edwin. "Could you please see that my wife get this" said Edwin handing the clerk a shopping bag. "She will need these things." Edwin left out from the hospital feeling defeated that he couldn't see Paris to tell her that he was going to Albany with her to this so-called art exhibit.

Edwin's cell phone rang as he open his car door and got in.

"Hey Edwin; it's Corona."

"Yeah Corona; what is going on?"

"Mommy wants to know when she can move in."

"Are you with her now?" Ask Edwin as he turns on the engine and the car radio started to blast.

"No." Said Corona; She is at home and I just left her a few minutes ago."

"Well." said Edwin, turning the car radio down and driving into traffic. "I just left the hospital and I haven't had a chance to talk with Paris as of yet."

"Why didn't mention it to her while you were at the hospital?" Ask Corona

"I couldn't." said Edwin

"What you mean you couldn't?" Ask Corona clearing her throat and interrupting Edwin before he could say another word. "That house is more your house than it is Paris' house after all it was your money that got the house."

"Look, I have to call you later" said Edwin driving.

"Where you at that you can't talk now?" Ask Corona

"I am leaving the hospital; and I am driving in heavy traffic. I'll give you a call later." Said Edwin clicking off his cell phone before Corona could protest.

Once Edwin arrived at home he fixed himself a drink; he couldn't help but to think about Paris going up to Albany to do painting. Who did she think she was anyway; she was always trying to be more important; and better than everybody else. Then he started to think about Jennifer running out the house like she was some kind a nut case. He sat down in the family room and decided to call Jennifer.

"Hello Edwin; I knew you were going to call; what took you so long?" ask Jennifer.

"Jennifer what is your problem?" Ask Edwin sipping his Gin and Coke.

"I want to know what your problem is." Said Jennifer

"I don't have a problem!" Exclaimed Edwin

"Oh yes you do!" Yell Jennifer taking a deep breath. "One minute you are limping around on that cane and then the next minute you can't walk without it. I feel like I am dealing with someone straight out of a Twilight Zones."

"I told you Jennifer that I can sometimes walk with the cane and sometimes my leg bothers me and I can't walk without it."

"You never told me that, you need to stop lying." Yell Jennifer.

"I broke my leg coming down the stairs in the house and now I am in physical therapy and I only have one more session and then I will get rid of the cane. Listen, I got another call coming in; I talk with you later. Edwin pressed a button on his phone.

"Hey man; what's going on?" Ask Bruce. "I hear Paris is in the hospital."

"Yeah, she is been in the hospital a while now. She is supposed to becoming home at the end of the week."

"What she in for?" Ask Bruce.

"She is in there for running down the streets naked." Said Edwin; taking a sip of his drink.

"What man, you got to be joking; tell me you are joking!" Exclaim Bruce trying to restrain himself from laughing.

Man, I am not joking Paris flipped her script right here in Hidden Valley and went to running naked down on Main Street. Said Edwin; getting up from his recliner and walking into the kitchen to make another drink.

"Nah man, don't tell me Paris was running down on Main Street there in Hidden Valley butt naked?" Laugh Bruce.

"And she was singing that Doris Day song she likes to sing." said Edwin laughing.

"Ah no man not that Que Sera Sera song." Laugh Bruce

"Yeah that's the song, and then the police came and arrested her and took her to the hospital." said Edwin, walking back into the family room and sitting down in his recliner.

"Well I know them white folks up there got an eye full they never forget!"

"Man you talking about being embarrassed; I didn't go to church for weeks behind that; in fact I left town for a day and went and visited a long lost cousin just to get away from it and my mother got sick and went into the hospital last week."

"Man oh man; what is wrong with her?" Ask Bruce.

"Well they think she had a mini stroke and they just kept her in the hospital for observation for a couple of days; but I am going to have to bring her here to live because she can't take care of herself."

"Wow man, did you talk to Paris about that?"

"Man Paris is still in the nut house and I tried to go and see her today; but they wouldn't let me in to see her." said Edwin.

"Why they wouldn't let you see her?" ask Bruce.

"I don't know man; they said something about her resting." said Edwin.

"So when will she be coming home." asked Bruce.

"She'll be home by the end of the week." said Edwin

"Man all I got to say is you got a lot on your plate." said Bruce.

"I sure do and you know I really don't want my moms to come live with us. Paris and my moms don't get along; but my sister thinks my mom's will be happy living here with us."

"Well you better talk to your wife about it; so do you think you and Paris is going to be showing up in Maryland for the jazz concert is next weekend?"

"Well I going." said Edwin "I don't think Paris is going to be able to make it."

"Do you think it's wise to leave Paris home alone?" ask Bruce.

"She will be alright and I know her friends will look in on her." said Edwin.

"Okay man, I got to run I'll see you next weekend." said Bruce.

Chapter 27

"What time is?" Ask Paris as she holds her arm up so the nurse can wrap the cuff around her arm to take her blood pressure."

"Its 6 pm said the nurse and the doctor has order more blood work to be done."

"I'm not giving up any more blood" said Paris. "You all have taken enough blood from me to fill up several blood banks."

"The doctor need the blood work done in order to find out what is bothering you Ms. Benson." said the nurse; taking the cuff off of Paris's arm.

"You can tell doctor whatever his name is I'm not giving up any more blood. I am tired of you all poking me and missing my veins." said Paris, getting up out of the bed and walking into the bathroom. "Excuse me I have to use the bathroom."

"Okay and by the way your dinner is here." Said the nurse and she exited the room.

The next morning Paris got up early and dressed and sat in the chair waiting for the doctor to come. Paris had breakfast and lunch finally the doctor came around four o'clock.

Ms. Benson; how are you feeling today?

"I am doing just fine" said Paris.

"I am Dr. Levy." He shakes hands with Paris "I apologize for being late; so I hear that you are not giving us permission to do anymore blood work?"

"That's right." said Paris turning down the volume on the television. "I have taken all kinds of test. Did you find anything wrong with me; did I have a mini stroke?"

"Well, the good news is no you didn't have a mini stroke what you had was a migraine." said Dr. Levy.

"That is all you found after keeping here for four days?" Ask Paris.

"Yes, however, you refused to let us continue examining you." said Dr. Levy

"Well, I can't do another blood test it's just too stressful for me with the nurses coming in to draw blood and missing my vein every hour. I am going home." said Paris.

"Okay." said Dr. Levy. But I want you to stop by my office tomorrow; here is my card. Call my office and let my nurse know the time you are coming in. It's very nice meeting you Ms. Benson and I will see you tomorrow. Wait for the nurse to give you the paperwork before leaving."

As soon as Dr. Levy left Paris picked up the phone and called Edwin on his cell phone."

"Hey Paris what's going on?" answer Edwin.

"Hi Edwin, I need you to come and get me." said Paris.

"I thought they were keeping you until the end of the week. I'm surprise they are letting you out soon." said Edwin getting up from his recliner and walking into the kitchen.

"Yeah, well I got tired of being the nurses treating me like pin cushion; so I am coming home." said Paris.

"I thought you weren't feeling well." said Edwin.

"I wasn't feeling well that is why I came to the hospital in the first place; remember!" yelled Paris.

"I came by the hospital yesterday and they wouldn't let me see you." said Edwin pacing back and forth. "Did you get your things I dropped off for you?"

"Yes I got them and thank you for finally bring them." said Paris impatiently looking at the clock on the nightstand next to the bed. "What time can you get here to pick me up?

"What was wrong with you that they wouldn't let me see you?" ask Edwin.

"The doctor had given me medication and he wanted me to rest." said Paris taking a deep breath. "So what time will you be here?"

"I'm running around doing some errands." said Edwin "I pick you up on the way back home around six thirty." said Edwin

"Yeah okay, I want to get home before dark Edwin and you know its starts to get dark around five o'clock."

Edwin didn't get to the hospital until seven o'clock and Paris was now waiting in the visitor's lounge. Edwin came limping in with his cane through the lobby and Paris just sat there and didn't say a word as she watch Edwin as he limps up to the visitor desk. "Excuse me; I am here to pick up my wife and take her home." said Edwin nonchalantly.

The freckle face blonde hair man wearing a checker red and black shirt looked up at Edwin.

"May I have her name sir?"

"Her name is Paris Benson." yell Edwin bang his open hand on the counter. "That's my wife name Paris Benson.

The man typed Paris' name in the computer and then he look over at Edwin. "Sir; your wife has already checked out."

"What you mean she already checked out?" yelled Edwin. "You mean I came all the way over here for nothing. If she was going to go home she should have had the decency to call me and let me know. What time did she check out?"

Paris didn't say a word she just sat there and watch Edwin make a total jackass out of himself like he has done so many times in the past.

"Just watch this fool." whisper Paris to the young couple sitting next to her.

"Well Sir; what I am trying to tell you is....." said the man.

Edwin interrupts the man yelling and banging on the visitor's desk. "Don't well sir me; if you folks knew she was checking out; why someone didn't call me. I am a busy man and I have more important things to do than coming over here and wasting my time."

Paris just sat there on the sofa and watches Edwin rant and rave. "He is an idiot!" whisper Paris.

"Wow, I feel sorry for his wife; I can't imagine what it must be like to live with someone like that." said the woman sitting next to Paris.

"Yeah, I feel sorry for her too." whisper Paris.

"Well where ever his wife maybe I hope she is alright." said the man sitting next to the woman.

"Sir, "I am trying to tell you .... said the desk clerk.

"What are you trying to tell me; you idiot?" Edwin screamed and pounded his fist on the desk.

"Your wife is sitting over there on the sofa. "Said the man pointing over to where Paris is sitting holding her pocketbook and shopping bag.

Edwin stands up straight and turns around and looks in the direction where the man is pointing and sees Paris sitting next to the couple laughing.

Oh man, I am sorry sir." Edwin extends his hand to shake the man's hand; but the man refused to shake hands with Edwin.

"Ah man, Paris, you left me a hanging like that?" Asked Edwin walking away from the visitor's desk toward Paris still sitting on the sofa, then he turns around and walks backward toward Paris talking to the desk clerk. "Man, I'm just anxious to get my wife home."

"It's okay. I understand; no harm done." said the man at the visitor desk shaking his head.

"Hey Paris; why you sitting letting me make a fool out of myself?"

"It's no different than any other day Edwin."

"You could have stopped me when I first came in the hospital; why didn't you say something?" ask Edwin.

"I am tired Edwin and I am ready to go home." Paris stood up and started walking toward the exit.

"I'm sorry I was late I had to do some things at the house; I didn't want it looking a mess when you came home then Corona call and said Butch got arrested for fighting again and she has to come up with $500.00 bail money to get him out of jail."

"I'm sorry to hear that Butch got into trouble again." Said Paris. "Where did you park the car?"

"You wait right here and I will bring the car around." Said Edwin and he limped down the street until he got out of Paris's sight and started walking faster. The night air was cold and windy; Edwin pull up in front of the hospital were Paris was talking with the security guard. Edwin presses on the horn and lower the passenger window and yells at her to get in the car.

"So what were you talking to the security guard about?" Ask Edwin waiting for her to answer before he pulled off.

"We were talking about weather; what did you think we were talking about Edwin?" Ask Paris.

"I just asked; no big deal. I got to go to the liquor store." said Edwin driving away from the hospital.

"Can you drop me off at home first?" ask Paris feeling cold and tired.

"I don't feel like stopping."

"Well home is on your way to the liquor store; can you just drop me off first?" Paris asked again and wishing she had called for car service.

"I'm not going into town. I am going to New Jersey to buy liquid." said Edwin

"Why do you have to go to New Jersey to buy a bottle of liquor?" ask Paris

"The liquor store here closes at seven thirty and they are already closed." said Edwin merging onto the highway.

"Well with all the running around you did; why didn't you stop by the liquor store before you picked me up?" Ask Paris.

"I didn't want to be late picking you up from the hospital." Said Edwin.

"But you were late Edwin; you are always late. You are late when you go to work; you are late whenever you decide to go to church and you are late when you go to family functions. Tell me Edwin do you think the world revolves around you?" Ask Paris feeling sick and tired.

"Look I am sorry I was late picking you up. I told you Corona called and was upset about Butch being arrested then I had to go and wire her $500.00 to bail him out of jail." said Edwin.

"You lent Corona $500.00 without discussing it with me; and where does this money come from? Ask Paris not wanting to believe that Edwin lent Corona money; more than likely he gave the money to Corona.

"Well Paris, I figured when you get paid you can pay the electric bill this month and the water bill and that would even everything out".

"And what are we suppose to eat being that I buy the food." Ask Paris.

"We have plenty of food in the freezer." said Edwin.

"I don't have anything else to say." Said Paris sliding down in her seat and closing her eyes; what is the point in arguing with this fool; the money is gone and nothing can be done about it. Paris felt sick and she was tired and couldn't understand why she had to go to New Jersey with Edwin to buy a bottle of liquor.

When they arrive at the liquor store in New Jersey Edwin got out the car with his cane and limps into the store. Paris sat in the car watching Edwin go into the store and a few minutes later he came limping out and got in the car.

"So where is the gin you bought?"

"It's in my coat pocket. " said Edwin pulling away from the curve.

"It's in your coat pocket!" Yell Paris sitting up in her seat. "You mean to tell me we came all the way to New Jersey to buy a small bottle of gin and what size did you buy?!"

"I brought a half a pint."

"A half a pint!" yells Paris looking at Edwin like he lost his mind. "I can't believe you came all the way to New Jersey to buy a half a pint of gin?"

I don't know what you are all excited about Paris. said Edwin

"I am not excited." said Paris speaking softly and slowly. "You couldn't drop me off at home with your stupid alcoholic, left back mentality. No you had to bring me all the way out here to New Jersey to buy a half pint of gin. That is why I am upset." Said Paris;

closing her eyes and easing back down in her seat. "Just wake me up when we get home."

Thirty minute later Paris wakes up and looks out the window and noticed that the surrounding were very dark and the only light that was coming through the window was the moon light. And she felt a chill come across her body an eerie feeling.

"What part of New Jersey is this Edwin?" ask Paris.

"This isn't New Jersey, this is Pennsylvania." said Edwin.

Paris looks out the window again; this time her face pressing up against the window pane and all she can see is trees and there is no houses or light poles and then she recognizes the area. "Edwin why on earth would you get off the highway and go through the forest, what is wrong with you?!" yells Paris.

"It's a nice night and I felt like a spin through the forest." said Edwin laughing.

All Paris could do is hear Ms. Becky's voice echoing in her mind. "It's everybody's business when you are being abuse." Paris went through her pocketbook fishing for her cell phone and she couldn't find it. "Where's that darn cell phone." Said Paris

"Why are you looking for your cell phone for?" asked Edwin.

"I want to see what time it is." Said Paris.

"Its nine o'clock" said Edwin looking over at Paris laughing.

Paris acts like she didn't hear Edwin. Paris finds her cell phone and it is actually eleven o'clock by the time on Paris's cell phone. She started to wonder how long has Edwin been driving around in the forest. Paris pressed some numbers on the phone and then put the phone up to her ear.

"Hello 91.1. Operator. How can I help you."

"My name is Paris Benson and my husband just picked me up from the hospital and now he is driving me through the forest and just in case someone finds my body I live in Hidden Valley, Pennsylvania at 1474 Buttermilk way and my cell phone number is 205-775-5515. I am just calling because I don't have anyone else to tell this to. Thank you for listening." Paris clicks her cell phone off. Paris looked over at Edwin driving and he acts like he didn't hear her make the phone call. Paris needed to talk with someone else to help her to keep calm; because it just didn't make any sense for Edwin to be driving in the forest; he must have been driving around in the forest for over an hour. Paris decided to make another phone call.

"Hello." said Ms Becky sounding like she just woke up.

"Hello, it is so good to hear a human voice.

Is this Paris? ask Ms. Becky.

"Yes it is"

Mr. Bonds told me you were in the hospital; how are you feeling?" Ask Ms. Becky.

"Yes I am out of the hospital now and my husband came and picked me up from the hospital and took me to New Jersey to buy a half a pint of gin and now he is driving me back home through the forest."

"You mean he is driving you through the State Forest Park; here in Pennsylvania?" Ask Ms. Becky sounding concern.

"Yes that's right." said Paris.

"Wow that is nowhere near your home." exclaimed Ms. Becky.

"Yes that's right and that is why I decided to call you; and I called 9.1.1 as well." said Paris looking over at Edwin driving.

"Alright, I am glad you called me Paris, but I want you to remain calm. You are going to be alright; he just probably trying to scare you. Did you have an argument?" ask Ms. Becky.

"Yes, I was upset because I just wanted to go straight home from the hospital but instead, Edwin couldn't drop me off. He had to go to the liquid store first in New Jersey. I called 911 to inform them of my situation." Said Paris still looking at Edwin driving and Edwin had no facial expression; he just continues driving as though he didn't hear Paris talking."

"Okay said Ms. Becky that's a good thing; he is probably not going to do anything to you. Just remain calm and let's talk about the anything. I will stay on the phone with you until you get home and you make sure you call me back the first thing tomorrow morning.

Ms Becky and Paris talk about the weather and they talk about how successful the art festival was and how many supporters the shelter had received since the festival. An hour later Edwin pulled up in the driveway and Ms. Becky reminded Paris to call her the first thing in the morning. Paris went into the house before Edwin and ran upstairs to the guest room and stayed the rest of the night and she didn't hear a word from Edwin. All Paris could think about is how she could get out of this house and survive. She has no relatives and no money saved for a rainy day; no more than what she gave Anthony to start college with.

Chapter 28

The next morning Paris didn't see Edwin; it was nine o'clock and Edwin was gone to work. Paris showered and dressed and was out of the house an hour later. She called Mr. Bonds and told him that she was out of the hospital and that she would be returning to work the next day. Then she called Dr. Levy's office and the nurse told her to come in the office at one o'clock. Paris then went to the library and sat down at the computer and realizes that she has a computer at home. She goes back home upstairs in her office and starts searching for apartments. All the apartments were too expensive. She then calls the department of Welfare.

"Hello this is the Assistance Office of Hidden Valley; how may I help you." asked the lady.

"I am in an abusive marriage said Paris and I need an apartment can you tell me how I can apply for housing and how long I would have to wait for an apartment? "Ask Paris.

"If you are in an abusive marriage you are going to have to get police reports to show that you are in an abusive marriage in order to get emergency assistance."

"I have no police reports but I am in a dangerous situation." Said Paris.

"I suggest that you call Housing Authority and perhaps they can help you." Said the lady.

"Thank you." Said Paris hanging up the phone and she turns

on the computer and went on line and found the phone number to Housing Authority. Then she decides to call the Housing Authority in New York City.

"Hello this is New York City Housing Authority; how may I help you." A woman answered with a Spanish accent.

Paris explained to the woman that she needs emergency housing and that she is a native New Yorker; but the woman told her the same thing that the woman at the Assistance Office told her. The woman also explained because Paris didn't have any under age children and she is not a senior citizen she is not eligible for housing. After hanging up Paris decided to call Ms. Becky.

"Oh Paris I am so glad you called I was worried about you." Paris thought to herself, you were so worried about me; but you didn't offer me a place to stay.

"I'm sorry I forgot to call you this morning. I am just trying to find a way out to escape from this insanity that I am living in." said Paris.

"You are going to have to call different agencies that might be able to offer you some assistance." said Ms. Becky.

"Yes I already made phone calls to a couple of places; but they were of no help." said Paris.

"Keep looking and I will call you later and see if I can come up with a place for you to live."

"Okay thanks Ms. Becky." said Paris and she hung up the phone and looked up at the clock on the wall and it was 12:30. Paris rushes down stairs; picks up her pocketbook off the bench by the front door and rushes out the house and gets into her car and drives to Dr. Levy's office.

Chapter 29

The medical building's stretch mall parking was filled up and Paris had to drive around in the circles until someone finally pulled out of a parking space. She went into the building and looks on the directory in the lobby and saw Dr. Levy's office was on the second floor. She had to walk down a long hallway past a dentist office, and the physical therapy office before she got on the elevator and went upstairs to the second floor. Dr. Levy's office was crowded with patients. Paris went up to the clerk sitting behind the window.

"Hi my name is Paris Benson and I have a one o'clock appointment with Dr. Levy." The clerk handed Paris some forms to fill out and told her have a seat and someone would call her. Before Paris could finish filling out the forms a nurse came out and called Paris.

"Yes that's me." Said Paris getting up from the chair and walking over to the door where the nurse was standing.

"Follow me Ms. Benson" said the nurse. Paris follows the nurse half way down the hall and then they a stopped in the middle of the hallway.

"Ms. Benson would please put your pocketbook down on the chair and take off your shoes and step on the scale.".

Paris followed the nurses' instructions and steps on the scale and waits for the nurse to read the scale.

"Okay you can step down." said the Nurse.

Paris steps off the scale and slips her shoes back on and picks up her pocketbook and follows the nurse into the exam room where her vitals are taken. The Nurse leaves the room and after waiting twenty minutes Dr. Levy enters the room.

"Hello Ms. Benson how are you feeling today?" Ask Dr. Levy sitting down on a stool in front of Paris.

"Just call me Paris. I'm feeling much better; just somewhat tired from being in the hospital."

"I see that you are married, do you have any children?" Ask Dr. Levy checking Paris' eyes with his little flash light.

"Open wide." Said Dr. Levy and then he look down Paris' throat and checks her ears.

"Yes I have one son." Said Paris

"Breath in and out I want to check your lungs and your heart." said Dr. Levy

"Dr. Levy steps back away from Paris "So how long have you been married?" Ask Dr. Levy walking behind Paris.

"Almost 30 years actually I've been married 25 years." said Paris.

"Take a deep breath." said Dr. Levy listening to Paris's back

"So tell me Paris how is everything at home." Asked the doctor smiling.

"Why do you want to know?" Ask Paris

"Well we did a lot of lab test on you while you were in the hospital and all the labs came back negative except we found that you are suffering from depression." said Dr. Levy looking concern.

"So are you saying something is mentally wrong with me and that is why I am feeling physically sick or that I am a hypochondriac?" Ask Paris frowning.

"No, I didn't say that. Would you mind sitting up on the exam table; I would like to check your reflexes."

Paris stands up and walks over to the exam table and pushes

herself up on the table in a sitting position. "So what are you saying Dr. Levy?" ask Paris

Dr. Levy pulls out a little hammer from his coat pocket and taps Paris on right knee and then on her left knee and he checks both her elbows. "Your reflexes are good." said Dr. Levy walking back to his stool and sliding it across the floor in front of Paris and then he sits down.

"I am just trying to find out how you are feeling so I can know how to treat you." Said Dr. Levy

Paris had to really think this out; how should she answer and what was the doctor looking for; Paris just sat and look at Dr. Levy trying to read his facial expressions should I tell him about the night mares or just go home and don't say anything. Is it possible that she has lost her mind after all she has been married into this crazy family for almost 30 years?

"Paris, how do you sleep at night?" ask Dr. Levy.

What do you mean how do I sleep? ask Paris.

"What I am asking is do you sleep throughout the night?" ask Dr. Levy.

Paris couldn't hold back the tears and she was scared to answer and now she knows the doctor knows something is seriously wrong. Dr. Levy turned around on his stool and stood up and walks across the room to the counter and picks up a box of tissues and walks back over and hands it Paris. Paris pulls out some tissues and wipes eyes.

"No, I don't sleep all night." said Paris; still wiping away her tears.

"So what do you do when you wake up?" ask Dr. Levy.

"I get up out of bed and walk around." answers Paris.

"When you say your walk around are you walking around in the house or do you go outside?" ask Dr. Levy

"I walk around in the house." said Paris still trying to figure out why Dr. Levy is asking her questions concerning her sleeping habits.

"Do you go back to bed right away?" ask Dr. Levy sitting back down on the stool.

"No." Said Paris.

"Why don't go right back to bed? ask Dr. Levy.

"Because I am scared...Okay, I am scared." cried Paris

"What are you scared of?" ask Dr. Levy.

I am scared of the nightmares, the nightmares scare me. said Paris with tears streaming down her face.

"What kind of nightmares are you having?" Ask Dr. Levy looking with deep concern.

Paris hesitated in answering Dr. Levy; she was scare that he would think she was crazy but at this point she felt she had no choice but to answer his question.

"I have these nightmares that someone is smothering me and I can't breathe. And then when I wake up there is no one standing next to me." cried Paris.

"You are being abused." Said Dr. Levy; making notes on his tablet. "I want you to attend a group therapy session for abused women once a week."

"No" said Paris shaking her head. "I won't go for group therapy."

"Why not; you need help in dealing with your situation." said Dr. Levy.

"I am a very private person and I just can't sit up in a room with a group of women airing out my life." said Paris.

"How about if I schedule you to with our social worker for abuse women; will you go then?"

"Yes." said Paris.

"Okay, I will have my nurse to contact the social worker to set an appointment with you.

Meanwhile, I will prescribe a medication for you to help you deal with depression.

"I prefer not to take medication for depression because my depression is due to my circumstances." said Paris sliding off the exam table and walking toward the door.

"But you need something to help you deal with the depression." said Dr. Levy.

"Okay; you can go ahead and write the prescription for me and I will fill it and think about it; but I am not promising to take the medication." said Paris.

"I will call the prescription in for you and you can pick it up." said Dr. Levy.

Doctor, tell me how am I supposed to get out of this bad situation? asked Paris.

"You are going to have to go through it; to get out of it." said Dr. Levy

"Oh my God; you sound like my mother; and what is that suppose to mean? Ask Paris rubbing her forehead.

"Just what I said, you are going to have to go through it to get out of it." repeated Dr. Levy opening the door. "Make sure you stop by nurse's station and set an appointment to see me in two weeks." Dr. Levy left the exam room with Paris whispering Dr. Levy's words. "You are going to have to go through it; to get out of it; I swear I thought I had already been through it."

After stopping at the nursing station Paris waited for the elevator and then she decided to walk down the stairs. The stairs was long and winding and Paris kept wondering how many steps she had to go down from the second floor just to get to the first floor. When she finally did get down to the first floor she open the door and Paris felt like she was lost. She didn't know which way to exit the building. She walks down the long hallway sees the physical therapy office and sees patients working out on the bicycles and doing stretches on tables and walking on treadmills. And she keeps walking down the long hallway; but then she thinks she is going the wrong way to exit the building. She turns around and walks back and all she can do is let out a loud gasp. She couldn't believe her eyes. There was Edwin in physical therapy. Paris walks around to the entrance of the clinic and opens the door and walks in. One of the therapists starts to walk toward her but Paris holds her hand up to stop him from approaching her.

"May I help you ma'am?" Ask a young man

"No" said Paris shaking her head. "Get away from me."

The young man turns and walks away and goes and sits behind the desk and starts talking to the woman sitting next to him.

Paris was in total disbelief at what she was seeing and hearing.

"Yeah baby I am your master and when I tell you to kneel down; you kneel" said Edwin slapping a white woman with blond hair on the behind with an elastic band.

"Yes Master." said the woman laughing and the woman turns around and bends over and starts twerking her buttock. The young man that is behind the desk sees Paris watching them and he walks over and speaks to Edwin and to the woman. Edwin looks over and sees Paris.

"Hey Honey;" said Edwin walking towards Paris "I am in therapy just like you wanted."

Paris turns around and walks out of the clinic and this time she had no problem finding the exit. She got into her car and went to crying and praying that she wasn't losing her mind messing around with crazy her husband and his family. And the nerve of Edwin lying to her telling her that he didn't need to go for physical therapy; he must have been smothering all this time and running.

Chapter 30

All Paris could do is drive not knowing where to go or what to do. She finally drove to Wal-Mart and got out the car and went into the store. "I might as well pick something up for dinner" Paris said to herself. She walks up and down the aisles in the supermarket pushing the cart but couldn't make up her mind what to get for dinner. Paris stops walking and just stood and stared.

"Hey Paris..."

Paris heard someone calling her and she looks around and screams with excitement.

"Papa....Oh Papa it is so good to see you."

Papa walks over and gives Paris a hug. "I just got back in town and parked my bus in the Main Street Terminal. I was going to call you as soon as I got finish picking up a few things from the store." So Paris what are you up to?"

"I was just standing here trying to figure what to cook for dinner." Said Paris smiling with a surprise look on her face.

"Well speaking of dinner lets go and have dinner. said Papa, putting his arm around Paris' shoulders and escorting her out of the supermarket.

"My car is over here in lane 23; where is your car?" ask Papa.

"My car is way in back over there somewhere." said Paris pointing.

"Well let's take my car and I'll drop you back here after we have dinner." said Papa smiling from ear to ear.

'Okay.' said Paris as she happily walks over with Papa and got in his car.

Paris and Papa laughs and talks about old times over dinner. Paris told Papa how she was going to Albany to work on a special project for the Boys and Girls club with her job.

"You want dessert?" Ask Papa looking for the waiter.

"Nah" said Paris "I am really trying to watch my weight; so I will just pass."

"Hey" said Papa "how many times do we get together and have dessert?"

"Okay; if I have to be bad I will have the cheese cake with pineapples." Said Paris, laughing.

"Now that's the way to go; how about some ice cream to go with it?" Asked Papa

"Sure why not and throw in a glass of brandy with it." said Paris.

Papa and Paris sat in the restaurant slowly eating their dessert and sipping on brandy and lighting up the restaurant with laugher; talking about old times.

"Paris can I ask you a serious question?" ask Papa.

"Sure you know you can ask me anything Papa." Said Paris wiping her mouth her napkin

Papa looks down at the table and he pick up his spoon and tapping it on the side of his plate and the waiter came over.

"Can I get you anything else Sir?" ask the waiter.

"No thank you." said Papa.

"I will bring you the check in a minute Sir." said the waiter as he walks away.

"Take your time, we are not in hurry." said Papa.

"So Paris tell me is everything at home alright?" asked Papa.

"Everything is fine." said Paris trying to sound convincing.

"Really, is it Paris?" Ask Papa with a puzzled look on his face.

"Yes really and why are you asking?"

"I am asking." said Papa speaking in a low tone and leaning across the table so the couple at the next table can't hear him. "Because when I saw you in the supermarket you were holding a gun."

"Oh no you didn't Papa see me in store with a gun." protested Paris shaking her head no. "You must have mistaken me for someone else. I was there with my shopping cart trying to decide what to cook for dinner."

"Paris, your shopping cart was empty!" whispered Papa.

"It was empty Papa because I was trying to decide what to cook for dinner." Said Paris raising her voice and the couple at the next table looked at her.

"What were you trying to decide Paris; whether to serve up a forty-five or a rifle for dinner? ask Papa in a low tone.

"I didn't realize I had a gun in my hand when you saw me Papa. Okay!" Exclaimed Paris

"Paris, you do realize that you were standing in Wal-Mart in front of the gun section?" Ask Papa.

"Yes." said Paris rolling eyes and looking around the restaurant.

"Now tell me what is going on with you?" Said Papa.

"I don't want to talk about it and besides I have to get early tomorrow morning to get ready for my trip." Said Paris she pushes her chair back away from the table to stand up.

"Paris" said Papa reaching across the table and holding Paris's hand and preventing her from standing up. "You must tell me so I can help you."

"I didn't realize I was holding a gun. I went into the supermarket to buy dinner; and then I decided to go over to the sports section to look at guns; but I didn't realize I was holding a gun when I saw you." said Paris.

"Excuse me Sir, would you like something else? Ask the Waiter.

"No thank you." said Papa.

"Here is your check Sir, you can pay on your way out and you may both have a nice evening." said Waiter putting the check face down on the table and walking away.

"Let's get out of here." said Papa.

"Okay. Said Paris I have to go to the ladies room."

Chapter 31

When Paris came out of the restaurant; Papa was sitting in his car waiting at front of the restaurant.

"Wow, talk about road side service." said Paris getting in the car.

"I wanted to make sure I didn't miss you coming out of the restaurant. Okay now, tell me why you were in the sporting goods department looking at guns." Said Papa.

Paris told Papa about Edwin being in a car accident and falling down the stairs in the house and him limping around on a cane and refusing to go for physical therapy and then seeing him in physical therapy clinic playing S&M games with his therapist and about the nightmares.

"So you were going to shoot your husband and his therapist for playing S&M games?" asked Papa looking at Paris like she had lost her mind.

"No, just Edwin because he is unfaithful and he is a liar; he been walking around all this time pretending he couldn't walk without his cane and now I know he has been smothering me in my sleep and running." said Paris.

"Whoa, this is way too much." Said Papa; pulling out of the restaurants' parking lot.

"Well you asked me." said Paris putting on her seatbelt.

"How long has this been going on?" Asked Papa

"I don't know, I know it was before he broke his leg; but the nightmares became more frequent after Edwin broke his leg and the cast was taken off his leg. said Paris.

"And you didn't know he was smothering you?"

"No; I am a deeper sleeper. said Paris.

"Okay; forgive me Paris if I sound stupid. I am just trying to understand what you are saying."

"I am telling you Papa I believe my husband has been smothering me and running. And when I told my doctor today about my nightmares; he said I was being abused. So my doctor believes me." replied Paris, trying to hold back the tears.

"I am sorry Paris I didn't mean to upset you but this a lot to take in; who else have you told about this? ask Papa.

"At first I didn't tell anyone but someone told me to tell everybody for my own protection; the more people that knew the safer I would be." explained Paris.

"They probably thought you were nuts Paris. Said Papa. At least that explains why you were in Wal-Mart holding a gun. Did you tell your husband that you knew he was smothering you?"

"I don't remember; I am so confused half the time with all the screaming and cussing me out that Edwin does and dealing with his crazy demonic mother and his trashy, low down dirty, whorish sister and whorish brother I don't which way is up anymore." said Paris.

"I have to tell you Paris killing your husband is not the answer and you need to get up and get out there before one of you end up dead." said Papa.

"I don't know how to escape." said Paris.

"Do you have any money save?" ask Papa

"No I don't, the last little money I did have save I gave it to Anthony to go to college. Said Paris.

"Do you have any relatives to go and stay with?"

"You know I don't have any family; I don't know why you ask me that Papa." said Paris with tears in her eye.

"Don't start crying." said Papa, as he drives into Wal-Mart parking lot. "Where is your car?"

"Its two lanes over to your left, near the front." said Paris.

Papa drives over and parks his car next to Paris' car. "I have to go into the store to get some items I want you to wait here until I get back." said Papa taking off his seatbelt and getting out of the car. "Don't leave Paris; wait for me."

"Okay, but hurry up because I am exhausted. Said Paris as she eased down in her seat and closed her eyes.

Papa comes back to the car twenty minutes later and Paris is sleep and he gets into the car and slams the door but Paris doesn't wake up.

"Wake up Paris, wake up." Said Papa nudging Paris on the shoulder

"Huh, where am I. Oh it's you." said Paris closing her mouth and sitting up in her chair.

"Girl you were out here snoring with your mouth wide open catching flies; and the dogs howling, folks standing all around my car looking in; I didn't know what was going on; when I came out of the store." Laughs Papa as he handed Paris a plastic shopping bag.

"You are very funny Papa." said Paris laughing and sitting up in her seat and wiping the saliva from the corners of her mouth with her fingers.

"Anyway I brought you a lock and a Phillips screw driver."

"What you get me a lock for Papa?" Asked Paris looking in the bag.

"You are going to move into another room in the house and sleep there and put this lock on the bedroom door and here is a money card with two hundred dollars on it for emergency purposes only if you should have to get up in the middle of the night and run to a hotel." Said Papa

Paris starts crying. "Thank you so much Papa; but all the bedrooms have locks."

"That's good; but make sure you use the lock I brought for you; and one other thing is I brought you a journal starting writing down everything that you do and your husband do; so you can start thinking clearly and stop crying girl; you don't have time to cry. You have to figure out a way to get out there and don't kill your husband. If you kill him you will kill yourself. Pray for him. Pray for a release." said Papa backing the car out of the parking space. He stops the car and pulls back into the parking space. "Paris stops crying and get out of my car and go home.

Paris starts laughing and crying at the same time; she gives Papa a hug and thanks him and then gets out of the car.

"I call you next week." said Papa shaking his head.

Okay; thank you Papa. Said Paris getting into her car; Papa waits for Paris to start her car and he watches her drive away and he prayed for God to protect her. When Paris pulls up in the driveway she sees Edwin's car and she sit a while in the car thinking that about Edwin playing S&M games with his therapist; however, Paris wasn't as mad about what she saw next to everything she had gone through with Edwin and his dysfunctional family; Edwin playing Slave & Master with his therapist was seemed almost normal. If Edwin would run off with another woman Paris wouldn't be upset; in fact he would be doing her a favor. Paris could hear Edwin big mouth all the way out in the driveway telling Corona everything is going to be alright. Paris took a deep breath and decided to get out the car and go in house. When Paris opens the door she looks down the foyer and saw Corona sitting at the kitchen table crying. Paris walks down the foyer and see the Butch and Tince sitting in the family room.

"What is going on here?" ask Paris No one would answer and Corona continue to cry and Edwin turn his back on Paris walks to the other side of the kitchen goes to the refrigerator and gets a bottle of beer.

Corona, why are you crying, what is wrong? ask Paris frowning. No one answered and Corona continued to cry. Paris began to get upset and she felt like cussing everyone out ;she was so tired of dealing with this deranged family. And here she comes home to find Corona sitting in her kitchen at her table crying and no one wants to tell her why.

"Would somebody; anybody please tell me why Corona is sitting here crying?" screamed Paris; she took a deep breath and walked over to Corona and kneels down apologizes for yelling and she hugs Corona and brushes Corona's hair away from her face and takes a napkin from the napkin holder that is in the middle of the table and gives it to Corona. "Corona, honey, please tell me why you are crying; is there something I can do to help you? ask Paris.

"Aunt Paris." said Tince. Walking out of the family room into the kitchen and looking scared. "Grandma tried to kill us this afternoon."

"WHAT!" Gasp Paris fell backwards on the floor. She couldn't believe what she had just heard. Paris looked over at Edwin standing next to the snack bar holding a can of beer looking upset and he made no effort to help Paris up off the floor.

"Okay, said Paris standing up; everything is going to be alright Corona at least you all made it out of there alive. Paris walked over to Tince and Butch both now standing in the kitchen looking like lost puppies. Paris gave Butch and Tince a hug and walk them back into the family room and three of them sat down on the sofa. "Tell me what happen?"

"Grandma came by the house this afternoon and I had come home from being in jail and she was mad." Said Butch, sitting next Paris looking scared, then Paris remembered that phone call from Edwin's cousin saying she wanted to kill one of the grandchildren.

"What was she mad about, was she mad because you were in jail?" Ask Paris looking at Butch.

"No," said Tince sitting on the other side of Paris. She was mad because she said mama stole her money."

"Okay so where is your grandmother now?" ask Paris.

"She tried to kill us with a butcher knife, Aunt Paris." Said Tince crying hysterically, Paris put her arms around Tince and hugs her. "She kept chasing us and chasing us all around the house trying to kill us and she was calling us all kinds of bad names."

"You are safe now honey, you going to be alright. So how on earth did you all get away from her?" Ask Paris frowning and Tince sat up on Paris's lap.

"Look it's late; you guys need to go to bed. Interrupted Edwin clearing his throat as if he was trying to signal the kids off to bed.

"They are talking to me and when we are finish talking then they can go to bed." Said Paris, knowing that Edwin and Corona didn't want her to know what had happen; she didn't see the point of them trying to hide anything she already knew Inez was a demonic nut. "So tell me how did you all manage to get away?"

"It's time them to for them to go to bed." said Corona, standing in the doorway of family room.

Oh hell no! Said Paris jumping up from the couch forgetting that Tince was sitting on her lap; Tince jump to her feet and she was holding onto Paris' arm. "These children are going to tell me what happen. I come home and find you sitting at my kitchen table crying and you think you can just brush me off and don't tell me anything; you both are out of your minds."

Now, you two jackasses go sit down and let these kids tell me what happen. Nobody and I mean nobody going to brush me off, you hear me nobody! screamed Paris shaking her finger at Edwin and Corona.

Paris sat back down and with Butch and Tince sitting on each side of her. "Now I want to know how you all got away and what happen to your grandmother; just take your time and tell me.

"I ran and pick up the phone to call the police and then....then." said Tince as she broke down and starts crying. "She tried to stab me but then Butch pulled me out of the way and mama got the phone and called the police."

Paris took Tince and held her in her arms and she hugged Butch. "It's okay baby, you are both safe now; so what happen how did you manage to keep her from killing you all before the police got there? Ask Paris still holding and rocking Tince in her arms.

"We ran in the bedroom and close the door and pushed the dresser in front of the door to keep her from coming in the room and when the police got there they had to knock down the door." said Butch.

"The police had to knock the door down?" Ask Paris frowning trying to imagine the scene.

"Yeah, they knock down the door with a bull horn."

"You mean a sledgehammer?" said Paris

"With a bull horn Aunt Paris, and then when we heard the police come in through the door we came out the bedroom and the police had pull out their guns and told grand mommy to drop the knife. She dropped the knife and fell down on the floor and went to crying and then the ambulance came with 2 men in white coats." said Butch.

"And they put grand mommy in a white bag and tied her up and took her away in the ambulance." cried Tince.

"I am so sorry Butch and Tince that you had to experience such an awful thing. Your grandmother is sick with a mental illness and she will be alright; the doctors are going to help her.

What is a mental illness Aunt Paris? Ask Tince.

"Well, it's when you are very sad and can't be happy for a very long time and sometime it makes people do things that they wouldn't normally do....." Paris lost her thought when she looks at Corona standing in the doorway of the family room. "Corona tells me what set your mother off? "I don't know what set her off" said Corona.

"You lying Corona; your mother was doing just fine on the new meds; so tell me why she did she off on a tantrum?"

"She ....she ...stuttered Tince grandma went off because she said mommy stole money from her again to get Butch out of jail; and the time before that mommy stole money from grand mommy to get her hair done."

"You talk too much Tince." yelled Corona. "You need to learn to keep your mouth shut."

"Don't get mad at the kids Corona all this mess could have been prevented; if you hadn't stolen your mother's money."

"I didn't steal mama's money. Mama is crazy and a liar. said Corona.

"Hey Butch and Tince are you all hungry?" Ask Paris ignoring Corona; she knew Corona had stolen Inez's money. That is what Corona would do every time Inez would go into the hospital and then

Corona would tell Inez that she was mistaken about the amount of money she had in the bank.

Are you kids' hungry? asked Paris.

Yeah." said Butch and Tince running into the kitchen.

Good I am going to throw on some food on the stove; and you guy go wash your hands. said Paris standing up and walking pass Edwin and Corona into the kitchen.

"Yeah make enough for us to eat too." said Edwin.

"So tell me where is your mother now Edwin and Corona?" Ask Paris.

"They took her away in a body bag." Said Tince

What? Yells Paris stopping in the kitchen and turning around and looking at Edwin and Corona "They had to kill Inez?"

"No, they didn't take mommy away in a body bag." Said Edwin

"Yes they did Uncle Edwin; yes they did too." Screams Tince.

"Girl, shut up and go wash your hands and stay out of grown folks business." Said Corona.

"Will somebody please tell me what happen to Inez?" ask Paris impatiently looking at Edwin and then back at Corona waiting for an answer.

"They took her to the hospital and then they are going to send her upstate New York to a mental institution." said Edwin.

"Well why is Tince talking about they carry Inez away in a body bag?" asked Paris.

She meant a straight jacket Aunt Paris. They put grand mommy in a straight jacket. said Butch sitting down at the table.

"Thank you Butch, for explaining that to me." said Paris, shaking her head and rolling her eyes at Edwin and Corona, and thinking that the paramedics should have taken Edwin and Corona away too.

"It's nine o'clock Edwin. How long have you all been here?" ask

Paris, taking cold cuts out of the refrigerator and walking over to the kitchen cabinet and looking over at Corona. Neither Corona nor Edwin answers Paris, "So Corona, how much money did your mother accused you of stealing?"

"A thousand dollars, but I didn't steal any of her money." Exclaim Corona.

Corona and the kids are going to stay the weekend with you Paris and I am going down to Maryland for the jazz concert.

"Ah ....Edwin darling, have you forgotten that I have to be in Albany in the morning and I won't be coming back until Monday evening." Said Paris sarcastically, as she made the sandwiches; so you can stay home and look after your family or they can stay here while we are gone.

"No; I don't like anybody in the house while I am gone. said Edwin. And can't they take someone else up to Albany? Why must you be the one to go?"

"It's my job Edwin and I am going. Said Paris; placing a platter of sandwiches and a container of milk on the table.

Its okay said Corona. I had plan on us going home in the morning.

"Edwin get the plates out the cabinet so everyone can eat; I have to go to bed and I have to get up early in the morning." Said Paris as she walked over and gave Butch and Tince a hug and assured them that everything is going to be alright. Paris picks up her pocketbook and the plastic bag with the lock and screw driver and the journal in it that Papa had given her and she climbed up the stairs which felt like she was climbing Mount Everest. Paris went into the guest bedroom put the bag in the back of the closet on the floor where she knew Edwin would never look. Paris was exhausted and the day seemed as though it was never going to end as she packed her suitcase for tomorrow's trip. She tried to visualize not being with Edwin; what would her life be like? Paris was so use to having a family; a husband someone to do things with and even thought Edwin wasn't good husband he still fit the basic description of a husband. Paris also knew she couldn't take too many more Inez's episodes of her losing her mind. Tonight was off the charts, coming home and finding Corona sitting at her kitchen table crying and the kids scared out of their minds because Inez tried to kill all three of them. The words of Dr. Levy came back to Paris "You have to go through it to get out it." "Well Lord, when am I going to be finish going through it; to get out of this mess?" whisper Paris.

Chapter 32

The alarm clock on Paris' cell phone rang and it was five thirty in the morning. Paris looked over at Edwin and he was still asleep. Paris shower and was dress in an half an hour in her blue jeans and sweat shirt. She started to wake Edwin to tell him goodbye. Then Paris thought she must be out of your mind to wake up Edwin. Paris was in her car by six thirty and by seven o'clock she was at the office helping Mr. Bonds load up the van with art supplies. By seven thirty Mr. Bonds and Paris was on the road to Albany.

Edwin wakes up at 8 o'clock and looks for Paris in the bathroom; no Paris. He goes downstairs and looks in the living room, in the dining room, the kitchen and in the family room. He then goes back to the front of the house and open the front door and sees that Paris car is gone. Edwin runs up stairs and puts his clothes on and runs back downstairs and out the kitchen door and get into his car and opens the garage door and drives down to Paris' job. There are only 2 employees that are in the office when Edwin walks in.

"Good Morning, I am looking for Paris Benson." said Edwin looking around the office.

"I am sorry Sir, but Paris is not in today; did you have an appointment with her?" Ask the Receptionist looking at Edwin up and down wondering who he is to Paris.

"I am her husband what do you mean she is not in today?" Ask Edwin

"I'm sorry Mr. Benson I just came in fifteen minutes ago and I have not seen Paris."

"She was supposed to be going to Albany, New York with your boss and they were supposed to be leaving today can you give me the address or the phone number to where they were going?" ask Edwin.

"It would be best if you call your wife on her cell phone and ask her for the information." said Receptionist becoming annoy with Edwin.

"What is wrong with you don't you know where they are going?" Ask Edwin.

"Sir I am sorry I can't help you. I am only the receptionist; they don't tell me everything."

"You are lying!" Screams Edwin turning around and walking out of the office.

As soon as Edwin left the office the receptionist pull out a list of phone numbers and look for Paris' cell number and calls her.

Paris took her cell phone out of her pocketbook and saw the office number flashing on her phone. "Hello."

"Hi Paris this is Linda ; I just wanted to inform you that your husband came by the office a few minutes ago looking for you."

"Did he say what he wanted?" ask Paris.

"He just wanted to know where you were going in Albany and I said I didn't know what to say. He left here raging mad. What if he comes back what should I say?." ask Linda

"What did you tell him?" Ask Paris.

"I told him I didn't know where you and Mr. Bonds went and he should call you." Said Linda.

"Okay, you did well. If he should come by again tell him the same thing you told him before and don't hesitate to call the 911.

But more and likely he won't be back. Thanks for calling me Linda." As soon as Paris clicked off her cell phone Edwin calls and Paris reluctantly answers the call.

"Hi Edwin"

"Hey Paris you left out this morning and didn't wake me up to say goodbye. What going on with you?" ask Edwin

"I didn't wake you up because you were up late with your sister last night and I got up at 5:30 this morning. I was going to give a call later this morning."

"So where you said you were going with boss?" asked Edwin.

"Well if you forgot Edwin, it must not been that important to you." Exclaimed Paris

"Look I just want to know where you are going; I got a right to know I am your husband you know."

"We are on our way up to Albany." said Paris.

"Who are we?" Ask Edwin.

"Look I am in the car with other people and I will call you later. "Said Paris and she turned off her cell phone off.

"How dare she hang up on me." said Edwin; as he gets out of his car and walks up the driveway to the house and the unlocking the door and going into the house and slams the front door. "Corona..... Corona. Yells Edwin walking up the stairs and he goes to the guest bedroom and bangs on the door.

"Corona.....Corona, wake up!"

Corona comes and opens the bedroom door looking daze and confused coughing and rubbing her eyes.

"What's wrong?" Ask Corona in a hoarse voice.

"I got to go to work and you and the kids got to go. Said Edwin; he turns around and walks down the hall to master bedroom.

"What time is it?" Ask Corona

"It's almost 9:30 and I am running late to work; so you and the kids got to go!"

"Where is Paris?" asked Corona

"Paris left for work and she won't be back until Monday." said Edwin.

"She has gone to work for the whole weekend?" asked Corona

"Yeah she working on a special project up in Albany for her job; so you and the kids need to get dress and I will drive you into town to get on a bus to take you back home." said Edwin picking up his cell phone and calling his job.

"Hi Shelby, this is Edwin I am going to be late for work; I had a family emergency and I won't be in until this afternoon."

"What time will you be in? "Ask Shelby.

"I will be there around twelve o'clock."

"Well don't forget today is my birthday and we are all going to the Cave to celebrate." Said Shelby.

"Okay thanks for reminding me" Said Edwin clicking off his cell phone as he walks back down the guest room where Corona is at. I don't know why Paris had to go off to Albany like she is some queen executive; she could have stayed here and took care of my sister and the kids. I don't want to be bothered with Corona and her stupid kids. That is the problem with Corona. Somebody always has to do something for her; she is like baggage; always a problem; her and her kids; that is why mommy tried to kill them because they are a problem. Edwin thought to himself as he approached the guest room.

"Did you get the kids up Corona I need to get to work today?"

"Yeah I am getting the kid up." Said Corona she walked slowly to Anthony's bedroom.

At eleven o'clock Edwin was driving Corona and kids into town to the Park and Ride to get on the bus to go back to New York and Edwin was tired and fed up with Corona and her kids; he didn't think they would ever get their slow behinds up and get out of the house.

"I am hungry Uncle Edwin." said Butch "Do you think we can stop and have breakfast?"

"No we don't have time to stop; I have to be at work by twelve o'clock; I have already spent too much time waiting for you to get up and get dress." said Edwin.

"You don't have to get nasty Edwin." said Corona sitting next to Edwin in the car.

"Please Uncle Edwin can we go to McDonalds for breakfast?" Begged Tince.

"Okay we will go to the drive-thru." said Edwin.

When they arrived at McDonalds the kids couldn't make up their minds what they wanted for breakfast and Edwin got mad and orders everybody an Egg McMuffin sandwich and a soft drink.

"Here you go!" Yell Edwin passing the food to Corona. "And don't eat in my car; I don't want crumbs all over my car seats and don't spill the drinks."

"You sure are in a bad mood this morning." said Corona passing the food to Butch. "Wait to we get to the bus station and we will eat there."

"I need money." said Corona. "I don't have any money for us to get back home."

"How come you never got any money Corona?" Ask Edwin not waiting for Corona to answer him. "This is exactly why mommy went off on you cause you always broke and begging for money. If you didn't steal a thousand dollars from mommy she wouldn't be in a state mental institution now; and on top of everything else you messed up our plans for setting Paris up."

"No I didn't and I told mama I was going to pay her back; but she didn't believe me." said Corona.

"Oh really." said Edwin pulling up into the Park and Ride and what about the three hundred and fifty dollars you took out of her bank account when she was in Bellevue Hospital?"

"I was going to put it back but before I knew it she was out the hospital." Said Corona; knowing she was lying and she had no intentions of paying her mother back. She needed the money because she behind on her rent again. She spent her rent money to get her and Tince weaves put in and she had to get herself a manicure, and Butch out of jail.

Edwin parks the car and got out and Corona and the kids got out the car and ran behind Edwin carrying their breakfast into the bus station. They sat down on a bench and went to eating their sandwiches. And Edwin went to the ticket window and brought tickets for Corona and the kids to take the bus back to New York City.

"Here you go Corona." said Edwin handing Corona three bus tickets.

"Thanks" said Corona; "but I don't have any money to get on the train once I get into New York."

"You know you are one sorry broad Corona." Said Edwin reaching in pocket and pulling out twenty dollars and giving it to Corona.

"I am tired of dealing with you always begging for money." said Edwin shaking his head. "That's why mommy tried to kill you Corona; don't you know people get tired of you begging."

"Don't keep reminding me." Said Corona walking over to the bench where the kids sitting. "What time is the bus coming?"

"The bus won't be here until two-thirty" said Edwin.

"You mean we have to sit here from twelve o'clock until two

thirty?" Ask Corona. "And what are we suppose to do until two thirty Edwin?"

"Sit here like everybody else. Edwin gave Corona a kiss on the forehead and walked away.

When Edwin drove up to his job his cell phone rang.

"So you decided to give me a call." said Edwin turning off the ignition in his car smiling from ear to ear.

"Hi Edwin." Said Jennifer, "I am sorry I ran out on you. It's just that....well you freak me out with that cane and then you turn around and be walking like nothing is wrong with you.

"I'm sorry baby I didn't mean to freak you out and just so you know I am finish with physical therapy and I kick the cane to the curb. So tell me what cha doing over the weekend?" Ask Edwin grinning from ear to ear.

"Well said Jennifer "I am free all weekend but I am not going to be in Pennsylvania especially since your wife is out of the hospital roaming around."

"Well, you will be happy to know she is back in the hospital." said Edwin.

"Really, what on earth happen this time?" Jennifer asks sarcastically.

"She went to my sister's apartment and tried to kill her and her children." said Edwin

"Oh my God that is awful Edwin; I am so sorry to hear that. How are they doing; your sister and the kids?" ask Jennifer

"They are doing okay; fortunately, the police arrived just in the nick of time. They had to knock down the door and then they had to wrestle her down to the floor to get the meat cleaver from her and then they put her in a straight-jacket and took her away to an insane asylum in upstate New York. said Edwin.

"What a horrible thing to happen to your family!" Exclaimed Jennifer wondering how Edwin is able to deal with the insanity that Paris put him through and he is able to maintain a job.

"The important thing is everybody is home safe and sound and Paris is upstate in the asylum where she belongs for a very long time." Said Edwin smiling and thinking how he can get Jennifer to come back to Pennsylvania for the weekend.

"Well; Edwin since you are free this weekend why don't you come on out to Detroit for the weekend." Said Jennifer.

"I would love to sweetheart; but after the incident with Paris and the police knocking down the door I had to shell out money to Corona to pay for the damages to her apartment."

"How much money do you need?" ask Jennifer

"Oh, I need about five hundred dollars." said Edwin.

"You need that much money to drive here." Ask Jennifer

"Hey I got to have money to travel or you can come here." said Edwin.

"No that is okay. It would be just like your wife to escape from the mental institution and kill me. I wire you the money and you can pick up in the morning from Western Union. said Jennifer.

"Love you baby." Said Edwin laughing and clicking the off button his cell phone then he hit the speed dial and calls Bruce and told him that he wouldn't be at the jazz concert and that Paris was back in the hospital and gave Bruce the same lie he told Jennifer that Paris tried to kill Corona and her kids.

Chapter 33

The trip to the Boys and Girls club is just what Paris needed and it was a lot of work to be done before they could put on the art show by the second week of December. Paris and Mr. Bonds arrived at their hotel early Friday afternoon and after checking in they went over to the Boys and Girls club and met the Project Director Mr. Felipe Nunez. Felipe Nunez was a very handsome man; Paris couldn't help but to stare at dark brown eyes and his short curly black hair with long side burns that matched his copper tan complexion. Felipe was 5"ll and he wore very fine thin cut mustache and with his shadow beard. Felipe look to be around 45 years old. Felipe gave Mr. Bonds and Paris a tour of the Boys and Girls Club. Felipe had spread out a meal for Mr. Bonds and Paris that was fit for a king. During their meal Felipe explained all the details how he wanted the art to portray the play that they the boys and girls will be performing.

"I don't know. I was under the impression that this was only going to take about 2 days and we would be assisting the boys and girls with their paintings; not us doing the actual paintings. said Mr. Bonds.

"I'm sorry you were misinformed, my assistant was not clear on the type of art that we need for the play." Said Felipe

"Well I am sorry too; but we have to be back at the office Monday morning." Said Mr. Bonds.

"I am sorry this has been a wasted trip for you both; but we need everything to be perfect in order to raise monies to keep out center open. If I had known you would not be able to give me more of your time I would not have invited you here." Said Mr. Felipe feeling disappointed; as he wipes his hands with his cloth napkin, and throws it in his plate fill with food.

"May I make a suggestion?" asked Paris taking a drink of water before she speaks in order to gather her thoughts.

"Of course my dear, feel free to express yourself." Said Felipe.

"Well first of all, said Paris taking a deep breath and looking at Felipe. How long do you think this project is going to take?"

"At least two to three weeks." said Felipe.

"It's no way we can stay two to three week." said Mr. Bonds.

"Why can I stay Mr. Bonds?" suggested Paris. "I mean I only work part time at the office and you have other people on your staff that can pick up my work load. And I can stay here and do the art work."

"I don't know." said Mr. Bonds.

"That is a perfect ideal." said Felipe.

"I am not covering your expense Paris; we were just supposed to be here for the weekend and this trip has already turned out to be very expensive." Said Mr. Bonds feeling annoyed.

"Well Mr. Bonds if you pay me my salary I can pay for my own expenses. "Said Paris.

"I doubt that will be enough Paris." Said Mr. Bonds.

"I can get Paris free room and board at the Bed and Breakfast that my sister and her husband own. Now you don't have to worry about her expenses and I will still pay for you for your time; then you should have enough money to pay Paris her salary for 3 weeks to work here." Suggested Filipe.

"Great, so we can start early tomorrow morning." said Paris standing up I am really exhausted; can we go back to the hotel now?"

"Yes said Mr. Bonds it is getting rather late. He stood up and shook Felipe's hand. It was a pleasure meeting you Felipe and we will be seeing you in the morning."

Paris was so excited about the project that's all she was able to talk about all the way back to hotel until Mr. Bond burst her bubble by asking her about Edwin.

"I got so excited about this project I forgot all about Edwin." said Paris taking a deep breath and shaking her head.

"So how are you going to deal with Edwin, Paris?" asked Mr. Bonds.

"What do you mean how am I going to deal with Edwin?" Paris was annoyed Mr. Bonds for asking her about Edwin. She wanted to tell Mr. Bonds to mind his business; but she knew Mr. Bonds was trying to look out for her.

"Look Paris, you know your husband was upset about you coming to Albany in the first place how are you going to deal with him?"

"Mr. Bonds this is my job and I have the privilege of working on this project for a very good cause and Monday I will call my husband and tell him I won't be back home for another three weeks and if he has a problem with it; then it will be just his problem. I have a job to do and I am going to do my job and he will just have to get over it." said Paris.

"Okay." Said Mr. Bond as though he didn't believe Paris would actually be that strong to stand up to Edwin.

Saturday morning Mr. Bonds and Paris met up in the hotel's restaurant for breakfast before going over to the Boys and Girls Club and Paris decided to ask Mr. Bonds for a raise; knowing that she would actually need more money to stay the extra three weeks.

"Paris you don't need any more money; Filipe and his family are going to take care all of your needs." Explain Mr. Bonds finishing off his coffee

"It's not fair; you are getting the pay for the work that I am doing on this special project and you are not giving me any extra monies for my expenses." said Paris; sitting across the table from Mr. Bonds.

"What extra expenses Paris you won't have to pay for your room and board or for transportation back and forth to the Boys and Girls Club." said Mr. Bonds eating his breakfast.

"Well Mr. Bonds ten dollars an hour is not enough money for me to stay; so I guess we will be leaving today." said Paris.

"But you promise Filipe that you are going to stay and do the work for him." said Mr. Bonds looking at Paris in disbelief and shaking his head.

Paris pulls out her cell phone. "What is Filipe's phone number so I can call him and explained to him that I won't be staying an extra three weeks; because even though he is paying you for my expenses for three weeks you won't pay me for doing the extra work and you know Mr. Bonds that is against the law to have me working and not paying me."

"Oh I am going to pay you for the extra hours you work but I am not giving you a raise for this project." said Mr. Bonds.

"Okay, I guess that's fair enough. Let's go; Filipe will be waiting for us." said Paris.

A half a hour later Mr. Bonds and Paris was at Boys and Girls Clubs.

"It's so good to see you both. Said Filipe shaking hands with Mr.

Bonds and Paris. "Would either of you like a cup of coffee before we get started?"

"No thank you." said Mr. Bonds. "We had breakfast at the hotel."

"No thank you;" said Paris looking sad.

"What is wrong Paris, you look so sad. Ask Filipe.

"It's not important." Said Paris. "Let get started!"

When Mr. Bonds found out that they had to go shopping for more art supplies because Filipe wanted mural painted in the foyer; Mr. Bonds got upset and said he had an emergency and had to go back home and asked Filipe for payment for the art work that Paris was going to do. Filipe only gave Mr. Bonds half the amount he promised and said he will pay the other half when the work was completed. Mr. Bonds thank Filipe and told Paris to stay in touch. Filipe and Paris went shopping for extra art supplies. After they finish shopping Filipe took Paris by to meet his sister Maria. The Bed and Bath was in a white colonial house with orange shutters Maria was about 5"4 and with long thick dark brown hair that she was wore in a pony tail and she was so skinny Paris couldn't help but to wonder if Maria had an over active thyroid. Maria took Paris to her room and all Paris could do was stare; the room look like something out of a fairy tale story with pink and white lace curtains and a pink matching bed spread. The bedroom had it own private bathroom which made Paris very happy that she didn't have to share a bathroom with the other guest. Maria cooked dinner and Paris met Maria's husband Raymond and Filipe's wife and children. Filipe talked about the festival and what type of paintings he wanted for the play and what the mural the mural should look like. The next day was Sunday and Filipe didn't believe in working on Sundays and that suited Paris just fine.

Filipe invited Paris to attend church with him and his family but

Paris refused and said she really needed the rest. The time along gave Paris time to think about Edwin how he claim not to be able to walk without his cane; him playing S&M games with his physical therapist and about Inez trying to kill Corona. If I was a man it would be no way would I put up with this dysfunctional family. I would be long gone. Paris thought to herself. But what would I do without a family? Paris had a hard time trying to visualize life without Edwin. Edwin and Anthony had been her whole life; in fact so have Inez, Corona and Steven without her even realizing it. Paris prayed a long prayer for God to show her the way out or make away out for her. Paris also took the alone time to look over Filipe's plans he had written out for the festival and the play which turn out to be a musical. Paris was not certain if Filipe was clear on what he wanted and that made this project more challenging than she could ever imagine. Paris cell phone rang and she hesitates to pick it up; when she looks at her phone she saw it was Papa calling.

"Hey Papa how are you?"

"Hey Lady Paris; I'm calling to see how things are going with you; did you make it up to Albany?" Ask Papa

"Yes, I made it and I am so glad to hear from Papa." Said Paris smiling.

"So did you put the lock on the bedroom door?" Ask Papa.

"No I didn't get a chance, but I already have a lock on the door." Said Paris

"Why didn't you put the extra lock on?" Ask Papa

Paris told Papa the horror story of Corona stealing Inez's money and Inez tried to kill Corona and the kids.

"Wow that is the wildest story I have ever heard." Said Papa.

"Well trust me when I tell you it is even wilder having to deal with it." Laughed Paris.

Papa laugh but he felt sorry for Paris because he knew she is in a bad situation. "I'm sorry for laughing Paris, but the stories you have told me about your husband and your in-laws sound so wild and crazy."

"That is because they are wild and crazy." laughs Paris.

"Well, I am going to be up in Albany in 2 weeks but I guess you will be gone by then."

"Actually, this turns out to be a two to three week project; so give me a call when you get here and we can meet-up."

"Hey that's sound great; I will talk with you then." Said Papa.

Paris clicks off her cell phone and went downstairs and saw some of the guest in the sitting room and she decided to just go out for a walk. It was a cool breeze that she found to be refreshing as she walked down the cobble stone street stepping on the leaves. Edwin hadn't called and that was fine with her; she could care less if he never calls her or if she never saw him again; but then again she misses Edwin with his loud mouth. Edwin was loud, in fact so was his family; except for Inez. Inez was a beautiful soft spoken women; it was just that she was mentally ill which she couldn't help. Paris didn't dislike Inez it was just that Inez had mental health problems. Paris felt Inez's wasn't getting the proper medical treatment for her illness; and that is what she kept trying to tell Edwin but of course he didn't want to hear a word she had to say; especially when it came to Inez.

"I just have to figure out how I can escape this madness." Paris thought to herself and the words of Dr. Levy words echoed again in her mind. "You got to go through it to get out of it." I just don't understand what he meant. whispered Paris.

Chapter 34

Monday morning after breakfast Maria drove Paris to the Boys and Girls club and she met the kids that she was to assist in painting the mural and the pictures for the festival and the play. Once Filipe was clear on what he wanted painted on the mural Paris and 4 of the art students was able to get start painting on the mural. In between painting the mural Paris gave instructions to the other art students on how to perfect their paintings that they had started.

How is it going? Ask Filipe standing in front of the canvas with his arms folded.

"Well I have to tell you Filipe; it going to take a miracle to get all this painting done in three weeks; but I have high hopes." Said Paris smiling. "And besides the art students that you have here are very talented and they are really doing a great job."

"I took the liberty of renting you a car Paris so you can go back and forth from the Bed and Breakfast to work every day." Said Filipe.

"Thank you Filipe that was very thoughtful of you." Said Paris smiling.

"No problem, if you should need anything just let my assistant know." Said Filipe as he exit the room

Paris felt like she living again working with the students on their art project; however, by lunch time she was tired and lunch was what she needed. The student was just as she expected bright and talented kids and Paris was glowing with happiness that she was able to talk Mr. Bonds into letting her stay and work on the project. At four o'clock when Paris was about to leave and go back to the Bed and Breakfast her cell phone rang and she saw it was Edwin. She forgot to call him and tell him that she wasn't coming home for another three weeks. Paris didn't pick up the call instead she went into Filipe's office and he was on the phone.

"Hold on for one second." Said Filipe speaking the person on the phone. "Can I help you with something Paris?"

"Yeah, I just came by to tell you I am leaving and I will need the key to the car." Said Paris.

"Oh yes;" said Filipe opening his desk drawer and taking the key out and giving it to Paris. "Here is the key to the Mazda 3 its sitting in the drive way."

"Thank you so much." said Paris.

Filipe was so involved with his conversation on the phone he didn't see Paris leave his office. Paris took the scenic route back to the Bed and Breakfast to enjoy the car which she felt was the perfect car for her. She pulls up in the driveway and she just sat in the car listening to Luther Vandross sing "A House Is Not a Home." She sat in the car thinking about how many years she had been married and thinking that she had a home and a family. She came to the realization it was all an illusion of impossibilities.

"What's you sitting in the driveway for; come on in the house?" yells Maria standing in the doorway.

"Oh, I was just enjoying the music and the car." said Paris as she got out the car and walks up the driveway to the house.

The house was empty with only Maria and her husband, Raymond. The house was warm with the aroma of stew chicken that filled the house.

"Yum" said Paris "What are you cooking?"

"I made stew chicken and beans with rice." said Maria walking a head of Paris into the kitchen "We have been waiting for you to have dinner with us; so you come and sit down and eat."

"Oh you didn't have to wait for me." said Paris.

"That is what we do here at the Bed and Breakfast all of the guests eat together."

Paris went into the bathroom and washes her hand and walks into the kitchen and she sees only Maria and Raymond.

"Where is the rest of your guest?" ask Paris sitting down at the table

"It's Monday and everybody goes home and when the weekend comes around again; everybody comes back again." said Raymond sitting down at the end of the table.

"Thank you so much for the dinner, everything was so good. said Paris as she finished her meal and getting up from the table.

"You must have some desert." said Maria.

"Thank you, but I really couldn't eat another bite and besides I have to make some phone calls."

"But I put a fresh pot of coffee on already and I made apple pie." Said Maria.

"You can't disappoint us by not having dessert." said Raymond."

"I tell you what, let me go and make a couple of phone calls and I will come back and have desert." said Paris walking away from the table.

"Okay, that's a deal" said Maria standing up. "Don't you take too long?"

Paris went upstairs to her room dreading to have to call Edwin; but she calls him anyway; after three rings Edwin answers his cell phone.

"Hello." answers Edwin clearing his throat.

"Hi Edwin, I'm sorry I didn't answer your call; but I was busy working." said Paris

"I thought you were coming back home this evening." said Edwin.

"I'm sorry; it has been so busy here and I thought I was going to make it back this evening; but it turns out the project is going to take three weeks." said Paris, trying to sound disappointed.

"You got to be kidding. Three weeks; that is a month. And what am I supposed to do with you being away a whole month?" asked Edwin.

"Three weeks is not a month; and besides I am quite sure you will find plenty to do with your physical therapist." said Paris wanting to hang up on Edwin.

"I am not in physical therapy no more." said Edwin sounding guilty.

"Well we didn't get to talk about you and the physical therapist playing your Slave and Master games because Corona was at the house crying and scared out of her mind because your mother tried to kill her and the kids."

"It was nothing to talk about." said Edwin.

"Oh really." said Paris sitting down on the bed. "There is plenty to talk about like you lying to me about the doctor saying you don't need physical therapy."

"Look Paris, I just wanted to surprise you." said Edwin laughing.

"Why don't you tell me Edwin how long have you been walking without your cane?"

"What difference does it make Paris; the important thing is I am not a cripple and I won't have to use a cane for the rest of my life?"

"It makes all the difference in the world especially since you have been smothering me and running and pretending that you couldn't walk." said Paris.

"You must have been having nightmares." said Edwin.

"I have been having nightmares a long time; because you had been smothering me and running a long time Edwin, even before you broke your leg. It's just that you messed up by smothering me more often after you broke your leg; and that is when I started to suspect you." said Paris speaking slowly in a low tone.

"You done lost your mind." yell Edwin. "You need your head check!"

"No, I don't need my head check Edwin; I know and God knows you have been smothering me."

"Something is wrong with you Paris accusing me of smothering you!" yells Edwin.

Paris became upset and thinks to herself. "*I can't allow this fool to take the "O" out of my joy by arguing with him. I can't let him interfere with my job; like he has done with so many other things I have been interested in. I can't even read a book without Edwin questioning me. I remember how he tried to interfere with me taking art classes at the university. Edwin questioned me every night about where I was going and he accused me of having an affair with the instructor and painting pictures of nude men. Edwin can't even stand to see me enjoying a concert, or a church social without him questioning me about why was I was laughing or singing; but not this time.*"

"I tell you what Edwin; when I get back home we will talk about this again. Good night." said Paris clicking off her cell phone.

Edwin was angry that Paris hung up on him so he press the re-dial button on his cell phone to call Paris back but the call went straight to voice mail. Edwin tried a second time to call; still no answer. Then his phone rang....

"Hey Corona, I was just on the phone with Paris and I can't believe she just hung on me. That skank thinks she is important because she got that five and dime job."

"Well at least you don't have to worry about her telling anyone that you are smothering her; because no one will believe her, especially since you were telling everyone she is crazy." said Corona. "Unless of course she has some kind of proof you been doing it."

"Yeah you right Corona, I better take a look around the bedrooms upstairs for cameras or other spyware devices. said Edwin sitting on the edge of his recliner scratching his head.

"Did you tell her Mommy is coming to live with you?" ask Corona

"No, I was going to tell her tonight over the phone but she hung up on me." said Edwin.

"You don't have to tell Paris Mommy is moving in. Just tell her Mommy is coming for a visit for a week and set Mommy off and let her kill Paris." said Corona laughing hysterically.

"Hey Corona, I getting a call from Jennifer; I'll talk to you later." said Edwin, clicking the cell phone over to speak with Jennifer.

"Hey Edwin honey, I sure miss you."

"I just left you this morning Jennifer."

"Yeah I know; but I still miss you; are you home now? ask Jennifer.

"Yeah I am home and I am tired from the trip back." Said Edwin and I need to get some rest.

"What wrong; you don't feel up to me loving you over the phone." Ask Jennifer

"It's just I got a lot on my mind."

"Don't tell me you having problems with that nut job of a wife?" ask Jennifer.

"Yep." said Edwin. "And I don't feel like talking about it".

"Yeah okay, I'll talk with you later; bye." said Jennifer.

"Good Morning Paris, you don't look to well this morning." said Raymond sitting down at the end of table while Maria sitting at the other end of the table passing a platter of bacon and eggs to Paris

"I am fine; just a little tired." said Paris passing the platter to Raymond.

"You're not hungry this morning?" asked Maria.

"I'll just have toast and coffee." said Paris.

After breakfast Paris hurried out the house and into her car and she took out her cell phone and dial. Within minutes a voice came over the phone.

Good Morning, Hidden Valley Medical Office may I help you.

Yes, said Paris taking a deep breath. Dr. Levy wanted me to schedule appointment with the Social worker for women going through domestic problems; may I speak with her."

"Oh yes, the social worker's name is Ms. Susan Palmer." The receptionist answered as if she was expecting Paris to call. "Ms. Palmer won't be in the office until later this morning; if you give me your name and number I will see that she gets your message. Paris gave the receptionist her name and phone number and by mid-morning Ms. Palmer called Paris.

"Hello." Said Paris answering her cell phone.

"Hello this is Susan Palmer may I speak with Paris Benson."

"Speaking." Said Paris putting down her paint brush and walked outside of the Boys and Girls club. "Dr. Levy wanted me to meet with you to discuss the problems I am having in my marriage but I am out of town for the next three weeks and I really need to address my problems before returning home. Is it any way we can have our sessions on the phone?"

"Yes it's no problem said Susan when would like to start?"

"Today, if that is possible." said Paris.

"Well today my schedule is full today; how about Thursday around two o'clock?"

"That will be fine." said Paris. I just really need to talk with someone who can help me to organize my thoughts so I can move forward in my life.

"Okay, I just need to get some information from you."

Paris stays on the phone for twenty minutes giving Susan her demographics; that evening Paris skipped dinner and Maria was upset with her. Paris was exhausted from working and from being depressed. She hated she had spoke with Edwin. Speaking with Edwin made her depressed and she could feel his presences even though she was miles away from him.

"I am sorry Maria but I am just exhausted, could you save my dinner and I will take it for lunch tomorrow?"

Maria went to rattling off in Spanish and went into the kitchen and Paris went upstairs and took a shower and went to bed only to wake up in the middle of the night upset that she had spoken to Edwin the night before and there were so many things she wanted to say to him. How she knew he was cheating on her. She wanted to explain to Edwin that all the problems that they were having was because of Inez and Corona was interfering in their marriage. And how they both needed counseling in order to deal with their problems. The fears of moving on with her life without him were starting to re-surface. She would be alone; no one to help her; what if she got sick there would be no one to come see about her. What if she ran out of money and couldn't afford to buy food and became homeless. The tears pour down Paris's face and she prayed for directions, for answers and for the strength to leave Edwin. God hates divorce kept echoing within Paris' mind but God also hates abuse, lying and adultery too. Paris whispers. "I got to pull it together. I must find a way out."

Thursday couldn't come around fast enough for Paris as she spent an hour telling Susan how Edwin would make up stories about smelling carbon monoxide and calling the gas and electric company and the nightmares and how she believe Edwin was smothering her and running and how Edwin was limping around on a cane acting like he couldn't walk. When Susan asked her about Edwin hitting her, Paris said Edwin had stopped hitting her because she had threatened to have him arrested. Or did he; Paris wasn't sure.

After talking to Susan; Paris felt like it was a waste of time because Susan didn't give her any advice on what she should do. Paris was disgusted with therapy session. Paris wish she could have spoke to Susan in person; just to see if Susan believes her or did Susan think she was crazy. The mural wasn't coming together fast enough and she only now had two weeks left. It was a good thing that Filipe was too busy to check on her because the last couple of days she had been distracted by her depression and her fears to move on with her life. When she went back into the building she saw the art student sitting around talking and not painting and Paris just felt so bad about falling down on this project and she needed to get focus and get the students focus.

"Okay I can see all of us need to get focus here." said Paris with a smile. "I tell you what let's go a walk." The four art students agreed and they went out for a walk and they talk about everything from art to their favorite television shows. When they got back Filipe was standing in front of the building waiting for them.

"Paris what are you doing, you come in here and look at this wall you haven't done anything." Said Filipe not waiting for Paris to answer him and turns and walks into the club with Paris, and the students slowly following behind him.

"That is not true." said Paris following in behind Filipe.

"Well you show me what have you been doing?" yelled Filipe waving his hands in front of the half painted wall.

"You don't really expect me to show you while you are yelling at me do you?" Ask Paris in her Mary Pippin's voice and batting her eyelashes. "When you have settled down, then and only then; I will be more than happy to discuss with you what we have been doing. Now if you excuse us Filipe; we have work to do; Come along now children; spit-spot we have work to do." Said Paris putting her arms the student's shoulders and she hurried away from Filipe before he realizes she just politely stubbed him off. Filipe stood there watching the kids being rushed off by Paris and laughing. Filipe shook his head and threw his hands up and went to rattling off in Spanish and walked back to his office. That afternoon Paris and the kids work hard to get the mural painted and by evening Paris felt like she was back on schedule. The rest of the evening Paris worked on some of the sketches for the mural and her cell phone rings; at first Paris is hesitant to pick up the phone thinking it might be Edwin; but she picks up the phone and see it is Ms. Becky calling.

"Hello Ms. Becky what a pleasant surprise to hear from you." said Paris.

"How are you doing Ms. Paris?"

"Oh I am doing just fine. I am up in Albany working on a special project for the Boys and Girls club." Said Paris.

"That sounds really great; but I just want you to know that I found a place for you to live." Said Ms. Becky.

"Oh really that is great; where is it the place located at?" Ask Paris.

"Well it's just up the road from the shelter and the woman is renting out her basement apartment." Said Ms. Becky. There was a long pause in the conversation and Ms. Becky was waiting to hear a response from Paris.

"Ms. Paris is you still there?" Ask Ms. Becky.

"Yes, I'm still here; how much is the rent?"

"The rent is $700 a month with utilities included." said Ms. Becky.

"Well that sounds really great but I can't move in the basement; I can't deal with to dust and mold and I don't like living in the woods." said Paris.

"Well it's a finish basement and you will have your own entrance." said Ms. Becky.

"I am sorry." said Paris rubbing her forehead. "I am just not interested in moving into that apartment."

"Okay." said Ms. Becky. "I just thought it might be something you would be interested in."

"Well thank you Ms. Becky I appreciate you looking into finding me an apartment; but it just that is not the apartment for me." said Paris.

"Oh you are welcome; give me a call when you get back in town."

"Okay, will do. Good night." Said Paris clicked off her cell phone. Paris knew she needed to move but that just wasn't the move for her. The next day Paris spoke to Susan and told her about Ms. Becky finding the apartment for her and she refused the apartment.

"Why did you refuse the apartment?" ask Susan.

"It's in the basement and I am claustrophobic."

"When did you become claustrophobic?" Ask Susan

"I don't know." said Paris "I just feel that with low ceiling and small rooms I would feel closed in."

"Have you seen the apartment?"

"No, I just feel I would be closed in living in the woods." said Paris.

"Well where would you like to live?" ask Susan

Paris didn't answer right away and she could not make up her mind where she wanted to live. It was too expensive to move back to New York and she had already try asking about moving into the public housing aka projects; but she didn't have any police records to help her to move into the public housing and she wasn't old enough to apply for senior housing and she didn't have any children either that would qualify her to move into public housing.

"I really don't know. I just want to have a home that I can be comfortable in and feel safe."

"I think you should really start thinking about where you want to move in order to make plans to move." suggested Susan.

"Yeah, I guess haven't given it much thought." said Paris; as she paced back and forth in front of the club house. "All I can think about is how am I going to survive and how I am going to survive all alone; by myself."

"You will get up every day and go to work and come home. Do you go to church?" Ask Susan

"Yes I do." Said Paris

"Well then when you are not working, you go to church and engage in church activities. And if you have any hobbies you will do them and you will meet new friends and spend time with them." Explain Susan.

"You make it sound all so simple." said Paris.

"Nothing is simple about change; but change is a part of life. And we all have to make changes as we grow older. It's how we view changes, how we deal with changes and how we accept changes. The more you are open to changes whether it is due to your circumstances or some unforeseen occurrence or due to the aging process; it's easier to deal with changes if you are open to changes. It not going to be an easy change for you Paris, but it is a necessary change that you are going to have to come to terms with in order for you to survive." explained Susan.

"Yes I know you are right; but how do I get there?"

"You are going to have to go through it to get there". said Susan taking a deep breath and looking at the time on the phone. Our hour is up. I will talk with you again the same day and time next week."

"Okay, good bye," Paris click off her cell phone and for the rest of the afternoon and evening all she could think about is how is she going to get to the point where she can see herself without Edwin; to see herself in a new home and as the days went by Paris kept trying to imagine and re-imagine with each stroke of her paint brush her life without Edwin. It was hard to imagine someone she spent 25 years with and they did have some good times and she still did love Edwin; but it was all was ousted out by the insanity of Inez Benson and the low down dirty schemes of Corona Benson.

Chapter 35

Two and half weeks have gone by and the mural on the foyer wall was completed with just a few needed touch ups. Paris instructed the art students on how to complete the touch ups while she help the other art students set their painting up on easels and hang their painting up in the library and in the recreation room. Paris's cell phone rang. She takes out her cell phone from her sweater pocket and saw it was Edwin calling. She turns the cell phone off and puts it back in her pocket. The girls wanted to go shopping for new clothes for the event and Paris decided to go along with them. Edwin calls several more times and he becomes annoyed that Paris isn't answering his calls.

When they came back to the club house Filipe's assistant had given Paris a note. After Paris read the note she ran into the back room and went into a closet and pull out paint cloths and the students came running in behind her. Paris drops the note on the floor as she runs down the hall carrying the paint cloths; and one of the students picks up the note and read it. The students ran down the hall behind Paris.

"Here, we have to hurry." said Paris passing out the paint cloths.

"One of you get the tacks out the supply closet." said Paris and I need a couple of you to go downstairs to the basement and bring up the 2 ladders. They hung up the paint cloths up over the mural and they draped the paint cloths over the other paintings that were on easels that stood in the library and recreation room.

"Oh I forgot about the paintings that are here on the walls. Could somebody go in Filipe's office and bring the roll of paper and tape." said Paris as she walks around in the library checking to see that all the painting on the easels were covered.

Two of the art students ran in Filipe's office and came back carrying rolls of paper under their arms and carrying scissors and a rolls tape. Paris and the students measure the paintings and cut the paper and the covered paintings on the walls.

"Oh my God here he comes." Said Paris excited and looking out the window. "I want everyone to go about their business and move those ladders. Two of the boys ran and move the ladders to the back of the house.

"Whatever you do don't look at him when he comes through that door!" said Paris

"Here he comes!" Yells one of the students running away from the window and ran into the recreation room. Paris ran and sat down behind the desk and pretending to be writing. The students pull out their cell phones, computers games and others pull out books and pretended to be reading. The front door squeaks open and the wind slams the door shut; the sound of wood floors squeaks with the sound of Filipe's footsteps. He walks down the foyer and sees the sheets hanging on the wall covering the mural. He walks in pass the mural and looked in the recreation room and saw the kids playing games and reading books and then he sees the covered paintings. He turns and walks across foyer to the library. He stood looking around and he sees more covered paintings and then he sees Paris sitting behind the desk writing and shuffling papers.

"Hello Paris."

"Oh hi Filipe; I'm sorry I didn't hear you come in; how are you today?" ask Paris.

"I'm just fine Paris; and may I ask what are you doing?" ask Filipe as he enters the room walking toward Paris sitting at the desk.

"Oh I am just making out some notes concerning the supplies I used on this project for Mr. Bonds." Said Paris; quickly gathering up the papers and placing them inside the desk drawer.

"I see." said Filipe "I gather that all the art work has been completed?"

"Yes indeed Sir it has." said Paris nodding and smiling.

"Okay let me see what everyone has done." said Filipe turning around and walking to the center of the room.

Paris quickly gets up from the desk and walks over to the entrance of the recreation room and invites the students into the library. The students stood next to their painting and unveil their paintings as Filipe inspects the paintings. Paris then invites Filipe into the recreation room. After an hour of Filipe inspecting all the paintings in the library and the recreation room Paris invited Filipe out into the foyer.

"Now for the unveiling of the masterpiece." announced Paris. The students unveil the twelve feet long by twelve feet wide mural. A sign hung in gold print above the mural "Clinton Avenue Historic District -The Mid 1800." The mural had brown, red, and green row houses; some with flowers on the window sill and with high steps that gave the illusion that one could climb up the steps into the history of Clinton Avenue homes; with its cobble stone streets, cafés and boutique shops. There are horse drawn buggies, box cars and women dressed up in long dresses, carrying handbags and some carrying gift boxes and others carrying umbrellas while others was wearing big hats with flowers. The men wearing overcoats with coats tails and ruffle shirts with bow ties and some with top hats and carrying canes An officer directing traffic, children running and little girls jumping rope, a little boy walking his dog, a mailman and a milk man making deliveries; an ice truck carrying a block of melting ice. The white never ending sidewalks with its street lights and traffic lights inviting you to walk the streets of history that leads to the little red school house and to the white church with a bronze color bell hanging from the church steeple that gives one the illusion of hearing the bell ringing.

Filipe stood in awe with his mouth open and he was speechless he walked closer to the picture as if he is going to enter into it, then he stops and turns around and looks at the students and at Paris. The foyer was filled with warm smiles as Filipe spoke with tears in his eyes.

"You all have done an outstanding, magnificent job. I am so proud of each and every one of you. It's just so beautiful. You all are so very talented. And thank you Paris for coming and helping us with this project and I hope you are going to stay for our special event."

"Of course I will and I just want to say Filipe you have very talented art students. I just want you to know that all the students came together and to make the mural a beautiful success and I think we owe ourselves a round of applause." Everyone cheer and applaud.

Chapter 36

The next morning Paris was excited and couldn't wait to tell Mr. Bonds about how successful the project had turned out. She sat in the dining room eating her breakfast and chatting away with Maria and Raymond about the mural and the other painting that students had done.

"Oh; would look at the time." said Paris looking up at the clock on the dining room wall and taking her last sip of coffee as she starts to gets up from the table. "It's already half past nine and Mr. Bonds must be coming in the office about right now and I can't wait to tell him about how successful we were in getting the paintings done."

Paris runs out of the dining room and back up to her bedroom and she picks up her cell phone and sees that Edwin has called again. "Well, I guess I have to call Edwin back........like later!" Said Paris giggling and walking over and bouncing down on the bed.

Mr. Bonds walks into his office and reaches over and picks up the receiver from his office phone. "Hello Mr. Bonds speaking how can I help you?"

"Good Morning Mr. Bonds how you are?"

"Paris." said Mr. Bonds sitting down on the corner of his desk. "How are you?"

"Oh I am just great." Exclaim Paris falling back on the bed and then sitting back up.

"Well that is great to hear; so tell me how is the project coming along?" Ask Mr. Bonds

"The project is completed!" Exclaim Paris.

"It's completed?!" ask Mr. Bonds standing up and walking behind his desk to look out the window. "That is fantastic and it has only been two and half weeks."

"Oh Mr. Bonds please can I stay for the event?" Ask Paris.

"I am sorry Paris but I am going to need you back here in the office." Said Mr. Bonds

"Why?" ask Paris standing up and pacing back and forth. "The event is just the week after next."

"Well our receptionist has found a new job and Jeff is taking his vacation next week". Said Mr. Bonds sitting down at his desk; and scratching his head; he felt bad telling Paris she couldn't stay for the event after she had worked so hard on the project.

"Well you don't need me I am only part time help." Said Paris.

"Not anymore you are not." Said Mr. Bonds. "How you would like a job as administrative assistant. You can be in charge of the office and set appointments for special projects."

"Wow that sounds great, I really can use a full time job and what is the salary?"

"We will discuss salary when you get back here and you need to get back here as soon as possible. And I tell you what; we can drive back up for the special event. Besides, I really want to see your art work. said Mr. Bonds.

"Oh thank you Mr. Bonds; I know you are going to be happy with all the work the students and I did for this event." I will head back first thing in the morning. Said Paris.

"That will be fine; I will see you tomorrow. Said Mr. Bonds.

As soon as Paris finish talking to Mr. Bonds another call came in and it was Edwin and he was the last person she wanted to talk to; but she had been avoiding him for the last few days so she decided to answer his call.

"Hello." Said Paris

"Hey Paris I have been trying to contact you." said Edwin pacing up and down in the foyer in the house.

"What's wrong?" Ask Paris.

"Nothing is wrong; I just want to know why you don't answer the phone when I call?" ask Edwin

"I am working. I need to be able to focus all my attention on my job. said Paris speaking slowly in a soft tone and rolling her eyes and clearing her throat. Sitting down in the rocking chair and rocking back and forth. "I am quite sure being the intelligent man that you are; you can understand that."

"I wanted to talk to you about my mother coming home from the hospital." said Edwin sitting down on steps in the foyer.

"Oh really." said Paris try to prepare herself for the horror-drama she is about to hear. "When is she coming home?"

"They are going to release her from the hospital in January and she is coming to live with us. said Edwin.

"Okay." Said Paris.

"Is that all you got to say is okay?" ask Edwin.

"That is all I have to say about it right now; I will be coming home tomorrow and then we can discuss it." Said Paris knowing there was nothing to discuss concerning Inez coming to live them; because at this point Paris was determine to find a way out; away from Edwin and all of the abuse and insanity that came along with being married into this dysfunctional family.

"Okay so what time do you think you will be home?" Ask Edwin

"I don't know because I have to stop by the office first." Paris said adamantly.

"Okay so call me when you get back in town." said Edwin

Yeah will do; talk to you then. Bye. Said Paris and clicking off her cell phone.

Paris refused to think about Edwin and about his mother coming to live with them. She drove to the Boys and Girls Club to see Filipe to let him know that she will be leaving in the morning. When she walks into the club house she see Filipe assistant.

"Oh hello Manuel I want to thank you for giving me the note that Filipe was coming. With your help, we were able to blow him away with our subtle presentation. Said Paris giggling.

"No problem; you done a very fine job with the students Paris and I was more than happy to be of assistance." said Manuel, helping Paris take off her jacket.

"Thank you Manuel; is Filipe in his office?" ask Paris.

"Yes he is and he has a surprise for you." said Manuel.

"Oh really now.... well do tell!" said Paris looking surprised.

"Oh no I will leave that to Filipe. I will let Filipe know you are here." Manuel walks down the hall to Filipe's office and Paris walks in front of the mural admire the art work done by the students.

"Hello; my dear Paris, how are you?" ask Filipe.

Filipe's voice startles Paris and she turns around and sees Filipe and Manuel standing behind her.

Hello Filipe, I am fine. Thank you." said Paris smiling. "How are you doing this morning, Filipi?

"I am doing just fine."

"I just want you to know I spoke with Mr. Bonds this morning and he is short staffed and he ask me to come back right away; so I will be leaving tomorrow morning. Said Paris.

"You can't leave said Filipe. Everyone will be disappointed and I have a surprise for you; so you can't go. Come let's go into my office. Manuel, please bring us some coffee."

"Oh no coffee for me; I had plenty this morning." said Paris waiting anxiously for the surprise.

"Then let us go into my office and you come too Manuel." said Filipe, as he walked to his office with Paris and Manuel following behind him.

"Have a seat." said Filipe as he walks behind his desk and sit down and opens the desk drawer and pull out some papers and places them on the desk facing Paris. Paris reads out loud the bold print Delaware Street Boys and Girls Club.

"You see this Paris we are opening a new Boys and Girls Club and I am offering you a full time job as a Recreational Director, you can teach art; play games with the kids, teach dancing and a thousand more things you can do. And the job pays twenty five dollars an hour for a forty hour week.

Paris sat there in shock; staring, she couldn't believe her ears. Two job offers in one morning. Filipe and Manuel both sat looking at Paris waiting for her answer.

"Well, will you take the job?" asked Manuel

Paris shook head no but she said yes at the same time.

"I am confuse Paris do you want the job or don't you?" Ask Filipe.

"Yes of course, I want the job." said Paris sitting there with her mouth open.

"Then why are you shaking you head no?" ask Manuel

"I am shaking my head because this has been an amazing experience; just being here and doing something I love and that is painting. It is just so good to have had this experience and then to be offered a job. Like Wow what a blessing!" Exclaim Paris.

"Good!" said Filipe "Then you don't have to go back home; you stay for the event."

I owe Mr. Bonds at least a two week notice and I some personal things to take care of and I told my husband I was coming home tomorrow. said Paris.

"Oh you are married." said Filipe throwing his hands up in the air. "How stupid of me; I didn't even consider the fact that you may have a family."

"That is not going to be a problem. And Mr. Bonds and I are coming back for the event but I need to go home and handle some personal affairs so I can move."

"So your family is not going to have a problem moving to Albany?"

"My son is away in college and my husband is very open to new beginnings; in fact we are originally from New York. I promise you it's not going to be a problem and Mr. Bonds and I will come back in time for the event. I wouldn't miss it for nothing in the world." said Paris smiling.

"Okay." said Filipe picking up the papers and putting them back into the drawer then the job is yours. Manuel you go get the application and all the forms she need to start work in two weeks. Paris was so excited about Filipe's job offer she forgot all about Mr. Bonds offering her a job as his assistant. She sat in the library filling out the application and her cell phone rings and she quickly searches through her pocketbook for her phone; she pulls it out of her pocket book and answers it.

Chapter 37

"Hello." answers Paris.

Hey Paris; what's going on?

"Oh Papa, I am doing just fine." said Paris. I am so glad you call I have a million and one things to tell you"

"Wow you sure sound like you are on top of the world today; I just want to let you know I have arrived here in Albany this morning and I am here just for the day and I will be leaving in the morning to go back into Pennsylvania; so how about you and I having lunch or dinner? Ask Papa.

"Let's do both. I have a million and one things to tell you." Said Paris smiling and excited to hear from Papa.

Paris gave Papa the address to Boys and Girls club to pick her up at noon and they went to a diner for lunch and then they tour downtown Albany. It wasn't until they went out to dinner that Paris told Papa about the job offers.

"That is fantastic Paris; who has two job offers in one day?" Ask Papa

"Correction my dear friend;" said Paris holding up her fingers. "Who has two job offers in one morning?"

"So which one did you accept?" Ask Papa.

"I accepted both of them." said Paris eating her dessert and smiling.

"You accepted both of them; don't tell me you are going to

commute back and forth between two jobs?" ask Papa, sarcastically waiting for Paris to answer. Paris sat there eating her coconut cream pie giggling and telling jokes about her driving up and down on the interstate five days a week to work part time for Mr. Bonds and Filipe. Papa didn't see the humor in Paris's jokes.

"No silly; it just that I don't know if I want to stay in Hidden Valley or just leave Edwin and move to Albany." said Paris wiping her mouth with her napkin.

"Whoa, wait a minute." said Papa clearing his throat and drinking water. "Are you still contemplating staying with Edwin?"

"Papa; I have been with him for 25 plus years and I don't know if I can actually live without him. I think I will be lost without Edwin."

"Paris." said Papa rubbing his forehead. "You have been living without Edwin for the last two and half weeks and you did just fine."

"You got a point Papa; but that was just two and a half weeks, it's not a life time. I knew Edwin was still here for me. And I really don't want to stay with Edwin especially since he plans on moving his mother in to live with us. I have to make sure; I know what I am doing before I walk away." Said Paris.

"Wait a minute Paris; he is going to move his mother in to live with you? Well let me tell you sis, you may not be able to walk away and haven't you been through enough already? I mean haven't you had enough of the insanity and the abuse?" ask Papa becoming upset with Paris.

Paris lean on the table with both of her elbows on the table and wiping her face with hands and then fold her hands and placed her hands on the table looking up at the ceiling as if she is about to say a prayer. "No." said Paris taking a deep breath. "I haven't gone completely through it because I need to come to terms with knowing that I have done everything I could possibly do to make my marriage work. I have to know within myself that I am right with God. You know God hates divorce unless it is on grounds of adultery."

"I hope you are not letting the folks at your church influence your thinking." said Papa.

"Well, they do make a good point; I do have to do what God wants me to do." said Paris.

"Look Paris, there is a difference in doing what God wants you to do and what religion wants you to do. Your relationship is with God and not a religion. What I mean is religion is an organization of people and you need to think about how God is viewing your situation and what Edwin is doing to you. A man is abusing his wife is not something God is not happy with; in fact God does not hears his prayers. And Edwin is cheating on you and that is only one of the reasons that he is physically, verbally, and emotionally abusing you." Said Papa.

"And what is the other reason he is abusing me? ask Paris.

Because he is crazy like his mama! exclaimed Papa.

"Well that much is true." laughs Paris taking a sip of water. The thing is this Papa; the day I married Edwin I made a vow to God and Edwin I would be married to him for better or worst. And I have to make sure I am doing the right thing. I love Edwin and he can't help that his mother is mentally ill and no more she can help it. I love Edwin; I just have to make sure when I leave I am doing the right thing. Because when I leave there won't be no going back.

Papa rear back in his seat and looked Paris. "Paris.....Paris, I hate to say it but you sound like you have lost your mind; how could you even think staying with him after all the abuse he has put you through.

Papa turns around and waves to the waiter.

"Yes Sir, what can I get for you?" Ask the Waiter.

"I will take a double scotch on the rocks." Said Papa looking at Paris feeling annoyed and in disbelief shaking his head.

"Would you like anything ma'am?" ask the Waiter

"Yes I will take a cup of tea with a shot of brandy." Thank you said Paris.

After the waiter walks away Papa turns back to Paris and looks at her and shaking his head. "I am so sorry Paris all that you have gone through and are still going through in this insane abusive marriage. I just want to tell you about a man on a deserted island out in the middle of nowhere."

The waiter comes back with the drinks and Papa thanks the waiter and takes a couple of sips his double scotch on the rocks.

"You see Paris; there was this man who was shipwreck on a deserted island with no way to get off. He prayed for God to send him someone to rescue him. Then one day someone came by on a raft and offer to take the man back to the main land where he could get food and water and transportation to go back home. The man told the person no because he wouldn't feel safe floating on a raft. So the person left him on the island. A day later another person came in a row boat and offered to take the man to the main land but the man refused because he said the row boat was too small. Some days later a steamship came by and the person offer him lift to the main land and the man refused because he said he knew he would not feel comfortable riding on a steamship. Then a day or two later a luxurious cruise liner came along and the captain offers to take him to the main land and the man again refuse because he said could never afford to pay back the monies to the captain for transporting him to the main land. The man never got off the deserted island and of course eventually he died."

"That's a very interesting story, Papa." said Paris smiling. "But until I can imagine my life without Edwin; I'm staying.

"Paris, God could be giving you a way out and by you not paying attention; you could end up never getting out of this abusive marriage and losing your life. I don't know which job you are going to choose but you have two good job offers and all you have to do is just choose one and get away from Edwin."

"I hear you Papa; so what time are we leaving in the morning? ask Paris.

"I will be rolling out at eight in the morning. Said Edwin feeling annoyed with Paris. "Let's go. I will pick you up at eight thirty." Paris gave Papa the address to the Bed and Breakfast and they left the restaurant.

Chapter 38

Edwin, Corona and Steven was at the house hangout and eating fried chicken wings, French fries, and boozing it up and while Corona's kids was upstairs in Anthony's room playing video games.

"So what did Paris say when you told her Mommy was coming here to live." Ask Steven.

"She wouldn't talk about it over the phone." Said Edwin.

"What you mean she wouldn't talk about it?" Ask Corona.

"Just what I said she wouldn't talk about it. She was at her job and said we can talk about it when she gets here tomorrow." said Edwin.

"Well I think the whole idea of bring Mommy here to live so she can lose her mind and kill Paris is crazy." said Steven.

"I would like to hear you say that when we collect that money from the insurance companies. said Corona chewing on a chicken bone. So Edwin, my dear brother how much money do you think we will get after mommy kills Paris?"

"She has one policy at Life Insurance for a $100,000.00 dollars and the same amount at the credit union life insurance policy and she has $2000.000 in her IRA. And we can just cremate her body and that will be dirt cheap." said Edwin.

"Yeah, but the problem with that is they will lock Mommy up forever, so you all can just count me out of your plains on killing

Paris." Said Steven; leaning back in his chair and waving of his hand at Edwin.

"They are going to lock her forever anyway; cause she nuts!" said Edwin laughing

"It's not like she would be going to jail; they would just put her back in that resort hospital where she is at now. They will only keep her for a couple of years and then she will be at home again. You know Steven you can always go and visit her." Exclaim Corona.

"Man, I got to go; I don't want to have anything to do with plotting to kill Paris and having Mommy locked up for the rest of her life." Said Steven; pushing away from the kitchen table and standing up. "I'm telling the two of you; you are not going to get away with it. I'm going home. Are you coming Corona?"

"Yeah I'm coming; you the only ride back I got back into New York." Said Corona; getting up from the kitchen table. She walked down the foyer to the stairs and yelled for Butch and Tince to come downstairs.

"Look man; don't say anything to nobody in the family and especially not to Paris about our plans to kill her." Said Edwin walking behind Steven

"I'm not saying anything; just don't count me in. I just don't see why you just don't divorce Paris that's better than killing her and involving Mommy. It just wrong!" said Steven walking to the front door.

"Come on yawl; I'm not waiting on you all night." Yells Corona.

"Don't you see man, if I divorce her then I will end up having to sell the house and splitting everything with her and I won't get the insurance money from her dying." Said Edwin putting his arm around Steven's shoulder.

"Man 200,000 dollars is not a lot of money man; and eventually you both will get found out." Said Steven looking at Edwin.

"How is anybody going to find out; Paris don't have any family or close friends and the folks at the church don't care anything about her. So who's going to ask questions?"

"Anthony. What are you going to tell him when he asks what happen to his mother? Ask Steven opening the front door.

"Man Anthony is my main man and he will believe anything I tell him; I already told him Paris crazy and a whore. And I told him that his mother had several abortions and I had to talk her out of aborting him and he believed every word." Said Edwin patting Steven on the back; "I'm telling you man; me and Corona got everything covered."

"Come on Corona let's go." said Steven shaking his head as he walked out the door and Butch and Tince came running down the stairs.

"Bye Uncle Edwin."

"Talk to you later Corona." said Edwin ignoring the kids and closing the door and walking back down the foyer to the kitchen; talking to his self. "I will get Mommy in here and set her off like a time bomb and I would be rid of Paris. She thinks she is so perfect and those dumb ugly paintings. I don't know what posses me marry that skank. said Edwin making himself a drink. She will try to talk me out of letting mommy move in; but I will break on her and shut her down. After Paris is dead and gone I get Jennifer to move in and make her paid the bills".

Chapter 39

The next morning the weather was horrible; it was cold and raining when Papa pulls up in his car in front of the Bed and Breakfast. He calls Paris on his cell phone.

"Hello." answers Paris

"Hey I'm outside are you ready?"

"I will be right out." said Paris clicking off her cell phone. "Oh Maria and Raymond thank you so much for your fine hospitality. I really enjoyed my stay here."

"Well you and your husband both can come and stay here until you find a home of your own." Suggested Raymond; he stood up from the table and walked over to Paris and gave her a hug.

"Oh thank you so much." said Paris and she walked over to the stove where Maria is standing and gives her a hug.

"Here" said Maria handing Paris a white paper bag. These are some muffins for you and your friend to eat on your way back to Pennsylvania."

Paris thanks Maria and Raymond again and runs to the door and picks up her pocketbook and suitcase. Papa sees Paris coming out of the house and he gets out of the car and rushes over to Paris and takes her suitcase and puts it in the back of the car and Paris gets in the front passenger seat.

"Are you sure you want to go back?" ask Papa.

"Yes I am sure."

"Why do you have to go back?" ask Papa.

I told you why last night. said Paris.

"You can call Edwin and say everything you want to over the phone." said Papa. He looked over at Paris and she had the big grin on her face. "You're nuts; Paris!"

"I know; but I still have to go back to get my personal belongings"

"Paris, you can always replace personal belongings." said Papa.

"No not everything. I have my collectable items and pictures of myself when I was a kid and my parents. I even have pictures of you and your family and those things I could never replace."

"You can't replace your life either Paris." said Papa pulling away from the curb and driving off into the traffic.

"Let's stop off at DDs and get some coffee to go with our muffins that Maria made for us."

"So what are you going to do when you get back to the house?" Ask Edwin pulling into the drive-thru at Dunkin Donuts.

"You know Papa you are starting to stress me out and I don't want to talk about it." Said Paris sounding annoyed

"Okay fine." Just don't you forget to put the lock on the bedroom door before you go to sleep tonight?"

By twelve o'clock Papa pull up in front of Paris' house; all the leaves had fallen from trees and the burning bushes that roped around the front yard and the house stood tall in front of the white frame and its red shutters. Paris thanked Papa for bring her home and he promised to call and check on her. Paris kissed Papa on the cheek and then she got out of the car. She didn't

see Edwin's car and she hoped he was at work. Paris slowly walks up the driveway to the front door and she turns around and sees Papa still sitting at the curb side. Paris waves goodbye to Papa and he just nods his head and prays that God will keep her safe. Paris unlocks the door and goes into the house and she looks in the dining room and in the living room and everything looks the same as she left it.

Paris walks down the foyer to the kitchen where dirty dishes were stack in the sink; and she thinks to herself that Edwin must have had Corona with her kids visiting. She looks into the family room Edwin's so-call man cave and then she walks back down the foyer and up the stairs and all the rooms upstairs were empty. She walked into the master bed and the ruminants 'of the nightmares of being smothered comes back to her; and chill runs through her body. Paris could hear Papa saying don't go back. "I am here now and I have to do what I feel I need to do." whispers Paris; as though she was answering Papa.

Paris goes into the guest room and puts her suitcase down and opens the closet door and she crawls into the back of the closet and pull out the plastic bag that holds the journal, lock and screw driver that Papa had brought for her. Then she runs downstairs to get a hammer out the kitchen drawer and she runs back upstairs.

It took Paris an hour after reading the instructions several times to get the lock on the door and she felt pretty proud of herself being that she has never used a hammer or screw driver before. Paris folds up the bag and the package that lock came in and put in her pocketbook and she sat her suitcase in the closet. It was now one forty five and that gave her enough time to get to the office and see Mr. Bonds before he left for the day.

Chapter 40

"Good Afternoon." said Paris as she walks into Mr. Bonds' office. Mr. Bonds look up from his desk.

"Well Good Afternoon Paris I am so happy you have flattered me with your presence. So how was your trip back home?" said Mr. Bonds.

"I just got back an hour ago and I went home to..... Paris stop and thought about what she was about to say.

"You stop by your home to do what Paris?"

"I stop to put my things away and to get my car; oh I almost forgot". said Paris looking into pocketbook and pulled out a check and handed to Mr. Bonds. "Filipe asked me to give to you this.

"Ah yes; thank you Paris." Said Mr. Bonds; he looked at the check and then placed it in the desk drawer. "So how did you enjoy yourself up at the Boys and Girls Club?"

"It was just wonderful and the kids were just fantastic and so talented." Said Paris smiling.

"Yes Filipe told me how much they like you; in fact he said he offered you a job and you accepted it and I just want to know when were you going to tell me that you had accepted this job or did you have plans in working for me and Filipe?" Ask Mr. Bonds.

"Mr. Bonds I just walk into your office and you didn't give me the chance to tell you." said Paris, clearing her throat and sitting down in the chair in front of Mr. Bonds' desk.

"You had the opportunity to tell me when you were in Albany." said Mr. Bonds.

"Mr. Bonds I really hadn't made up my mind about working for Filipe. Besides you had made your offer first before Filipe had even spoken to me. And to be quite honest because I have been going through some problems at home I don't know where I want to be so I ask Filipe to give me two weeks before I start."

"So you did make up your mind to work for Filipe?" Ask Mr. Bonds

"No I didn't."

"Well Filipe is under the impression that you are coming back to the Boys and Girls Club to work Paris; so which is it? Are you going to work for me or for Filipe?"

"Please give me two weeks to make up my mind?" ask Paris.

"Okay I will give you two weeks and that is all; now we got a thousand things to do." Said Mr. Bonds standing up and walking over to his file cabinet and pulling out folders. Mr. Bonds wasn't kidding when he said he had a thousand things for Paris to do. At the end of the day when Paris arrived at home she was exhausted and could've went to sleep in the driveway; which might not have been a bad idea as she pull up behind Edwin's car and saw Edwin was getting in his car.

Chapter 41

"Hey Edwin" yells Paris as she let's down the car window on the passenger side of the car and she pulls her car up next to Edwin's car where you going?"

"Hi Paris." said Edwin getting out of his car and walking over to the driver's side of Paris car. "Are you just getting back from Albany?

"No; I got back earlier;" Said Paris getting out of the car. "I had to go to work once I got back in town; so where are you going?"

"I have to go and pick Steven up his car broke down in Buttstown, New Jersey. I'll be back soon."

"Okay. I am going to bed; I am whipped." said Paris. Paris was so tired all she could do was go upstairs and take a shower and the movie Psycho came into her mind as she was taking a shower and all she could think about was Papa telling her not to go back home. Paris hurried out of the shower and got into bed and then she got out of the bed and went into the guest room and got in the bed. Then got up and closed the door and lock it. When Paris woke up it was five o'clock in the morning and she gets up and goes the linen closet and pulls out a bath towel and face cloth and went into Anthony's bathroom and took a shower. When she came out into the hallway Edwin was standing there waiting for her.

"What's up with you Paris; I came home last night looking to spend some time with you and you lock yourself in the guest bedroom; how dare you put an extra lock on the bedroom door." Said Edwin.

"I was exhausted so I went and took a shower and went to sleep." Said Paris ignoring Edwin remarks about the lock she put on door.

"So you still think I was smothering you?" ask Edwin following Paris into the master bedroom.

"That's right." said Paris.

"You know something Paris you always telling me I need therapy but you are the one that needs therapy."

"I agree with you Edwin that is why I go for therapy every week." said Paris getting dress. "And I think we can both use some therapy; perhaps we should go to see a marriage counselor so we can work our problems out."

Edwin just stood watched Paris dressing with disgust written all over his face. Paris finishes dressing; combing her hair and applying makeup, and went into the guest room and picks up her pocketbook, cell phone, keys and goes downstairs. And Edwin follows behind her.

"So Edwin, How do you feel about going to see a marriage counselor?" Ask Paris.

"I have to think about it" said Edwin

"Well that's a good start at least you are willing to think about it." said Paris as she filled the tea pot with water and placed it on the stove. "I see you had company."

"Yeah Corona and the kids were here last night and Steven was here too" said Edwin.

"Huh, that must have been very interesting time; you all being here and even Steven found time to visit." Said Paris as she turned on the stove and walked over to the kitchen table and sat down.

"We talked about Mommy coming to here to live." Said Edwin sitting down at the kitchen table..

"Okay." said Paris

"Okay, is that all you can say is okay?" asked Edwin he was in shock that Paris was so easy to convince; in fact he didn't have to convince her at all. He was actually disappointed in Paris response; he was ready to argue and beat her down if necessary.

"Yes I said Okay. First we have to meet with her doctor to find out what her needs are; like what medications she is taking and what she can and can't eat; you know things like that." said Paris

The tea pot kettle whistle and Paris took the tea pot off the stove and got a cup out the cabinet and a tea bag. It didn't matter to Paris about Inez moving in; coming back to the house just made her realize that she wanted to be as far away from Edwin as his crazy deranged family. But Paris knew at this point she couldn't tell Edwin she was leaving him; she knew she would just have to get up and leave.

"Furthermore," said Paris walking to the table and sitting down. "You will have to be the one to take care of her."

Edwin was shock by Paris' reaction to his mother coming to live with them. "Why do I have to be the one to take care of her?"

Edwin she is your mother and it is your responsibility and Corona's as well as Steven's responsibility to take care of your mother. Now when is she coming home? Ask Paris sipping her tea.

"The first week in January" said Edwin thinking to his self that Paris is acting like she was a white woman and so cool and calm about his mother coming to live with them.

"Okay now; you call the hospital and set an appointment with her doctors so we can go up there together and talk with the doctors about your mother's condition." suggested Paris

"I don't want you talking to my mother's doctors." yells Edwin

"Don't start yelling Edwin it's too early in the morning for you to be acting like a fool. Said Paris calmly and sipping her tea. "I just want you to realize that once your mother moves in you won't have time to go hanging out with your friends and seeing your old lady on the side." Paris had to hold back the laughter as she watch Edwin go into shock over her being so calm and mentioning his mistress.

"What old lady on the side, I am not seeing nobody. yells Edwin, slamming his fist down on the table.

"Yes you are Edwin the same one you were in the car accident with having sex." said Paris getting up from the table and picking up her pocket book and getting her jacket out of the hall closet. I think I will go over to the diner for breakfast too bad you are not dress you could've join me."

Edwin was feeling so out done and humiliated by Paris' calm and nonchalant attitude about him having an affair. How did she know anyway?

"I am not having an affair!" exclaimed Edwin

"Oh yes you are Edwin and I know you don't want to be with me; and frankly speaking, which I quote I don't give a damn; you should have just man-up and told me. Said Paris as she put on her jacket.

"Somebody at the church must have told you that. yells Edwin.

"Oh; do the church folk know too?" asked Paris laughing.

"No" said Edwin.

"Oh so you are admitting that you are having an affair?" asks

Paris, putting on her and gloves and walking down the foyer and opening the front door and stepping outside.

"I am not having an affair; and whoever told you that is lying!" yells Edwin

"Yes, you are Edwin that is why you are smothering me and running. Said Paris. She turned around and looked back at Edwin with a smile on her face and then walking to her car. That is why you have been cursing at me and calling me all kinds of names because that is what all you low down dirty men do that cheat on their wives. In fact you have been seeing other women for years even when we lived in New York. I have to go; I must have my breakfast before I go to work. Said Paris she smiled at Edwin and got in her car and then she let the window down.

"And by the way Edwin being that you have been whoring around you better get yourself checked out to make sure you have not contracted A.I.D.S."

Paris closed the car window and drove away leaving Edwin standing in the driveway with his eyes bulging out of his eye sockets looking like a buffoon. Paris felt good about her conversation she had with Edwin; and he couldn't handle it. Now all she had to do was make up her mind which job she was going to take. She never did discuss salary with Mr. Bonds and she suspected it would not match Filipe offer. And the idea of moving to Albany was challenging to her after all she didn't know anyone there but Filipe and his family and the art students; but Papa did say Robin lived there; her thoughts were interrupted by her cell phone ringing. Paris didn't answer the phone; she thought it was Edwin calling. When she pulls up into diner's parking lot she opens her pocketbook and pulls out her cell phone and sees that it was Papa calling. Paris called him back.

"Hi Papa, I am sorry I miss your call I was driving."

"Hey how are you doing; what's going on?" Ask Papa

"Papa, I am doing just fine." said Paris getting out the car. "After you dropped me off I went upstairs and put lock on the bedroom door and then I went to work; are you still here in PA?"

"No, I'm down in Maryland." said Papa wondering if Paris made a decision about leaving Edwin and what job she has chosen to accept.

"When are you coming back up this way?"

"I won't know until they give me my new schedule next month, have you made up your mind where you going to work at?" asked Papa

"No; I still haven't made up my mind." Said Paris, as she walked into the diner.

"Keep me posted" said Papa I talk with you later.

"Loves you much." Said Paris.

"Love you too. Said Papa.

That evening Paris went to a little café in town and sat down and had dinner; she didn't feel like going back to the house and dealing with Edwin; in fact she felt a somewhat uneasy in the house with Edwin but she had to go back and she didn't understand why. When she finished dinner she open her wallet and looks at the money card that Papa had given her and she felt like going to a hotel but no. She told herself she had to go back to the house. When Paris got home Edwin was on the phone with Corona.

"I talk to you later." said Edwin

Paris walks down the foyer through the kitchen and to family room where Edwin is sitting.

"Hi Edwin" Paris was surprise Edwin wasn't still mad from the conversation they had earlier; but that was fine with her she was tired and really didn't feel like talking to Edwin; yet alone looking at him.

"Hey Paris; how are you doing?"

"I'm very tired." said Paris.

"You never told me about how you made out with your job in Albany." said Edwin.

What is this some kind of trick question; he is not even bringing up the conversation we had this morning; obviously it's because he is cheating; but it don't matter because I don't care who he seeing, the woman can have him and his crazy family. I wish I could meet her and thank her for taking this jackass off my hands. Paris thinks to herself.

"It went well. I will tell you about it another time. I am dead tired and I have to go to bed."

Paris goes upstairs into the master bedroom bathroom and turns on the shower and takes her clothes off and then changes her mind and turns off the shower; she didn't feel safe with Edwin in the house. She walks back into the bedroom and opens her dresser drawer pulls out a night gown and put it on; then she takes it off and takes out a sweat shirt, a pair of sweat pants and a pair socks she put them on and gets into bed; then she gets back up, walk down stairs and picks up her pocketbook, and keys off the bench in the foyer by the front door and goes back up stairs but this time she goes into the guest room and locks the bedroom door and she looks in her pocketbook for her cell phone. She sets her cell phone alarm to ring at six thirty in the morning and gets into bed and turns off the lights and turns on the television and she falls asleep.

Chapter 42

Paris awakens by someone yelling and screaming. At first she thought it was someone on the television but it was a life insurance commercial on; then she realized it was Edwin. Paris got up and unlocks and slowly opens the bedroom door. She walks out into the hallway and walks around to the balcony of the stairs and she looks down and sees Edwin hitting the walls with his fist and knocking over the kitchen chairs. Paris runs back in the bedroom and locks the door and put on her sneakers and pick up pocketbook, and picks up her cell phone and her keys off the nightstand. She slowly opens the bedroom door and tip toe down the stairs and she could hear Edwin crying and yelling "she's dead....Mommy is dead..... She died."

"Oh my God" said Paris standing by the front door in the foyer looking at Edwin. Edwin turns around and sees Paris and screams; "It's your fault Paris mommy is dead. You wished her to death!" Cries Edwin.

Paris took a couple of steps backward to the door and turns around and unlocks and opens the front door and runs and gets in the car and turn on the ignition and Edwin came running out of the house yelling at Paris accusing her of killing his mother.

Its pitch black outside and the moon light is the only light and Paris can barely see her way backing out of the drive way. She backs out of the driveway but then she realizes that she is driving in the wrong direction, she comes to the culdesac; she locks the car doors and drives in the circle of the culdesac and stops. Being upset and afraid and she had to pull herself together; she didn't know what to think or where to drive. Then she remember the money card that Papa gave her; she steps on the gas and takes off and she sees Edwin standing in the middle of the road waving his fist screaming and yelling.

"You killed my Mommy!" screams Edwin shaking his fist in the air.

The neighbors turn on their house lights and peered out through their slightly crack windows and doors. Paris slams on the breaks and her car screeches and spends out of control. Paris is shaken up and puts her head down on the steering wheel and she starts praying "God please make this fool move out of my way; protect Edwin God. Don't let me kill him." Edwin runs up to the car and starts banging on the hood of the car. Paris backs the car up and turns it around and tries to go around Edwin but he runs in front of the car.

"Get out of way Edwin!" Paris hits the brakes.

Edwin runs up to the car and starts beating on the hood of the car again and yelling.

"You kill my Mommy and I'm going to kill you Paris!"

Paris backs the car up and takes off. Edwin jumps in front of the car again yelling and waving his fist.

"You kill her....you killed her Paris...you kill my Mommy!"

Paris hit the brakes hard and the car comes to a screeching stop almost hitting Edwin. Paris backs the car up and pulls down the window. I am not going to stop next time Edwin; I'm telling you .....Don't run in front of my car again! Paris closed her window and backs the car up again and stops. Edwin runs up to the side of the car and tries to grab hold of the door handle and banged on the car window. Paris steps on the accelerators and takes off; leaving Edwin running behind the car yelling and screaming that she killed his mommy. Paris pulls off on the side road and she takes out her cell phone and dial 911 and a recording comes on. Paris looked up and saw a police car passing by and going in the direction of her house.

Chapter 43

Paris click off her cell phone and follows the police car back to the house and there she saw Edwin sitting on the steps in front of their home with a neighbor sitting beside him with his arm around Edwin's shoulders; the two officers got out the car and walked up the driveway to the house and Paris followed behind them.

"We got a call from a Mr. Edwin Benson?" Ask the officer.

"Yes, I'm him." said Edwin standing up and pointing at Paris standing behind the officers. "She killed my mother!"

The officers turned around and looked at Paris and Paris was shock at Edwin accusations and she stepped back away from the officers. "He is telling a lie officer. I was nowhere near his mother when she died I was......."

"What's your name miss?" Interrupted the other office who was a female which caught Paris by surprise, in all the fifteen years Paris lived in Hidden Valley she had never seen a female officer.

"Paris Benson and I am Edwin's wife and I did not kill his mother. I was at home in the bed when Edwin got a phone call that his mother died."

"She lying!" screamed Edwin; "I'm telling you she is lying!"

"Who are you?" Asked the female officer; speaking to the little half bald headed white man with glasses that was sitting next to Edwin on the steps.

"Oh, I am just a neighbor from next door." Said the man now, standing up next to Edwin with his robe and slippers on. "I heard all the commotion and I just came out to see if I could help Edwin when I saw him down on his knees in the middle of the street crying. So I just came out to help him up and walked him back over to his house." Said the neighbor. I am the one that called you.

"What is your name sir? asked the Officer pulling out her pad.

"Thomas Ford and I live right next door." Pointed in the direction of his house.

"What is your address?" asked the officer

"1476 Buttermilk Way" said Thomas, if you don't need me any longer I would like to go back to bed; I have to go to work in the morning."

"Do you have a number we can reach you at?" Asked the other officer.

"Yes you can call me on my cell at (702) 552-5552.

"Thank you Mr. Ford, for your help and we will contact you if we need any more information." said the female office still writing.

"My name is Officer Dixon said the male officer and this is my partner Officer Clayton"

"Nice to meet you; can I go now? Ask Thomas.

"Yeah you can go" said Officer Clayton. "We won't need you right now."

"I'm sorry to hear about your mother Edwin and if you should need anything don't hesitate to call me." Said Thomas looking at Paris as if she was a murderer and rushing off to his house.

"Can we go in the house?" asked Officer Dixon

Edwin turned around and walked up the steps and opens the door; and went in and held the door open for Paris and the officers as they entered into the house. They stopped in the foyer and the officers looked in the living room and then in the dining room.

"So where is the body?" asked Officer Clayton

"Paris killed my mother upstate New York and then she ran back here and act like nothing had happen" said Edwin.

"You need to stop lying Edwin!" Screamed Paris and crying. "You know I was nowhere near your mother when she died."

"Calm down." Said Officer Clayton.

"Calm down?" "How can I be calm and he is accusing me of murdering his mother. His mother was upstate New York in an insane asylum!" said Paris screamed and pointed at Edwin.

"We are going to ask you again Mrs. Benson to calm down and stop screaming." Said Officer Dixon.

"How did you find out that was mother had been murdered?" ask Officer Clayton

"My sister called me and said someone from the hospital called her and told her that Paris came by the hospital and took my mother out on a day pass and Paris never returned with my mother. And two days later after Paris came back home they found my mother dead with head bashed in laying face up dead in an alley." cried Edwin.

"I'm telling you he is lying." cried Paris as she walks into the living room and turns on the light and walks over to the coach and sat down.

"Oh I'm telling a lie Paris?" said Edwin walking over to the coach and standing up in front of Paris. Weren't you upstate New York?

"Yes I was upstate; but I don't even know what hospital your mother was in" cried Paris.

"What were you doing upstate Paris?" asked Officer Dixon.

"I was working on a project for my job at the Boys and Girls club in Albany, New York."

"What was the name of the hospital was mother was in?" asked Officer Dixon

"Hudson Valley Hospital" Said Edwin now standing up in front of the officers.

"Isn't that an insane asylum in Poughkeepsie, New York?" Asked Officer Clayton, writing in her note pad.

"She was in the hospital and Paris took her out on a day pass and killed her." answer Edwin.

"His mother was a basket case and so is Edwin." yells Paris; wiping the tears from her eyes.

"Do you mind if I look around asked Officer Dixon.

"Go right ahead." Said Edwin as he walks across the room and sitting in the chair across from Paris. "I don't have anything to hide."

Officer Clayton sat down next to Paris on the sofa and tries to comfort her and ask her questions about how long was she up in Albany and questions concerning her job. Office Dixon returned to the living room with more questions and they told Paris they have to take her in for questioning. The officers handcuff Paris when she refused to go to the precinct. Paris cried, screamed and yelled at Edwin and told him how she should've run him over with her car as they took her out the house and put her in the back of the squad car.

-One Year Later-

"You are the best Papa, coming to see me and bring me my favorite chocolates and flowers too. What is a girl suppose to do?" Ask Paris laughing.

"You know I have to come see about you and make sure you are staying out of trouble. And besides when I spoke to you on the phone you never did tell me what happen when the police arrested you or how you ended up here." said Papa.

"I tried to explain to the officers that Inez was in an insane asylum in upstate New York when she died; and I was home in the bed when Edwin received the phone call; but they didn't believe me and officers took me down to the police precinct and held me there until they could verify my story. They found out that Inez had escaped along with two other patients from the asylum and as they were running across the highway, Inez got ran over by a truck and died. How wild is that Papa?"

"That is straight up wild and crazy!" said Papa.

"Well anyway, when they let me go; I use that money card you gave me and went to a hotel and later that day I went back to the precinct and took out an order of protection against Edwin and

I asked the police to come back to the house with me so I could get my things. I manage not only to get my clothes; a couple of my paintings which I sold for extra money, pictures and couple of my collectable items. I also took a couple of Edwin's blank checks and went to the bank and withdrew three thousand dollars." said

Paris laughing. I use that money to cover some of my expenses and to hire a divorce lawyer and now I am Ms. Paris Love again. Then I came back here to work at the Boys and Girls Club as a Recreational Director and I stayed at the Bed and Breakfast for a couple of months until I found this house to rent."

"Well congratulations on your escape from the island of insanity and abuse. And may I ask what grounds did you divorce Edwin on?

"You know Papa I gave that marriage one hundred and twenty percent and my biggest problem was listening to the church folks. I knew deep down inside that he was committing adultery and I had to stop listening to people and start listening to what was going on around me. I had to start thinking for myself and paying attention to what I was reading in the bible. God would not want me to stay in a dysfunctional family environment with folks trying to kill me. I had to remember that I worship God and not man and I had to start putting more faith in God and trusting Him to help me to come to terms with what was going on in my so-called marriage. Later on one of the church members told me that Edwin was seeing another woman that lived in Detroit. By that time I was already divorced. You know Papa, when I left there to come here to Albany to work on the project at the Boy and Girls Club my thinking was so distorted and confused from listening to others and I was hurt and angry. When I went back home I knew I didn't want to be there and when Edwin went berserk he confirmed everything I felt and needed to know. So I just needed to go through it to get out of it." You know Papa it's crazy; it's like I need Edwin's consent to leave him and I got it when he went straight to nut city on me."

So what grounds did you get divorced? Ask Papa.

"On grounds of domestic violence; it wasn't until after I divorced him I found out from one of the church members that he was having an affair. I didn't fight him about the house because I didn't want him stalking me. I just want to get on with my life and be happy and in peace. Okay?!"

"Okay; I'm proud of you Paris; you did the right thing." said Papa.

"And you know Papa; looking back on things that Edwin would do like always running us to the hotels and saying he smells carbon monoxide. I realize that was a plot to kill me; he figured if he did it enough times then one day he could release carbon monoxide when him and Anthony would be out together and it would kill me. And he use to smother me and run. He use to do it once in a while and turn over and pretend he was sleeping; all the gagging and coughing I would do he would never wake up and ask me was I okay. Then when he had that car accident and he was going to the physical therapist all that time and pretending that he wasn't going and he needed a cane to walk and he was smothering me. I guess he figure walking with a cane no one would suspect him of killing me."

"But he was hesitant for some reason." Said Papa "He could have just killed you when Anthony went off to college; but for some reason he held back from killing you; maybe he was just trying to drive you crazy like his mama."

"Yeah maybe," said Paris. "I never forget the night I came out of the hospital and he refused to drive me home but took me to New Jersey to buy a half a pint of Gin and I went to sleep on the way back home and when I woke up he was driving through the forest real slow. He was going to kill me then; but I called 911 and told the operator that Edwin was driving me through the forest and I called Ms. Becky and she stayed on the phone with me until we got home."

"Why didn't you leave then Paris? Ask Papa frowning.

"I didn't leave Papa, because I was in denial of what was

happening. I couldn't believe or accept this man that I was married to for twenty five years that would go to church with me three times a week and we raised a child together was trying to kill me." "Come on let's get off this porch and go in the house."

Papa and Paris went into the house and she went into the kitchen with Papa following behind her. Papa pulled out the chair from the kitchen table and sat down. Paris took out a bottle of wine and placed on the table.

"Someone might have been coercing him to kill you Paris and perhaps he was having reservations about it." Suggested Papa. "It was good that you made those phone calls."

"Yeah well, Ms. Becky told me it was everybody business to know that I was being abuse; the more people that knew I was being abused the safer I would be." Paris took wine glasses from the cabinet and placed them on the table. "Yeah, I wouldn't be surprised if Corona and Steven was in on the plan to kill me as well." Said Paris raising her eyebrows and taking sweet potato pie out of the refrigerator and placing it on the table.

"I have to tell you Papa, the gossiping and the ridicule from some of my spiritual brothers and sisters made me feel bad and Brother Lentil; not believing a word I said. They all took part in abusing me right along with Edwin. But Ms. Becky said when someone is being abuse it's everybody's business." Said Paris as she put the dishes on the table and cutting the pie."

"Yeah well; you just have to ignore those busybodies." Said Papa as Paris passes him a slice of sweet potato pie. "Pie sure looks good Paris."

"And you know Papa, just thinking about all those times that he said he had to go to Detroit for his job he was seeing another woman and probably in the car having sex with her when he had that car accident. And just think he would put on his suit and go to church and pretend to be an up-standing Christian and all that time he was plotting to kill me. And Edwin, Corona, and Steven knew their mother had problems with demons on top of being crazy; but they kept it a secret from me and if she hadn't slipped and went to talking about it I would have never known. And Edwin wanting to bring Inez to live with us and that was probably to get Inez to kill me."

"I am surprise you didn't run him over that night when he told you he was going to kill you." said Papa pouring the wine.

"You know Papa I had to pray for God to protect Edwin from me; because there were times he would make me so angry that I wanted to kill him. But I pray a many a day that God would change my heart; because if I would have kill him and that would have taken my own life; even if I didn't go jail. So I am so happy and thankful to God for sending you into Wal-Mart "Said Paris smiling.

"Yeah little sister, you were a mean, tough looking citizen that day I saw you!" Laughs Papa. "In fact I was scared when I saw you."

"Yeah right" said Paris laughing.

So Ms. Paris Love how did come you to choosing where you want to work? ask Papa.

"First of all I hated Hidden Valley." laughs Paris. "Lord knows somebody ought to hide that left-back place. Putting all jokes aside, I love kids and as a Recreational Director I get paid to paint, play games, organized events and parties. I can re-imagine my dream, my life as an artist. Tears weld up in Paris' eyes. You know Papa I went through many years of abuse and didn't realize it because I was trying to help Edwin with his mother because I loved him; but all the time I was trying to help I was being abused. But when people like you and Mr. Bonds and Ms. Becky, the social worker and my doctors' helped me it made all the difference in the world. Thank you so much Papa for making it your business to help me.

Papa reached across the table and held Paris' hand. Hey, Paris it everybody's business when someone is being abuse and besides I got to keep looking out for you so I can get some more of these here sweet potato pies.

-The End-

About the Author

Charlotte Raybon a Native New Yorker.
Author of "*Meet the Veggies- What Happens in Miss Mae's Kitchen.*"

Printed in the United States
by Bookmasters

Printed in the United States
By Bookmasters